D0069410

MUSEUMS
AND WOMEN
AND OTHER STORIES

John Updike

MUSEUMS
AND WOMEN

AND OTHER STORIES

VINTAGE BOOKS

A DIVISION OF RANDOM HOUSE

NEW YORK

First Vintage Books Edition, August 1981
Copyright © 1960, 1965, 1966, 1967, 1968, 1969, 1970, 1971, 1972
by John Updike
All rights reserved under International and Pan-American
Copyright Conventions. Published in the United States
by Random House, Inc., New York and simultaneously
in Canada by Random House of Canada Limited, Toronto.
Originally published by Alfred A. Knopf, Inc.,
New York, in October 1972.

Library of Congress Cataloging in Publication Data
Updike, John.
Museums and women and other stories.
I. Title.
PS3571.P4M78 1981   813'.54   81-40080
ISBN 0-394-74762-3   AACR2

Manufactured in the United States of America

Grateful acknowledgment is made to the following publications, which first printed the stories specified:

THE NEW YORKER: "Marching Through Boston," "The Witnesses," "The Pro" (1966); "The Taste of Metal," "Museums and Women" (1967); "Man and Daughter in the Cold" (1968); "The Corner," "The Day of the Dying Rabbit," "I Will Not Let Thee Go, Except Thou Bless Me," "One of My Generation," "The Hillies" (1969); "The Deacon," "The Orphaned Swimming Pool," "The Carol Sing" (1970); "Plumbing," "The Baluchitherium," "Jesus on Honshu" (1971); "Solitaire" (1972).

HARPER'S MAGAZINE: "Your Lover Just Called" (1966); "Eros Rampant" (1968); "Sublimating" (1971).

THE TRANSATLANTIC REVIEW: "During the Jurassic" (1966); "Under the Microscope" (1968); "The Invention of the Horse Collar" (1972).

ESQUIRE: "God Speaks" [under the title "Deus Dixit"] (1965); "The Slump" (1968).

PLAYBOY: "I Am Dying, Egypt, Dying" (1969).

AUDIENCE: "When Everyone Was Pregnant" (1971).

NEW WORLD WRITING: "The Sea's Green Sameness" (1960).

Illustration credits will be found on page 281.

TO ALFRED AND HELEN KNOPF

He has made everything beautiful in its time; also he has put eternity into man's mind, yet so that he cannot find out what God has done from the beginning to the end.

I know that there is nothing better for them than to be happy and enjoy themselves as long as they live;

also that it is God's gift to man that every one should eat and drink and take pleasure in all his toil.

—ECCLESIASTES 3.11–13

Revised Standard Version

Contents

CONTENTS

MUSEUMS
AND WOMEN

Museums and Women

SET TOGETHER, the two words are seen to be mutually transparent; the E's, the M's blend—the M's framing and squaring the structure lend resonance and a curious formal weight to the M central in the creature, which it dominates like a dark core winged with flitting syllables. Both words hum. Both suggest radiance, antiquity, mystery, and duty.

My first museum I would visit with my mother. It was a provincial museum, a stately pride to the third-class inland city it ornamented. It was approached through paradisaical grounds of raked gravel walks, humus-fed plantings of exotic flora, and trees wearing tags, as if freshly dubbed by Adam. The museum's contents were disturbingly various, its cases stocked with whatever scraps of foreign civilization had fallen to it from the imperious fortunes of the steel and textile barons of the province. A shredding kayak shared a room with a rack of Polynesian paddles. A mummy, its skull half masked in gold, lay in an antechamber like one more of the open-casket funerals common in my childhood. Miniature Mexican villages lit up when a switch was flicked, and a pyramid was being built by dogged brown dolls who never pulled their papier-mâché stone a fraction of an inch. An infinitely patient Chinaman, as remote from me as the resident of a star, had carved a yellow rhinoceros horn into an upright crescental city, pagoda-tipped, of balconies, vines, and thimble-sized people wearing microscopic expressions of pain.

This was downstairs. Upstairs, up a double flight of marble climaxed by a green fountain splashing greenly, the works of art were displayed. Upstairs, every fall, the county amateur artists exhibited four hundred watercolors of peonies and stone barns. The rest of the year, sombrely professional oils of rotting, tangled woodland had the walls to themselves, sharing the great cool rooms with cases of Philadelphia silver, chests decorated with hearts, tulips, and bleeding pelicans by Mennonite folk artists, thick aqua glassware left bubbled by the blowing process, quaint quilts, and strange small statues. Strange it may be, only in the impression they made on me. They were bronze statuettes, randomly burnished here and there as if by a caressing hand, of nudes or groups of nudes. The excuse for nudity varied; some of the figures were American Indians, some were mythical Greeks. One lady, wearing a refined, aloof expression, was having her clothes torn from her by a squat man with horns and hairy hooved legs hinged the wrong way. Another statue bodied forth two naked boys wrestling. Another was of an Indian, dressed in only a knife belt, sitting astride a horse bareback, his chin bowed to his chest in sorrow, his exquisitely toed feet hanging down both hard and limp, begging to be touched. I think it was the smallness of these figures that carried them so penetratingly into my mind. Each, if it could have been released into life, would have stood about twenty inches high and weighed in my arms perhaps as much as a cat. I itched to finger them, to interact with them, to insert myself into their mysterious silent world of strenuous contention— their bulged tendons burnished, their hushed violence detailed down to the fingernails. They were in their smallness like secret thoughts of mine projected into dimension and permanence, and they returned to me as a response that carried strangely into parts of my body. I felt myself a furtive animal stirring in the shadow of my mother.

My mother: like the museum, she filled her category. I knew no other, and accepted her as the index, inclusive and definitive, of women. Now I see that she too was provincial, containing much that was beautiful, but somewhat jumbled, and distorted by great gaps. She was an unsearchable mixture of knowledge and ignorance, openness and reserve; though she took me many Sundays to the museum, I do not remember our discussing anything in it except once when, noticing how the small statues fascinated me, she said, "Billy, they seem such unhappy little people." In her glancing way she had hit something true. The defeated Indian was not alone in melancholy; all the statuettes, as they engaged in the struggles or frolics that gave each group the metallic unity of a single casting, seemed caught in a tarnished fate from which I yearned to rescue them. I wanted to touch them to comfort them, yet I held my hand back, afraid of breaking the seal on their sullen, furious underworld.

My mood of dread in those high cool galleries condensed upon the small statues but did not emanate from them; it seemed to originate above and behind me, as if from another living person in the room. Often my mother, wordlessly browsing by the wall on the paintings of woods and shaggy meadows, was the only other person in the room. Who she was was a mystery so deep it never formed into a question.

She had descended to me from thin clouds of preëxistent time, enveloped me, and set me moving toward an unseen goal with a vague expectation that in the beginning was more hers than mine. She was not content. I felt that the motion which brought us again and again to the museum was an agitated one, that she was pointing me through these corridors toward a radiant place she had despaired of reaching. The fountain at the head of the stairs splashed unseen; my mother's footsteps rustled and she drew me into another room, where a case of silver stood aflame with reflections like the mouth of a dragon of beauty. She let me go forward to meet it alone. I was her son and the center of her expectations. I dutifully absorbed the light-struck terror of the hushed high chambers, and went through each doorway with a kind of timid rapacity.

This museum, my first, I associate with another, less ghostly hunt; for this was one of the places—others being the telephone company, the pretzel factory, and the county fair—where schoolchildren were taken on educational expeditions. I would usually be toward the end of the line, among the unpaired stragglers, and up front, in the loud nucleus of leaders, the freckled girl I had decided I loved. The decision, perhaps, was as much my mother's as mine. The girl lived in our neighborhood, one of a pack of sisters, and from the time she could walk past our front hedge my mother had taken one of her quixotic fancies to her. She spoke admiringly of her "spirit"; this admiration surprised me, for the girl was what was known locally as "bold," and as she grew older fell in with a crowd of children whose doings would certainly have struck my mother as "unhappy." My mother always invited her to my birthday parties, where she, misplaced but rapidly forgiving the situation, animated for a few dazzling hours my circle of shadowy-faced, sheltered friends.

Museums and Women

When I try to picture my school days, I seem to be embedded among boiling clouds straining to catch a glimpse of her, or trapped in a movie theatre behind a row of huge heads while fragmented arcs of the screen confusingly flicker. The alphabet separated us; she sat near the front of the classroom and I, William Young, toward the rear. Where the alphabet no longer obtained, other systems of distinction intervened. In the museum, a ruthless law propelled her forward to gather with the other bold spirits, tittering, around the defenseless little statues while I hung back, on the edge of the fountain, envious, angry, and brimming with things to say. I never said them. It seemed a simple matter of position; I was never in a position to declare, let alone act upon, my love. No distinction cuts as deep as the one between the worshipped and the worshipping. I am condemned by nature to be dutiful and reverent.

The girl who was to become my wife was standing at the top of some stone museum steps that I was climbing. Though it was bitterly cold, with crusts of snow packed into the stone, she wore threadbare sneakers from which her little toes stuck out, and she was smoking. Awesome sheets of smoke and frozen vapor flew from her mouth and she seemed, posed against a fluted pilaster, a white-faced priestess immolating herself in the worship of tobacco. "Aren't your feet cold?" I asked her.

"A little. I don't mind it."

"A stoic."

"Maybe I'm a masochist."

"Who isn't?"

She said nothing. Had I said something curious?

I lit a cigarette, though inhaling the raw air rasped my

throat, and asked her, "Aren't you in Medieval Art? You sit near the front."

"Yes. Do you sit in the back?"

"I feel I should. I'm a history major."

"This is your first fine-arts course?"

"Yeah. It met at a good hour—late enough for a late breakfast and early enough for an early lunch. I'm trying to have a sophomore slump."

"Are you succeeding?"

"Not really. When the chips are down, I tend to grind."

"How do you like Medieval Art?"

"I love it. It's like going to a movie in the morning, which is my idea of sin."

"You have funny ideas."

"No. They're very conventional. It would never occur to me, for example, to stand outside in the snow in bare feet."

"They're not really bare."

Nevertheless, I yearned to touch them, to comfort them. There was in this girl, this pale creature of the college museum, a withdrawing that drew me forward. I felt in her an innocent sad blankness where I must stamp my name. I pursued her through the museum. It was, as museums go, rather intimate. Architecturally, it was radiantly hollow, being built around a skylight-roofed replica of a sixteenth-century Italian courtyard. At the four corners of the flagstone courtyard floor, four great gray terra-cotta statues of the seasons stood. Bigger than life, they were French, and reduced the four epic passages of the year to four charming aristocrats, two male and two female, who had chosen to attend a costume ball piquantly attired in grapes and ribbons. I remember that Spring wore a floppy hat and carried a basket of rigid flowers. The stairways and galleries that enabled the museum to communicate with itself around the courtyard were distinctly medieval in feeling, and the vagaries of benefaction had left the museum's medieval and Oriental collections disproportionately strong, though a worthy attempt had been made to piece together the history of art since the Renaissance with a painting or at least a drawing by each master. But the rooms that contained these later works—including some Cézannes and Renoirs that, because they were rarely reproduced in art books, had the secret sweetness of flowers in a forest—were off the route of the course we were both taking, so my courtship primarily led down stone corridors, past Romanesque capitals, through low gray archways giving on gilded altar panels.

I remember stalking her around a capital from Avignon; it illustrated Samson and his deeds. On one side he was bearing off the gates of Gaza, while around the corner his massive head was lying aswoon in Delilah's lap as she clumsily sawed his hair. The class had been assigned a paper on this capital, and as I rehearsed my interpretation, elaborately linear and accompanied by many agitated indications of my hands, the girl said thoughtfully, "You see awfully much in it, don't you?"

My hands froze and crept back, embarrassed; the terminology of fine-arts analysis was new to me, and in fact I did doubt that an illiterate carver of semi-barbaric Europe could have been as aesthetically ingenious as I was. "What do *you* see in it?" I asked in self-defense.

"Not very much," she said. "I wonder why they assigned it. It's not that lovely. I think the Cluny ones are much nicer."

It thrilled me to hear her speak with such careless authority. She was a fine-arts major, and there was a sense in which she contained the museum, had mastered all the priceless and timeless things that would become, in my possessing her, mine as well. She had first appeared to me as someone guarding the gates.

Once I accompanied her into Boston, to the museum there, to study, in connection with another course she was taking, an ancient Attic sphinx. This she liked, though it was just a headless winged body of white marble, very simple, sitting stiffly on its haunches, its broad breast glowing under the nicks of stylized feathers. She showed me the S-curve of its body, repeated in the tail and again, presumably, in the vanished head.

"It's a very proud little statue, isn't it?" I ventured, seeking to join her in her little careless heaven of appreciation. Again, I seemed to have said something curious.

"I love it" was all she replied, with a dent of stubbornness in her mouth and an inviting blankness in her eyes.

Outside, the weather was winter, the trees medieval presences arching gray through gray. We walked and walked, and for a time the only shelter we shared was the museum. My courtship progressed; we talked solemnly; the childhood I had spent in such angry silence and timid foreboding had left me with much to say. She could listen; she was like a room of vases: you enter and find your sense of yourself abruptly sharpened by a vague, tranquil expectancy in the air. I see her sitting on the broad cold balustrade that at second-story height ran around the courtyard. Beyond her head, the flagstones shone as if wet and Printemps in her wide hat was baroquely foreshortened. An apprehension of height seized me; this girl seemed poised on the edge of a fall. I heard the volume of emptiness calling to her, calling her away from me, so full of talk. There was in her something mute and remote which spoke only once, once when, after our lying side by side an entire evening, she told me calmly, "You know I don't love you yet."

I took this as a challenge, though it may have been meant as a release. I carried the chase through exams (we both got A-minuses) and into another course, a spring-term course called, simply, Prints. My mother, surprisingly, wrote warning me that I mustn't spread myself too thin—she thought now that that had been *her* mistake at college. I was offended, for I thought that without my telling her anything she would know I was in the process of capturing the very gatekeeper of the temple of learning that must be the radiant place she had pointed me toward so long ago. The absence of her blessing seemed a tacit curse.

Here I must quickly insert, like a thin keystone, an imaginary woman I found in a faraway museum. It was another university museum, ancient and sprawling and resolutely masculine, full of battered weapons of war and unearthed agricultural tools and dull maps of diggings. All its contents seemed to need a dusting and a tasteful rearrangement by a female hand. But upstairs, in an out-of-the-way chamber, under a case of brilliantly polished glass, I one day discovered a smooth statuette of a nude asleep on a mattress. She was a dainty white dream, an eighteenth-century fancy; only that century would have thought to render a mattress in marble. Not that every stitch and seam was given the dignity of stone; but the corners were rounded, the buttoned squares of plumpness shown, and the creases of "give" lovingly sculpted. In short, it was clear that the woman was comfortable, and not posed on an arbitrary slab, or slaughtered on an altar. She was asleep, not dead; the delicate aroma of her slumber seemed to rise through the glass. She was the size of the small straining figures that had fascinated my childhood, and, as with them, smallness intensified sensual content. As I stood gazing into the eternal privacy of her sleep—her one hand resting palm up beside her averted head, one knee lifted in a light suggestion of restlessness—I was disturbed by dread and a premonition of loss. Why? Was not my wife also fair, and finely formed, and mute? Perhaps it was the mattress that brought this ideal other woman so close; it was a raft on which she had floated out of the inaccessible past and which brought her, small and intangible as a thought, ashore on the island of my bounded present. We seemed about to release each other from twin enchantments. Was not my huge face the oppressive dream that was making her stir? And was not I, out of all the thousands who had visited this museum, the first to find her here asleep? What we seek in museums is the opposite of what we seek in churches—the consoling sense of previous visitation. In museums, rather, we seek the untouched, the never-before-discovered; and it is their final unsearchability that leads us to hope, and return.

Two more, two more of each, each nameless. None have names. Museums are in the end nameless and continuous; we turn a corner in the Louvre and meet the head of a sphinx whose body is displayed in Boston. So, too, the women were broken arcs of one curve.

She was the friend of a friend, and she and I, having had lunch with the mutual friend, bade him goodbye and, both being loose in New York for the afternoon, went to a museum together. It was a new one, recently completed after the plan of a recently dead American wizard. It was shaped like a truncated top and its floor was a continuous spiral around an overweening core of empty vertical space.

From the leaning, shining walls immense rectangles of torn and spattered canvas projected on thin arms of bent pipe. Menacing magnifications of textural accidents, they needed to be viewed at a distance greater than the architecture afforded. The floor width was limited by a rather slender and low concrete guard wall that more invited than discouraged a plunge into the cathedralic depths below. Too reverent to scoff and too dizzy to judge, my unexpected companion and I dutifully unwound our way down the exitless ramp, locked in a wizard's spell. Suddenly, as she lurched backward from one especially explosive painting, her high heels were tricked by the slope, and she fell against me and squeezed my arm. Ferocious gumbos splashed on one side of us; the siren chasm called on the other. She righted herself but did not let go of my arm. Pointing my eyes ahead, inhaling the presence of perfume, feeling like a cliff-climber whose companion has panicked on the sheerest part of the face, I accommodated my arm to her grip and, thus secured, we carefully descended the remainder of the museum. Not until our feet attained the safety of street level were we released. Our bodies then separated and did not touch again. Yet the spell was imperfectly broken, like the door of a chamber which, once unsealed, can never be closed quite tight.

Not far down the same avenue there is a museum which was once a mansion and still retains a homelike quality, if one can imagine people rich enough in self-esteem to inhabit walls so overripe with masterpieces, to dine from tureens by Cellini, and afterward to seat their bodies complacently on furniture invested with the blood of empires. There once were people so self-confident, and on the day of my visit I was one of them, for the woman I was with and I were perfectly in love. We had come from love-making, and were to return to it, and the museum, visited between the evaporation and the recondensation of desire, was like a bridge whose either end is dissolved in mist—its suspension miraculous, its purpose remembered only by the murmuring stream running in the invisible ravine below. Homeless, we had found a home worthy of us. We seemed hosts; surely we had walked these Persian rugs before, appraised this amphora with an eye to its purchase, debated the position of this marble-topped table whose veins foamed like gently surfing aquamarine. The woman's sensibility was more an interior decorator's than an art student's, and through her I felt furnishings unfold into a world of gilded scrolls, rubbed stuffs, cherished surfaces, painstakingly inlaid veneers, varnished cadenzas of line and curve lovingly carved by men whose hands were haunted by the memory of women. Rustling beside me, her body, which I had seen asleep on a mattress, seemed to wear clothes as a needless luxuriance, an ultra-extravagance heaped upon what was already, like the museum, both priceless and free. Room after room we entered and owned. A lingering look, a shared smile was enough to secure our claim. Once she said, of a chest whose panels were painted with pubescent cherubs after Boucher, that she didn't find it terribly "attractive." The one word, pronounced with a worried twist of her eyebrows, delighted me like the first polysyllable pronounced by an infant daughter. In this museum I was more the guide; it was I who could name the modes and deliver the appreciations. Her muteness was not a reserve but an expectancy; she and the museum were perfectly open and mutually transparent. As we passed a dark-red tapestry, her bare-shouldered summer dress, of a similar red, blended with it, isolating her head and shoulders like a bust. The stuffs of every laden room conspired to flatter her, to elicit with tinted reflective shadows the shy structure of her face, to accent with sumptuous textures her demure skin. My knowledge of how she looked asleep gave a tender nap to the alert surface of her wakefulness now. My woman, fully searched, and my museum, fully possessed; for this translucent interval—like the instant of translucence that shows in a wave between its peaking and its curling under—I had come to the limits of unsearchability. From this beautiful boundary I could imagine no retreat.

The last time I saw this woman was in another museum, where she had taken a job. I found her in a small room lined with pale books and journals, and her face as it looked up in surprise was also pale. She took me into the corridors and showed me the furniture it was her job to catalogue. When we had reached the last room of her special province, and her gay, rather matter-of-fact lecture had ended, she asked me, "Why have you come? To upset me?"

"I don't mean to upset you. I wanted to see if you're all right."

"I'm all right. Please, William. If anything's left of what you felt for me, let me alone. Don't come teasing me."

"I'm sorry. It doesn't feel like teasing to me."

Her chin reddened and the rims of her eyes went pink as tears seized her eyes. Our bodies ached to comfort each other, but at any moment someone—a professor, a nun—might wander into the room. "You know," she said, "we really had it." A sob bowed her head and rebounded from the polished surfaces around us.

"I know. I know we did."

She looked up at me, the anger of her eyes blurred. "Then why—?"

I shrugged. "Cowardice. I've always been timid. A sense of duty. I don't know. I can't do it to her. Not yet."

"Not yet," she said. "That's your little song, isn't it? That's the little song you've been singing me all along."

"Would you rather the song had been, Not ever? That would have been no song at all."

With two careful swipes of her fingers, as if she were sculpting her own face, she wiped the tears from below her eyes. "It's my fault. It's my fault for falling in love with you. In a funny way, it was unfair to you."

"Let's walk," I said.

Blind to all beauty, we walked through halls of paintings and statues and urns. A fountain splashed unseen off to our left. Through a doorway I glimpsed, still proud, its broad chest still glowing, the headless sphinx.

"No, it's my fault," I said. "I was in no position to love you. I guess I never have been." Her eyes went bold and her freckles leaped up childishly as she grinned, as if to console me.

Yet what she said was not consolatory. "Well just don't do it to anybody else."

"Lady, there is nobody else. You're all of it. You have no idea, how beautiful you are."

"You made me believe it at the time. I'm grateful for that."

"And for nothing else?"

"Oh, for lots of things, really. You got me into the museum. It's fun."

"You came here to please me?"

"Yes."

"God, it's terrible to love what you can't have. Maybe that's why you love it."

"No, I don't think so. I think that's the way you work. But not everybody works that way."

"Well, maybe one of those others will find you now."

"No. You were it. You saw something in me nobody else ever saw. I didn't know it was there myself. Now go away, unless you want to see me cry some more."

We parted and I descended marble stairs. Before pushing through the revolving doors, I looked back, and it came to me that nothing about museums is as splendid as their entrances—the sudden vault, the shapely cornices, the motionless uniformed guard like a wittily disguised archangel, the broad stairs leading upward into heaven knows what mansions of expectantly hushed treasure. And it appeared to me that now I was condemned, in my search for the radiance that had faded behind me, to enter more and more museums, and to be a little less exalted by each new entrance, and a little more quickly disenchanted by the familiar contents beyond.

The Hillies

THE TOWN OF TARBOX was founded, in 1634, on the way
north from Plymouth, by men fearful of attack. They built
their fortified meetinghouse on a rocky outcropping com-
manding a defensive view of the river valley, where a flotilla
of canoes might materialize and where commerce and industry, when they peaceably came, settled of their own
gravity. Just as the functions of the meetinghouse slowly
split between a town hall and a Congregational church, the
town itself evolved two centers: the hilltop green and the
downtown. On the green stands the present church, the sixth
successive religious edifice on this site, a marvel (or outrage,
depending upon your architectural politics) of poured concrete, encircled by venerable clapboarded homes that include
the tiny old tilting post office (built 1741, decommissioned
1839) and its companion the onetime town jail, recently
transformed into a kinetic-art gallery by a young couple from
Colorado. Downtown, a block or more of false fronts and
show windows straggles toward the factory—once productive
of textiles, now of plastic "recreational products" such as

inflatable rafts and seamless footballs. The street holds two hardware stores, three banks, a Woolworth's with a new façade of corrugated Fiberglas, the granite post office (built 1933) with its Japanese cherry trees outside and its Pilgrim murals inside, the new two-story Town Hall of pre-rusted steel and thick brown glass, and a host of retail enterprises self-proclaimed by signs ranging in style from the heartily garish to the timidly tasteful, from 3-D neo-Superman to mimicry of the pallid script incised on Colonial tombstones. This downtown is no uglier than most, and its denizens can alleviate their prospect by lifting their eyes to the hill, where the church's parabolic peak gleams through the feathery foliage of the surviving elms. Between the green and the downtown lies an awkward steep area that has never been, until recently, settled at all. Solid ledge, this slope repelled buildings in the early days and by default became a half-hearted park, a waste tract diagonally skewered by several small streets, dotted with various memorial attempts—obelisks and urns—that have fallen short of impressiveness, and feebly utilized by a set of benches where, until recently, no one ever sat. For lately these leaden, eerily veined rocks and triangular patches of parched grass *have* been settled, by flocks of young people; they sit and lie here overlooking downtown Tarbox as if the spectacle is as fascinating as Dante's rose. Dawn finds them already in position, and midnight merely intensifies the murmur of their conversation, marred by screams and smashed bottles. The town, with the wit anonymously secreted within the most pedestrian of populations, has christened them "the hillies."

They are less exotic than hippies. Many are the offspring of prominent citizens; the son of the bank president is one, and the daughter of the meatmarket man is another. But even children one recognizes from the sidewalk days when they peddled lemonade or pedalled a tricycle stare now from the rocks with the hostile strangeness of marauders. Their solidarity appears absolute. Their faces, whose pallor is accented by smears of dirt, repel scrutiny; returning their collective stare is as difficult as gazing into a furnace or the face of a grieving widow. In honesty, some of these effects—of intense embarrassment, of menace—may be "read into" the faces of the hillies; apart from lifting their voices in vague mockery, they make no threatening moves. They claim they want only to be left alone.

When did they arrive? Their advent merges with the occasional vagrant sleeping on a bench, and with the children who used to play here while their mothers shopped. At first, they seemed to be sunning; the town is famous for its beach, and acquiring a tan falls within our code of coherent behavior. Then, as the hillies were seen to be sitting up and clothed in floppy costumes that covered all but their hands and faces, it was supposed that their congregation was sexual in motive; the rocks were a pickup point for the lovers' lanes among the ponds and pines and quarries on the dark edges of town. True, the toughs of neighboring villages swarmed in, racing their Hondas and Mustangs in a preening, suggestive fashion. But our flaxen beauties, if they succumbed, always returned to dream on the hill; and then it seemed that the real reason was drugs. Certainly their torpitude transcends normal physiology. And certainly the afternoon air is sweet with pot, and pushers of harder stuff come down from Boston at appointed times. None of our suppositions has proved entirely false, even the first, for on bright days some of the young men do shuck their shirts and lie spread-eagled under the sun, on the brown grass by the Civil

The Hillies

War obelisk. Yet the sun burns best at the beach, and sex and dope can be enjoyed elsewhere, even—so anxious are we parents to please—in the hillies' own homes.

With the swift pragmatism that is triumphantly American, the town now tolerates drugs in its midst. Once a scandalous rumor on the rim of possibility, drugs moved inward, became a scandal that must be faced, and now loom as a commonplace reality. The local hospital proficiently treats fifteen-year-old girls deranged by barbiturates, and our family doctors matter-of-factly counsel their adolescent patients against the dangers, such as infectious hepatitis, of dirty needles. That surprising phrase woven into our flag, "the pursuit of happiness," waves above the shaggy, dazed heads on the hill; a local parson has suggested that the community sponsor a "turn-on" center for rainy days and cold weather. Yet the hillies respond with silence. They pointedly decline to sit on the green that holds the church, though they have been offered sanctuary from police harassment there. The town discovers itself scorned by a mystery beyond drugs, by an implacable "no" spoken between its two traditional centers. And the numbers grow; as many as seventy were counted the other evening.

We have spies. The clergy mingle and bring back reports of intelligent, uplifting conversations; the only rudeness they encounter is the angry shouting ("Animals!" "Enlist!") from the passing carfuls of middle-aged bourgeoisie. The guidance director at the high school, wearing a three days' beard and blotched bluejeans, passes out questionnaires. Two daring young housewives have spent an entire night on the hill, with a tape recorder concealed in a picnic hamper. The police, those bone-chilled sentries on the boundaries of chaos, have developed their expertise by the intimate light of warfare.

They sweep the rocks clean every second hour all night, which discourages cooking fires, and have instituted, via a few quisling hillies, a form of self-policing. Containment, briefly, is their present policy. The selectmen cling to the concept of the green as "common land," intended for public pasturage. By this interpretation, the hillies graze, rather than trespass. Nothing is simple. Apparently there are strata and class animosities within the hillies—the "grassies," for example, who smoke marijuana in the middle area of the slope, detest the "beeries," who inhabit the high rocks, where they smash their no-return bottles, fistfight, and bring the wrath of the town down upon them all. The grassies also dislike the "pillies," who loll beneath them, near the curb, and who take harder drugs, and who deal with the sinister salesmen from Boston. It is these pillies, stretched bemused between the Spanish-American War memorial urns, who could tell us, if we wished to know, how the trashy façades of Poirier's Liquor Mart and Leonard's Pharmaceutical Store appear when deep-dyed by LSD and ballooned by the Eternal. In a sense, they see an America whose glory is hidden from the rest of us. The guidance director's questionnaires reveal some surprising statistics. Twelve per cent of the hillies favor the Vietnam war. Thirty-four per cent have not enjoyed sexual intercourse. Sixty-one per cent own their own automobiles. Eighty-six per cent hope to attend some sort of graduate school.

Each week, the Tarbox *Star* prints more of the vivacious correspondence occasioned by the hillies. One taxpayer writes to say that God has forsaken the country, that these young people are fungi on a fallen tree. Another, a veteran of the Second World War, replies that on the contrary they are harbingers of hope, super-Americans dedicated to saving a mad world from self-destruction; if he didn't have a family to support, he would go and join them. A housewife writes to complain of loud obscenities that wing outward from the hill. Another housewife promptly rebuts all such "credit-card hypocrites, installment-plan lechers, and Pharisees in plastic curlers." A hillie writes to assert that he was driven from his own home by "the stench of ego" and "heartbreaking lasciviousness." The father of a hillie, in phrases broken and twisted by the force of his passion, describes circumstantially his child's upbringing in an atmosphere of love and plenty and in conclusion hopes that other parents will benefit from the hard lesson of his present disgrace—a punishment he "nightly embraces with grateful prayer." Various old men write in to reminisce about their youths. Some remember hard work, bitter winters, and penny-pinching; others depict a lyrically empty land where a boy's natural prankishness and tendency to idle had room to "run their course." One "old-timer" states that "there is nothing new under the sun"; another sharply retorts that *everything* is new under the sun, that these youngsters are "subconsciously seeking accommodation" with unprecedented overpopulation and "hypertechnology." The Colorado couple write from their gallery to agree, and to suggest that salvation lies in Hindu reposefulness, "free-form creativity," and wheat germ. A downtown businessman observes that the hillies have become something of a tourist attraction and should not be disbanded "without careful preliminary study." A minister cautions readers to "let him who is without sin cast the first stone." The editor editorializes to the effect that "our" generation has made a "mess" of the world and that the hillies are registering a "legitimate protest"; a letter signed by sixteen hillies responds that they protest nothing, they just want to sit and "dig." "Life as it is," the letter (a document mimeographed and distributed by the local chapter of PAX) concludes, "truly grooves."

The printed correspondence reflects only a fraction of the opinions expressed orally. The local sociologist has told a luncheon meeting of the Rotary Club that the hillies are seeking "to reëmploy human-ness as a non-relative category." The local Negro, a crack golfer and horseman whose seat on his chestnut mare is the pride of the local hunt club, cryptically told the Kiwanis that "when you create a slave population, you must expect a slave mentality." The local Jesuit informed an evening meeting of the Lions that drugs are "the logical end product of the pernicious Protestant heresy of the 'inner light.' " The waitresses at the local restaurant tell customers that the sight of the hillies through the plate-glass windows gives them "the creeps." "Why don't they go to *work?*" they ask; their own legs are blue-veined from the strain of work, of waiting and hustling. The local Indian, who might be thought sympathetic, since some of the hillies affect Pocahontas bands and bead necklaces, is savage on the subject: "Clean the garbage out," he tells the seedy crowd that hangs around the liquor mart. "Push 'em back where they came from." But this ancient formula, so often invoked in our history, no longer applies. They came from our own homes. And in honesty do we want them back? How much a rural myth is parental love? The Prodigal Son no doubt became a useful overseer; they needed his hands. We need our self-respect. That is what is eroding on the hill—the foundations of our lives, the identities our industry and acquisitiveness have heaped up beneath the flag's blessing. The local derelict is the only adult who wanders among them without self-consciousness and without fear.

For fear is the mood. People are bringing the shutters down from their attics and putting them back on their windows. Fences are appearing where children used to stray freely from back yard to back yard, through loose hedges of forsythia and box. Locksmiths are working overtime. Once we parked our cars with the keys dangling from the dashboard, and a dog could sleep undisturbed in the middle of the street. No more. Fear reigns, and impatience. The downtown seems to be tightening like a fist, a glistening clot of apoplectic signs and sunstruck, stalled automobiles. And the hillies are slowly withdrawing upward, and clustering around the becrics, and accepting them as leaders. They are getting ready for our attack.

The Day of the Dying Rabbit

THE SHUTTER CLICKS, and what is captured is mostly accident —that happy foreground diagonal, the telling expression for-ever pinned in mid-flight between two plateaus of vacuity. Margaret and I didn't exactly intend to have six children. At first, we were trying until we got a boy. Then, after Jimmy arrived, it was half our trying to give him a brother so he wouldn't turn queer under all those sisters, and half our missing, the both of us, the way new babies are. You know how they are—delicate as film, wrapped in bunting instead of lead foil, but coiled with that same miraculous brimming whatever-it-is: *susceptibility*, let's say. That wobbly hot head. Those navy-blue eyes with the pupils set at $f/2$. The wrists hinged on silk and the soles of the feet as tender as the eyelids: film that fine-grained would show a doghouse roof from five miles up.

Also, I'm a photographer by trade and one trick of the trade is a lot of takes. In fact, all six kids have turned out pretty well, now that we've got the baby's feet to stop looking at each other and Deirdre fitted out with glasses. Having so many works smoothly enough in the city, where I go off to the studio and they go off to school, but on vacations things tend to jam. We rent the same four-room shack every August. When the cat dragged in as a love-present this mauled rabbit it had caught, it was minutes before I could get close enough even to *see*.

Henrietta—she's the second youngest, the last girl—screamed. There are screams like flashbulbs—just that cold. This one brought Linda out from her murder mystery and Cora up from her Beatles magazine, and they crowded into the corridor that goes with the bedrooms the landlord added to the shack to make it more rentable and that isn't wide enough for two pairs of shoulders. Off this corridor into the outdoors is a salt-pimpled aluminum screen door with a misadjusted pneumatic attachment that snaps like lightning the first two-thirds of its arc and then closes the last third slow as a clock, ticking. That's how the cat got in. It wasn't our cat exactly, just a tattered calico stray the children had been feeding salami scraps to out in the field between our yard and the freshwater pond. Deirdre had been helping Margaret with the dishes, and they piled into the corridor just ahead of me, in time to hear Linda let crash with a collection of those four-letter words that come out of her face more and more. The more pop out, the more angelic her face grows. She is thirteen, and in a few years I suppose it will be liquor and drugs, going in. I don't know where she gets the words, or how to stop them coming. Her cheeks are trimming down, her nose bones edging up, her mouth getting witty in the corners, and her eyes gathering depth; and I don't know how to stop that coming, either. Faces, when you look at them through a lens, are passageways for angels, sometimes whole clouds of them. Jimmy told me the other day—he's been reading books of records, mostly sports—about a man so fat he had been buried in a piano case for a casket, and he asked me what a casket was, and I told him, and a dozen angels overlapped in his face as he mentally matched up casket with fatness, and piano, and earth; and got the picture. Click.

After Linda's swearing, there was the sound of a slap and a second's silence while it developed who had been hit: Henrietta. Her crying clawed the corridor walls, and down among our legs the cat reconsidered its offer to negotiate and streaked back out the screen door, those last ticking inches, leaving the rabbit with us. Now I could see it: a half-grown rabbit huddled like a fur doorstop in the doorway to the bigger girls' room. No one dared touch it. We froze around it in a circle. Henrietta was still sobbing, and Cora's transistor was keeping the beat with static, like a heart stuffed with steel wool. Then God came down the hall from the smaller children's room.

Godfrey is the baby, the second boy. We were getting harder up for names, which was one reason we stopped. Another was, the club feet seemed a warning. He was slow to walk after they took the casts off, and at age four he marches along with an unstoppable sort of deliberate dignity, on these undeformed but somehow distinctly rectangular big feet. He pushed his way through our legs and without hesitation squatted and picked up the rabbit. Cora, the most squeamish of the children—the others are always putting worms down her back—squealed, and God twitched and flipped the bunny back to the floor; it hit neck first, and lay there looking bent. Linda punched Cora, and Henrietta jabbed God, but still none of the rest of us was willing to touch the rabbit, which might be dead this time, so we let God try again. We needed Jimmy. He and Deirdre have the natural touch—middle children tend to. But all month he's been out of the shack, out of our way, playing catch with himself, rowing in the pond, brooding on what it means to be a boy. He's ten. I've missed him. A father is like a dog— he needs a boy for a friend.

This time in God's arms, the rabbit made a sudden motion that felt ticklish, and got dropped again, but the sign of life was reassuring, and Deirdre pushed through at last, and all evening there we were, paying sick calls on this shoebox, whispering, while Deirdre and Henrietta alternately dribbled milk in a dropper, and God kept trying to turn it into a Steiff stuffed animal, and Cora kept screwing up her nerve to look the bunny in its left eye, which had been a little chewed, so it looked like isinglass. Jimmy came in from the pond after dark and stood at the foot of Deirdre's bed, watching her try to nurse the rabbit back to health with a dropper of stale milk. She was crooning and crying. No fuss; just the tears. The rabbit was lying panting on its right side, the bad eye up. Linda was on the next bed, reading her mystery, above it all. God was asleep. Jimmy's nostrils pinched in, and he turned his back on the whole business. He had got the picture. The rabbit was going to die. At the back of my brain I felt tired, damp, and cold.

What was it in the next twenty-four hours that slowly flooded me, that makes me want to get the day on some kind of film? I don't know exactly, so I must put everything in, however underexposed.

Linda and Cora were still awake when headlights boomed in the driveway—we're a city block from the nearest house and a half mile from the road—and the Pingrees came by. Ian works for an ad agency I've photographed some nudes shampooing in the shower for, and on vacation he lives in boat-neck shirts and cherry-red Bermudas and blue sunglasses, and grows a salt-and-pepper beard—a Verichrome fathead, and nearsighted at that. But his wife, Jenny, is nifty: low forehead, like a fox. Freckles. Thick red sun-dulled hair ironed flat down her back. Hips. And an angle about her legs, the way they're put together, slightly bowed but with the something big and bland and smooth and unimpeachable about the thighs that you usually find only in the fenders of new cars. Though she's very serious and liberal and agitated these days, I could look at her forever, she's such fun for the eyes. Which isn't the same as being photogenic. The few shots I've taken of her show a staring woman with baby fat, whereas some skinny snit who isn't even a name to me comes over in the magazines as my personal version of Eros. The camera does lie, all the time. It has to.

Margaret doesn't mind the Pingrees, which isn't the same as liking them, but in recent years she doesn't much admit to liking anybody; so it was midnight when they left, all of us giddy with drink and talk under the stars, that seem so presiding and reproachful when you're drunk, shouting goodbye in the driveway, and agreeing on tennis tomorrow. I remembered the rabbit. Deirdre, Linda, and Cora were asleep, Linda with the light still on and the mystery rising and falling on her chest, Cora floating above her, in the upper bunk bed. The rabbit was in the shoebox under a protective lean-to of cookout grilles, in case the cat came back. We moved a grille aside and lit a match, expecting the rabbit to be dead. Photograph by sulphur-glow: undertakers at work. But though the rabbit wasn't hopping, the whiskers were moving, back and forth no more than a millimeter or two at the tips, but enough to signify breathing, life, hope, what else? Eternal solicitude brooding above us, also holding a match, and burning Its fingers. Our detection of life, magnified by liquor, emboldened us to make love for the first time in, oh, days beyond counting. She's always tired, and says the Pill depresses her, and a kind of arms race of avoidance has grown up around her complaints. Moonlight muted by window screens. Great eyesockets beneath me, looking up. To the shack smells of mist and cedar and salt we added musk. Margaret slipped into sleep quick as a fish afterward, but for an uncertain length of time—the hours after midnight lose their numbers, if you don't remind them with a luminous dial—I lay there, the rabbit swollen huge and oppressive, blanketing all of us, a clenching of the nerves snatching me back from sleep by a whisker, the breathing and rustling all around me precarious, the rumbling and swaying of a ship that at any moment, the next or then the next, might hit an iceberg.

Morning. The rabbit took some milk, and his isinglass eye slightly widened. The children triumphantly crowed. Jubilant sun-sparkle on the sea beyond the sand beyond the pond. We rowed across, six in the rowboat and two in the kayak. The tides had been high in the night, delivering debris dropped between here and Portugal. Jimmy walked far down the beach, collecting light bulbs jettisoned from ships—they are vacuums and will float forever, if you let them. I had put the 135mm. telephoto on the Nikon and loaded in a roll of Plus-X and took some shots of the children (Cora's face, horrified and ecstatic, caught in the translucent wall of a breaker about to submerge her; Godfrey, his close-cut blond hair shiny as a helmet, a Tritonesque strand of kelp slung across his shoulders) but most of grass and sand and shadows, close-up, using the ultraviolet filter, trying to get, what may be ungettable, the way the shadow edges stagger from grain to grain on the sand, and the way some bent-over grass blades draw circles around themselves, to keep time away.

Jimmy brought the bulbs back and arranged them in order of size, and before I could get to him had methodically smashed two. All I could see was bleeding feet but I didn't mean to grab him so hard. The marks of my hand were still red on his arm a half hour later. Our fight depressed Henrietta; like a seismograph, she feels all violence as hers. God said he was hungry and Deirdre began to worry about the rabbit: there is this puffy look children's faces get that I associate with guilt but that can also signal grief. Deirdre and Jimmy took the kayak, to be there first, and Linda, who maybe thinks the exercise will improve her bosom, rowed the rest of us to our dock. We walked to the house, heads down. Our path is full of poison ivy, our scorched lawn full of flat thistles. In our absence, the rabbit, still lying on its side, had created a tidy little heap of pellet-like feces. The children were ecstatic; they had a dirty joke and a miracle all in one. The rabbit's recovery was assured. But the eye looked cloudier to me, and the arc of the whisker tips even more fractional.

Lunch: soup and sandwiches. In the sky, the clouding over from the west that often arrives around noon. The level of light moved down, and the hands of the year swept forward a month. It was autumn, every blade of grass shining. August has this tinny, shifty quality, the only month without a holiday to pin it down. Our tennis date was at two. You can picture for yourself Jenny Pingree in tennis whites: those rounded guileless thighs, and the bobbing, flying hair tied behind with a kerkchief of blue gauze, and that humorless, utterly intent clumsiness—especially when catching the balls tossed to her as server—that we love in children, trained animals, and women who are normally graceful. She and I, thanks to my predatory net play, took Ian and Margaret, 6–3, and the next set was called at 4–4, when our hour on the court ran out. A moral triumph for Margaret, who played like the swinger of fifteen years ago, and passed me in the alley half a dozen times. Dazzling with sweat, she took the car and went shopping with the four children who had come along to the courts; Linda had stayed in the shack with another book, and Jimmy had walked to a neighboring house, where there was a boy his age. The Pingrees dropped me off at our mailbox. Since they were going back to the city Sunday, we had agreed on a beach picnic tonight. The mail consisted of forwarded bills, pencil-printed letters to the children from their friends on other islands or beside lakes, and *Life*. While walking down our dirt road I flicked through an overgorgeous photographic essay on Afghanistan. Hurrying blurred women in peacock-colored saris, mud palaces, rose dust, silver rivers high in the Hindu Kush. An entire valley—misted, forested earth—filled the center page spread. The *lenses* those people have! Nothing beautiful on earth is as selfless as a beautiful lens.

Entering the shack, I shouted out to Linda, "It's just me," thinking she would be afraid of rapists. I went into her room and looked in the shoebox. The eye was lustreless and the whiskers had stopped moving, even infinitesimally.

"I think the bunny's had it," I said.

"Don't make me look," she said, propped up in the lower bunk, keeping her eyes deep in a paperback titled *A Stitch in*

Time Kills Nine. The cover showed a dressmaker's dummy pierced by a stiletto, and bleeding. "I couldn't *stand it*," she said.

"What should I do?" I asked her.

"Bury it." She might have been reading from the book. Her profile, I noticed, was becoming a cameo, with a lovely gentle bulge to the forehead, high like Margaret's. I hoped being intelligent wouldn't cramp her life.

"Deirdre will want to see it," I argued. "It's her baby."

"It will only make her *sad*," Linda said. "And dis*gust* me. Already it must be *full* of *ver*min."

Nothing goads me to courage like some woman's taking a high tone. Afraid to touch the rabbit's body while life was haunting it, I touched it now, and found it tepid, and lifted it from the box. The body, far from stiff, felt unhinged; its back or neck must have been broken since the moment the cat pounced. Blood had dried in the ear—an intricate tunnel leading brainwards, velvety at the tip, oddly muscular at the root. The eye not of isinglass was an opaque black bead. Linda was right; there was no need for Deirdre to see. I took the rabbit out beyond the prickly yard, into the field, and laid it beneath the least stunted swamp oak, where any child who wanted to be sure that I hadn't buried it alive could come and find it. I put a marsh marigold by its nose, in case it was resurrected and needed to eat, and paused above the composition—fur, flower, the arty shape of fallen oak leaves—with a self-congratulatory sensation that must have carried on my face back to the shack, for Margaret, in the kitchen loading the refrigerator, looked up at me and said, "Say. I don't mind your being partners with Jenny, but you don't have to toss the balls to her in that cute confiding way."

"The poor bitch can't catch them otherwise. You saw that."

"I saw more than I wanted to. I nearly threw up."

"That second set," I said, "your backhand was terrific. The Maggie-O of old."

Deirdre came down the hall from the bedrooms. Her eyes seemed enormous; I went to her and kneeled to hold her around the waist, and began, "Sweetie, I have some sad news."

"Linda told me," she said, and walked by me into the kitchen. "Mommy, can I make the cocoa?"

"You did everything you could," I called after her. "You were a wonderful nurse and made the bunny's last day very happy."

"I know," she called in answer. "Mommy, I *promise* I won't let the milk boil over this time."

Of the children, only Henrietta and Godfrey let me lead them to where the rabbit rested. Henrietta skittishly hung back, and never came closer than ten yards. God marched close, gazed down sternly, and said, "Get up." Nothing happened, except the ordinary motions of the day: the gulls and stately geese beating home above the pond, the traffic roaring invisible along the highway. He squatted down, and I prevented him from picking up the rabbit, before I saw it was the flower he was after.

Jimmy, then, was the only one who cried. He came home a half hour after we had meant to set out rowing across the pond to the beach picnic, and rushed into the field toward the tree with the tallest silhouette and came back carrying on his cheeks stains he tried to hide by thumping God. "If *you* hadn't dropped him," he said. "You *baby*."

"It was nobody's fault," Margaret told him, impatiently cradling her basket of hot dogs and raw hamburger.

"I'm going to kill that cat," Jimmy said. He added, cleverly, an old grievance: "Other kids my age have BB guns."

"Oh, our big man," Cora said. He flew at her in a flurry of fists and sobs, and ran away and hid. At the dock I let Linda and Cora take the kayak, and the rest of us waited a good ten minutes with the rowboat before Jimmy ran down the path in the dusk, himself a silhouette, like the stunted trees and the dark bar of dunes between two sheets of reflected sunset. Ever notice how sunsets upside down look like stairs?

"Somehow," Margaret said to me, as we waited, "you've deliberately dramatized this." But nothing could fleck the happiness widening within me, to capture the dying light.

The Pingrees had brought swordfish and another, older couple—the man was perhaps an advertising client. Though he was tanned like a tobacco leaf and wore the smartest summer playclothes, a pleading uncertainty in his manner seemed to crave the support of advertisement. His wife had once been beautiful and held herself lightly, lithely at attention—a soldier in the war of self-preservation. With them came two teen-age boys clad in jeans and buttonless vests and hair so long their summer complexions had remained sallow. One was their son, the other his friend. We all collected driftwood—a wandering, lonely, prehistoric task that frightens me. Darkness descended too soon, as it does in the tropics, where the warmth leads us to expect an endless June evening from childhood. We made a game of popping champagne corks, the kids trying to catch them on the fly. Startling, how high they soared, in the open air. The two boys gathered around Linda, and I protectively eavesdropped, and was shamed by the innocence and long childish pauses of what I overheard: "Philadelphia . . . just been in the airport, on our way to my uncle's, he lives in Virginia . . . wonderful horses, super . . . it's not actually blue, just bluey-green, blue only I guess by comparison . . . was in France once, and went to the races . . . never been . . . I want to go." Margaret and Jenny, kneeling in the sand to cook, setting out paper plates on tables that were merely wide pieces of driftwood, seemed sisters. The woman of the strange couple tried to flirt with me, talking of foreign places: "Paris is so dead, suddenly . . . the girls fly over to London to buy their clothes, and then their mothers won't let them wear them . . . Malta . . . Istanbul . . . life . . . sincerity . . . the *people* . . . the poor Greeks . . . a friend absolutely assures me, the C.I.A. engineered . . . apparently used the NATO contingency plan." Another champagne cork sailed in the air, hesitated, and drifted down, Jimmy diving but missing, having misjudged. A remote light, a lightship, or the promontory of a continent hidden in daylight, materialized on the horizon, beyond the shushing of the surf. Margaret and Jenny served us. Hamburgers and swordfish full of woodsmoke. Celery and sand. God, sticky with things he had spilled upon himself, sucked his thumb and rubbed against Margaret's legs. Jimmy came to me, furious because the big boys wouldn't Indian-wrestle with him, only with Linda and Cora: "Showing off for their boyfriends . . . whacked me for no reason . . . just because I said 'sex bomb.' "

We sat in a ring, survivors, around the fire, the heart of a collapsing star, fed anew by paper plates. The man of the older couple, in whose breath the champagne had undergone an acrid chemical transformation, told me about his money— how as a youth just out of business school, in the depths of the Depression, he had made a million dollars in some deal involving Stalin and surplus wheat. He had liked Stalin, and Stalin had liked him. "The thing we must realize about your Communist is that he's just another kind of businessman." Across the fire I watched his wife, spurned by me, ardently gesturing with the teen-age boy who was not her son, and wondered how I would take their picture. Tri-X, wide-open, at 1/60; but the shadows would be lost, the subtle events within them, and the highlights would be vapid blobs. There is no adjustment, no darkroom trickery, equivalent to the elastic tolerance of our eyes as they travel.

As my new friend murmured on and on about his money, and the champagne warming in my hand released carbon dioxide to the air, exposures flickered in and out around the fire: glances, inklings, angels. Margaret gazing, the nick of a frown erect between her brows. Henrietta's face vertically compressing above an ear of corn she was devouring. The well-preserved woman's face a mask of bronze with cunningly welded seams, but her hand an exclamatory white as it touched her son's friend's arm in some conversational urgency lost in the crackle of driftwood. The halo of hair around Ian's knees, innocent as babies' pates. Jenny's hair an elongated flurry as she turned to speak to the older couple's son; his bearded face was a blur in the shadows, melancholy, the eyes seeming closed, like the Jesus on a faded, drooping veronica. I heard Jenny say, ". . . must destroy the system! We've forgotten how to love!" Deirdre's glasses, catching the light, leaped like moth wings toward the fire, escaping perspective. Beside me, the old man's face went silent, and suffered a deflation wherein nothing held firm but the reflected glitter of firelight on a tooth his grimace had absentmindedly left exposed. Beyond him, on the edge of the light, Cora and Linda were revealed sitting together, their legs stretched out long before them, warming, their faces in shadow, sexless and solemn, as if attentive to the sensations of the revolution of the earth beneath them. Godfrey was asleep, his head pillowed on Margaret's thigh, his body suddenly wrenched by a dream sob, and a heavy succeeding sigh.

It was strange, after these fragmentary illuminations, to stumble through the unseen sand and grass, with our blankets and belongings, to the boats on the shore of the pond. Margaret and five children took the rowboat; I nominated Jimmy to come with me in the kayak. The night was starless. The pond, between the retreating campfire and the slowly nearing lights of our neighbors' houses, was black. I could scarcely see his silhouette as it struggled for the rhythm of the stroke: left, a little turn with the wrists, right, the little turn reversed, left. Our paddles occasionally clashed, or snagged on the weeds that clog this pond. But the kayak sits lightly, and soon we put the confused conversation of the rowers, and their wildly careening flashlight beam, behind. Silence widened around us. Steering the rudder with the foot pedals, I let Jimmy paddle alone, and stared upward until I had produced, in the hazed sky overhead, a single, unsteady star. It winked out. I returned to paddling and received an astonishing impression of phosphorescence: every stroke, right and left, called into visibility a rich arc of sparks, animalcula hailing our passage with bright shouts. The pond was more populous than China. My son and I were afloat on a firmament warmer than the heavens.

"Hey, Dad."

His voice broke the silence carefully; my benevolence engulfed him, my fellow-wanderer, my leader, my gentle, secretive future. "What, Jimmy?"

"I think we're about to hit something."

We stopped paddling, and a mass, gray etched on gray, higher than a man, glided swiftly toward us and struck the prow of the kayak. With this bump, and my awakening laugh, the day of the dying rabbit ended. Exulting in homogenous glory, I had steered us into the bank. We pushed off, and by the lights of our neighbors' houses navigated to the dock, and waited for the rowboat with its tangle of voices and impatience and things that would snag. The days since have been merely happy days. This day was singular in its, let's say, *gallantry:* between the cat's gallant intentions and my son's gallantly calm warning, the dying rabbit sank like film in the developing pan, and preserved us all.

The Deacon

HE PASSES THE PLATE, and counts the money afterward—a large dogged-looking man, wearing metal-framed glasses that seem tight across his face and that bite into the flesh around his eyes. He wears for Sunday morning a clean white shirt, but a glance downward, as you lay on your thin envelope and pass the golden plate back to him, discovers fallen socks and scuffed shoes. And as he with his fellow-deacons strides forward toward the altar, his suit is revealed as the pants of one suit (gray) and the coat of another (brown). He is too much at home here. During the sermon, he stares toward a corner of the nave ceiling, which needs repair, and slowly, reverently, yet unmistakably chews gum. He lingers in the vestibule, with his barking, possessive laugh, when the rest of the congregation has passed into the sunshine and the dry-mouthed minister is fidgeting to be out of his cassock and home to lunch. The deacon's car, a dusty Dodge, is parked outside the parish hall most evenings. He himself wonders why he is there so often, how he slipped into this ceaseless round of men's suppers, of Christian Education Committee meetings, choir rehearsals, emergency sessions of the Board of Finance where hours churn by in irrelevant argument and prayerful silences that produce nothing. "Nothing," he says to his wife on returning, waking her. "The old fool refuses to amortize the debt." He means the treasurer. "His Eminence tells us foreign missions can't be applied to the oil bill even if we make it up in the summer at five per cent interest." He means the minister. "It was on the tip of my tongue to ask whence he derives all his business expertise."

"Why don't you resign?" she asks. "Let the young people get involved before they drop away."

"One more peace in Vietnam sermon, they'll drop away anyway." He falls heavily into bed, smelling of chewing gum. As with men who spend nights away from home drinking in bars, he feels guilty, but the motion, the brightness and excitement of the place where he has been continues in him: the varnished old tables, the yellowing Sunday-school charts, the folding chairs and pocked linoleum, the cork bulletin board, the giggles of the children's choir leaving, the strange constant sense of dark sacred space surrounding their lit meeting room like the void upholding a bright planet. "One more blessing on the damn Vietcong," he mumbles, and the young minister's face, white and worriedly sucking a pipestem, skids like a vision of the Devil across his plagued mind. He has a headache. The sides of his nose, the tops of his cheeks, the space above his ears—wherever the frames of his glasses dig —dully hurt. His wife snores, neglected. In less than seven hours, the alarm clock will ring. This must stop. He must turn over a new leaf.

His name is Miles. He is over fifty, an electrical engineer. Every seven years or so, he changes employers and locations. He has been a member of the board of deacons of a prosperous Methodist church in Iowa, a complex of dashing blond brick-and-glass buildings set in acres of parking lot carved from a cornfield; then of a Presbyterian church in San Francisco, gold-rush Gothic clinging to the back of Nob Hill, attended on Sundays by a handful of Chinese businessmen and prostitutes in sunglasses and whiskery, dazed dropout youths looking for a warm place in which to wind up their Saturday-night trips; then of another Presbyterian church in New York State, a dour granite chapel in a suburb of Schenectady; and most recently, in southeastern Pennsylvania, of a cryptlike Reformed church sunk among clouds of foliage so dense that the lights are kept burning in midday and the cobwebbed balconies swarm all summer with wasps. Though Miles has travelled far, he has never broken out of the loose net of Calvinist denominations that places almost every American within sight of a spire. He wonders why. He was raised in Ohio, in a village that had lost the tang of the frontier but kept its bleak narrowness, and was confirmed in the same colorless, bean-eating creed that millions in his generation have dismissed forever. He was not, as he understood the term, religious. Ceremony bored him. Closing his eyes to pray made him dizzy. He distinctly heard in the devotional service the overamplified tone of voice that in business matters would signal either ignorance or dishonesty. His profession prepared him to believe that our minds, with their crackle of self-importance, are merely collections of electrical circuits. He saw nothing about his body worth resurrecting. God, concretely considered, had a way of merging with that corner of the church ceiling that showed signs of water leakage. That men should be good, he did not doubt, or that social order demands personal sacrifice; but the Heavenly hypothesis, as it had fallen upon his ears these forty years of

Sundays, crushes us all to the same level of unworthiness, and redeems us all indiscriminately, elevating especially, these days, the irresponsible—the unemployable, the riotous, the outrageous, the one in one hundred that strays. Neither God nor His ministers displayed love for deacons—indeed, Pharisees were the first objects of their wrath. Why persist, then, in work so thoroughly thankless, begging for pledges, pinching and scraping to save degenerate old buildings, facing rings of Sunday-school faces baked to adamant cynicism by hours of television-watching, attending fruitless meetings where the senile and the frustrated dominate, arguing, yawning, missing sleep, the company of his wife, the small, certain joys of home. Why? He had wanted to offer his children the Christian option, to begin them as citizens as he had begun; but all have left home now, are in college or married, and, as far as he can tactfully gather, are unchurched. So be it. He has done his part.

A new job offer arrives, irresistible, inviting him to New England. In Pennsylvania the Fellowship Society gives him a farewell dinner; his squad of Sunday-school teachers presents him with a pen set; he hands in his laborious financial records, his neat minutes of vague proceedings. He bows his head for the last time in that dark sanctuary smelling of moldering plaster and buzzing with captive wasps. He is free. Their new house is smaller, their new town is white. He does not join a church; he stays home reading the Sunday paper. Wincing, he flicks past religious news. He drives his wife north to admire the turning foliage. His evenings are immense. He reads through Winston Churchill's history of the Second World War; he installs elaborate electrical gadgets around the house, which now and then give his wife a shock. They go to drive-in movies, and sit islanded in a sea of fornication. They go bowling and square dancing, and feel ridiculous, too ponderous and slow. His wife, these years of evenings alone, has developed a time-passing pattern—television shows spaced with spells of sewing and dozing—into which he fits awkwardly. She listens to him grunt and sigh and grope for words. But Sunday mornings are the worst—blighted times haunted by the giddy swish and roar of churchward traffic on the road outside. He stands by the window; the sight of three little girls, in white beribboned hats, bluebird coats, and dresses of starched organdie, scampering home from Sunday school gives him a pang unholy in its keenness.

Behind him his wife says, "Why don't you go to church?"

"No, I think I'll wash the Dodge."

"You washed it last Sunday."

"Maybe I should take up golf."

"You want to go to church. Go. It's no sin."

"Not the Methodists. Those bastards in Iowa nearly worked me to death."

"What's the pretty white one in the middle of town? Congregational. We've never been Congregationalists; they'd let you alone."

"Are you sure you wouldn't like to take a drive?"

"I get carsick with all that starting and stopping. To tell the truth, it would be a relief to have you out of the house."

Already he is pulling off his sweater, to make way for a clean shirt. He puts on a coat that doesn't match his pants. "I'll go," he says, "but I'll be damned if I'll join."

He arrives late, and sits staring at the ceiling. It is a wooden church, and the beams and ceiling boards in drying out have pulled apart. Above every clear-glass window he sees the dried-apple-colored stains of leakage. At the door, the minis-

ter, a very young pale man with a round moon face and a
know-it-all pucker to his lips, clasps Miles' hand as if never
to let it go. "We've been looking for you, Miles. We received
a splendid letter about you from your Reformed pastor in
Pennsylvania. As you know, since the U.C.C. merger you
don't even need to be reconfirmed. There's a men's supper
this Thursday. We'll hope to see you there." Some minister's
hands, Miles has noticed, grow fatty under the pressure of
being so often shaken, and others dwindle to the bones; this
one's, for all his fat face, is mostly bones.

The church as a whole is threadbare and scrawny; it makes
no resistance to his helpless infiltration of the Men's Club, the
Board of Finance, the Debt Liquidation and Building Mainte-
nance Committee. He and a few shaggy Pilgrim Youth paint
the Sunday-school chairs Chinese red. He and one grimy
codger and three bottles of beer clean the furnace room of
forgotten furniture and pageant props, of warped hymnals
and unused programs still tied in the printer's bundles, of the
gilded remnants of a dozen abandoned projects. Once he
attends a committee meeting to which no one else comes. It
is a gusty winter night, a night of cold rain from the sea,
freezing on the roads. The minister has been up all night with
the family of a suicide and cannot himself attend; he has
dropped off the church keys with Miles.

The front door key, no bigger than a car key, seems
magically small for so large a building. Is it the only one?
Miles makes a mental note: have duplicates made. He turns on
a light and waits for the other committee members—a retired
banker and two maiden ladies. The furnace is running
gamely, but with an audible limp in its stride. It is a coal
burner converted to oil twenty years ago. The old cast-iron

clinker grates are still heaped in a corner, too heavy to throw
out. Should be sold for scrap. Every penny counts. Pinching
and scraping. Miles thinks, as upon a mystery, upon the
prodigality of heating a huge vacant barn like this with such
an inefficient burner. Hot air rises direct from the basement
to the ceiling, drying and spreading the wood. Fuel needle
half gummed up. Waste. Nothing but waste, salvage and
waste. And weariness.

Miles removes his glasses and rubs the chafed spots at the
bridge of his nose. He replaces them to look at his watch.
His watch has stopped, its small face wet from the storm like
an excited child's. The electric clock in the minister's study
has been unplugged. Bogus thrift. There are books: con-
cordances, daily helps, through the year verse by verse, great
sermons, best sermons, sermon hints, all second-hand, no,
third-hand, worse, hundredth-hand, thousandth-hand, a coin
rubbed blank. The books are leaning on their sides and half
the shelves are empty. Empty. The desk is clean. No business
conducted on it. He tests the minister's fountain-pen and it is
dry. Dry as an old snakeskin, dry as a locust husk that still
clings to a tree.

In search of the time, Miles goes into the sanctuary. The
1880 pendulum clock on the choir balustrade still ticks. He
can hear it in the dark, overhead. He switches on the nave
lights. A moment passes before they come on. Some shaky
connection in the toggle, the wiring doubtless rotten through-
out the walls, a wonder it hasn't burnt down. Miles has never
belonged to a wooden church before. Around and above him,
like a stiff white forest, the hewn frame creaks and groans
in conversation with the wind. The high black windows,
lashed as if by handfuls of sand, seem to flinch, yet do not
break, and Miles feels the timbers of this ark, with its ballast

of tattered pews, give and sway with the fierce weather, yet hold; and this is why he has come, to share the pride of this ancient thing that will not quite die, to have it all to himself. Warm air from a grilled duct breathes on his ankles. Miles can see upward past the clock and the organ to the corner of the unused gallery where souvenirs of the church's past— Puritan pew doors, tin footwarmers, velvet collection bags, Victorian commemorative albums, cracking portraits of wigged pastors, oval photographs of deceased deacons, and inexplicable unlabelled ferrotypes of chubby cross children and picnics past—repose in dusty glass cases that are in themselves antiques. All this anonymous treasure Miles possesses by being here, like a Pharaoh hidden with his life's rich furniture, while the rain like a robber rattles to get in.

Yes, the deacon sees, it is indeed a preparation for death— an emptiness where many others have been, which is what death will be. It is good to be at home here. Nothing now exists but himself, this shell, and the storm. The windows clatter; the sand has turned to gravel, the rain has turned to sleet. The storm seizes the church by its steeple and shakes, but the walls were built with love, and withstand. The others are very late, they will not be coming; he is not displeased, he is serene. He turns out the lights. He locks the door.

I Will Not Let Thee Go,
Except Thou Bless Me

AT THE FAREWELL PARTY for the Bridesons, the Bridesons themselves were very tired. Lou (for Louise) had been sorting and packing and destroying for days, and her sleep was gouged by nightmares of trunks that would not close, of doors that opened to reveal forgotten secret rooms crammed with yet more debris of ten years' residence—with unmended furniture and outgrown toys and stacked *Lifes* and *National Geographics* and hundreds, thousands, of children's drawings, each one a moment, a memory, impossible to keep, impossible to discard. And there was another dream, recurrent, in which she and the children arrived in Texas. Brown horizon on all sides enclosed a houseless plain. They wheeled the airplane stairway away, and Tom was not there, he was not with them. Of course: he had left them. He had stayed behind, in green Connecticut. "Now, children"—she seemed to be shouting into a sandstorm—"we must keep together, together. . . ." Lou would awake, and the dark body beside hers in the bed was an alien presence, a visitor from another world.

And Tom, hurriedly tying up loose ends in the city, lunching one day with his old employers and the next day with representatives of his new, returning each evening to an emptier house and increasingly apprehensive children, slept badly also. The familiar lulling noises—car horn and dog bark, the freight train's echoing shunt and the main drag's murmur—had become irritants; the town had unravelled into tugging threads of love. Departure rehearses death. He lay staring with open sockets, a void where thoughts swirled until the spell was broken by the tinkle of the milkman, who also, it seemed, had loved him. Fatigue lent to everything the febrile import of an apparition. At the farewell party, his friends of nearly a decade seemed remote, yet garish. Linda Cotteral, that mouse, was wearing green eyeshadow. Bugs Leonard had gone Mod—turquoise shirt, wide pink tie—and had come already drunk from cocktails somewhere else. Maggie Aldridge, as Tom was carrying the two coats to the bedroom, swung down the hall in a white dress with astonishingly wide sleeves. Taken unawares, Tom uttered the word "Lovely!" to hide his loud heartbeat. She grinned, and then sniffed, as if to erase the grin. Her grin, white above white, had been a momentary flash of old warmth, but in the next moment, as she brushed by him, her eyes were cast ahead in stony pretense of being just another woman. He recognized his impulse to touch her, to seize her wrist, as that of a madman, deranged by lack of sleep.

Drinks yielded to dinner, dinner to dancing. Gamely they tried to Frug (or was it Monkey?) to the plangent anthems of a younger generation. Then the rock music yielded, as their host dug deeper into his strata of accumulated records,

to the reeds and muted brass and foggy sighing that had
voiced the furtive allegiances of their own, strange, in-
between generation—too young to be warriors, too old to be
rebels. Too tired to talk, Tom danced. The men with whom
he had shared hundreds of athletic Sunday afternoons had
become hollow-voiced ghosts inhabiting an infinite recession
of weekends when he would not be here. His field was computer software (indeed, he *was* the software); theirs was
advertising or securities or the law, and though they all
helped uphold the Manhattan tent pole of a nationwide canopy
of rockets and promises, they spoke different languages
when there was no score to shout. "If I was John Lindsay,"
a man began, and rather than listen Tom seized a woman, who
whirled him around. These women: he had seen their beauty
pass from the smooth bodily complacence of young mother-
hood to the angular self-possession, slightly gray and wry, of
veteran wives. To have witnessed this, to have seen in the
sides of his vision so many pregnancies and births and quarrels
and near-divorces and divorces and affairs and near-affairs and
arrivals in vans and departures in vans, loomed, in retrospect,
as the one accomplishment of his tenancy here—a heap of
organic incident that in a village of old would have moldered
into wisdom. But he was not wise, merely older. The thought
of Texas frightened him: a desert of strangers, barbecues on
parched lawns, in the gaunt shade of oil rigs and radar dishes.

"We'll miss you," Linda Cotteral dutifully said. Mouselike,
she nestled when dancing; all men must look alike to her—a
wall of damp shirt.

"I doubt it," he responded, stumbling. It surprised him that
he didn't dance very well. He had danced a lot in Connecticut,
rather than make conversation, yet his finesse had flattened
along one of those hyperbolic curves that computers delight

in projecting. Men had been wrong ever to imagine the universe as a set of circles; in reality, nothing closes, everything
approaches, but never quite touches, its asymptote.

"Have you danced with Maggie?"

"Not for years. As you know."

"Don't you think you should?"

"She'd refuse."

"Ask her," Linda said, and left him for the arms of a man
who would be here next weekend, who was real.

Maggie liked living rooms; they flattered her sense of
courtesy and display. She had spread herself with her sleeves
on the big curved white sofa, white on white. Lou's voice
tinkled from the kitchen. Lou always gravitated, at parties,
to the kitchen, just as others, along personal magnetic lines,
drifted outside to the screened porch, or sought safety in the
bathroom. Picturing his wife perched on a kitchen stool,
comfortably showing her thighs and tapping her ashes into
the sink, Tom approached Maggie and, numb as a moth, asked
her to dance.

She looked up. Her eyes had been painted to look startled.
"Really?" she asked, and added, "I'm terribly tired."

"Me too."

She looked down to where her hands were folded in her
white lap. Her contemplative posture appeared to express the
hope that he, like an unharmonious thought, would melt
away.

Tom told her, "I'll never ask you again."

With a sigh, then sniffing as if to erase the sigh, Maggie
rose and went with him into the darkened playroom, where
other adults were dancing, folding each other into old remembered music. She lifted her arms to accept him; her wide sleeves

made her difficult to grasp. Her body in his arms, unexpectedly, felt wrong: something had unbalanced her—her third drink, or time. Her hand in his felt overheated.

"You're taller," she said.

"I am?"

"I believe you've grown, Tom."

"No, it's just that your memory of me has shrunk."

"Please, let's not talk memories. You asked me to dance."

"I've discovered I don't dance very well."

"Do your best."

"I always have."

"No."

"Don't you believe it was my best?"

"Of course I don't believe that."

Her hot hand was limp, but her body, as he tried to contain and steer it, seemed faintly resistant, as perhaps any idea does when it is embodied. He did not feel that she was rigid deliberately, as a rebuke to him, but that they both, once again, were encountering certain basic factors of gravity and inertia. She did not resist when, trying to solve their bad fit —trying to devise, as it were, an interface—he hugged her closer to his chest. Nor, however, did he feel her infuse this submission with conscious willingness, as lovers do when they transmute their bodies into pure sensitivity and volition. She held mute. While he sought for words to fill their grappling silence, she sniffed.

He said, "You have a cold."

She nodded.

He asked, "A fever?"

Again she nodded, more tersely, with a touch of the automatic, a touch he remembered as intrinsic to her manner of consent.

Surer of himself, he glided them across waxed squares of vinyl and heard his voice emerge enriched by a paternal, protective echo. "You shouldn't have come if you're sick."

"I wanted to."

"Why?" He knew the answer: because of him. He feared he was holding her so close she had felt his heart thump; he might injure her with his heart. He relaxed his right arm, and she accepted the inch of freedom as she had surrendered it, without spirit—a merely metric adjustment. And her voice, when she used it, swooped at the start and scratched, like an old record.

"Oh Tom," Maggie said, "you know me. I can't say no. If I'm invited to a party, I come." And she must have felt, as did he, that her shrug insufficiently broke the hold his silence would have clinched, for she snapped her head and said with angry emphasis, "Anyway, I *had* to come and say good*bye* to the Bridesons."

His silence had become a helpless holding on.

"Who have been so *kind*," Maggie finished. The music stopped. She tried to back out of his arms, but he held her until, in the little hi-fi cabinet with its sleepless incubatory glow, another record flopped from the stack. Softly fighting to be free, Maggie felt to him, with her great sleeves, like a sumptuous heavy bird that has evolved into innocence on an island, that can be seized by any passing sailor, and that will shortly become extinct. Facing downward to avoid her beating wings, he saw her thighs, fat in net tights, and had to laugh, not so much at this befuddled struggle as at the comedy of the female body, that kind white clown, all greasepaint and bounce. To have seized her again, to feel her contending, was simply jolly.

"Tom, let go of me."

I Will Not Let Thee Go, Except Thou Bless Me

"I can't."

Music released them from struggle. An antique record carried them back to wartime radio they had listened to as children, children a thousand miles apart. Maggie smoothed her fluffed cloth and formally permitted herself to be danced with. Her voice had become, with its faint bronchial rasp, a weapon cutting across the involuntary tendency of her body to melt, to glide. She held her face averted and downcast, so that her shoulders were not quite square with his; if he could adjust this nagging misalignment, perhaps by bringing her feverish hand closer to his shoulder, the fit would be again perfect, after a gap of years. He timidly tugged her hand, and she said harshly, "What do you want me to say?"

"Nothing. Something inoffensive."

"There's nothing to say, Tommy."

"O.K."

"You said it all, five years ago."

"Was it five?"

"Five."

"It doesn't seem that long."

"It does if you live it, minute after minute."

"I lived it too."

"No."

"O.K. Listen—"

"No. You promised we'd just dance."

But only a few bars of music, blurred saxophones and a ruminating clarinet, passed before she said, in a dangerously small and dreaming voice, "I was thinking, how funny . . . Five years ago you were my life and my death, and now . . ."

"Yes?"

"No, it wouldn't be fair. You're leaving."

"Come on, sweet Maggie, say it."

". . . you're just nothing."

He was paralyzed, but his body continued to move, and the music flowed on, out of some infinitely remote U.S.O. where doomed sailors swayed with their clinging girls.

She sniffed and repeated, "You're *nothing*, Tommy."

He heard himself laugh. "Thank you. I received the bit the first time."

Being nothing, he supposed, excused him from speech; his silence wrested an embarrassed giggle from her. She said, "Well, I suppose it proves I've grown."

"Yes," he agreed, trying to be inoffensive, "you are a beautifully growing girl."

"You were always full of compliments, Tommy."

Turquoise and pink flickered in the side of his vision; his shoulder was touched. Bugs Leonard asked to cut in. Tom backed off from Maggie, relieved to let go, yet hoping, as he yielded her, for a yielding glance. But her stare was stony, as it had been in the hall, except that there it had been directed past him, and here fell full upon him. He bowed.

Those hours after midnight, usually weightless, bent his bones in a strained curve that pressed against the inside of his forehead. Too weary to leave, he stood in the darkened playroom watching the others dance, and observed that Bugs and Maggie danced close, in wide confident circles that lifted her sleeves like true wings. A man sidled up to him and said, "If I was John Lindsay, I'd build a ten-foot wall across Ninety-sixth Street and forget it," and lurched away. Tom had known this man once. He went into the living room and offered here and there to say goodbye, startling conspiracies of people deep in conversation. They had forgotten he was leaving. He went into the kitchen to collect Lou; she recognized him, and doused her cigarette in the sink, and stepped down from the stool, smoothing her skirt. On his way from the bedroom with their coats, he ducked into the bathroom to see if he had aged; he was one of those who gravitated, at parties, to the bathroom. Of these Connecticut homes he would remember best the bright caves of porcelain fixtures: the shower curtains patterned in antique automobiles, the pastel towelling, the shaggy toilet-seat coverlets, the inevitable cartoon anthology on the water closet. The lecherous gleam of hygiene. Goodbye, Crane. Goodbye, Kleenex. See you in Houston.

Lou was waiting in the foyer. A well-rehearsed team, they pecked the hostess farewell, apologized in unison for being party poops, and went into the green darkness. Their headlights ransacked the bushes along this driveway for the final time.

Safely on the road, Lou asked, "Did Maggie kiss you goodbye?"

"No. She was quite unfriendly."

"Why shouldn't she be?"

"No reason. She should be. She should be awful and she was." He was going to agree, agree, all the way to Texas.

"She kissed *me*," Lou said.

"When?"

"When you were in the bathroom."

"Where did she kiss you?"

"I was standing in the foyer waiting for you to get done admiring yourself or whatever you were doing. She swooped out of the living room."

"I mean where *on* you?"

: 57 :

"On the mouth."

"Warmly?"

"Very. I didn't know how to respond. I'd never been kissed like that, by another woman."

"*Did* you respond?"

"Well, a little. It happened so quickly."

He must not appear too interested, or seem to gloat. "Well," Tom said, "she may have been drunk."

"Or else very tired," said Lou, "like the rest of us."

The Corner

THE TOWN is one of those that people pass through on the way to somewhere else; so its inhabitants have become expert in giving directions. Ray Blandy cannot be on his porch five minutes before a car, baffled by the lack of signs at the corner, will shout to him, "Is this the way to the wharf?" or "Am I on the right road to East Mather?" Using words and gestures that have become rote, Ray heads it on its way, with something of the satisfaction with which he mails a letter, or flushes a toilet, or puts in another week at Unitek Electronics. Catty-corner across the awkward intersection (Wharf Street swerves south and meets Reservoir Road and Prudence Avenue at acute, half-blind angles), Mr. Latroy, a milkman who is home from noon on, and who is also an auxiliary policeman, directs automobiles uncertain if, to reach the famous old textile mill in Lacetown, they should bear left around the traffic island or go straight up the hill. There is nothing on the corner to hold cars here except the small variety store run by an old Dutch couple, the Van Der Bijns. Its modest size and dim, rusted advertisements are geared to foot traffic. Children going to school stop here for candy, and townspeople after work stop for cigarettes and bread, but for long tracts of the day there is little for Mr. Van Der Bijn to do but sit behind his display windows and grieve that the cars passing through take the corner too fast.

There have been accidents. Eight years ago, around eleven o'clock of a muggy July morning, when Susan Craven had been standing on her sidewalk wondering whether she should go to the playground or give Linda Latroy's back yard one more try, a clam truck speedily rounding the corner snapped a kingbolt, went right up over the banking, swung— while the driver wildly twisted the slack steering wheel— within a foot of unblinking, preoccupied Susan, bounced back down the banking, straight across Prudence Street, and smack, in a shower of shingles, into the house then owned by Miss Beulah Cogswell. She has since died, after living for years on her telling of the accident: "*Well*, I was in the kitchen making my morning *tea* and naturally thought it was just *another* of those dreadful sonic booms. But, *when* I go with my cup and saucer into the front parlor here *right* where my television set had been was this dirty windshield with a man's absolutely *white* face, mouthing like a fish, the carpet *drenched* with shingles and plaster and the corner cupboard three feet into the room and not one, would you be*lieve* it, not a single piece of bone china so much as *cracked!*" Now her house is occupied by a young couple with a baby that cries all night. The Cravens have moved to Falmouth, selling their house to the Blandys. And the Latroy girls have heard that Susan is married, to an Air Force man from Otis Base; it's hard to believe. It seems just yesterday she was brushed by death, a rude little girl with fat legs.

Long before this, so long ago only the Van Der Bijns and

Mrs. Billy Hannaford witnessed the wreckage, a drunken driver took the corner too fast in the opposite direction from the truck and skidded up over the curb into the left-hand display window of the variety store. No one was hurt; the Van Der Bijns were asleep upstairs and the drunk, well known locally, remained relaxed and amused. But the accident left a delicate scar on the corner, in the perceptible disparity between the two large plate-glass panes: the left one is less wavery and golden in tint than the right, and its frame is of newer molding, which does not perfectly match.

Somewhere between these two accidents there is an old man down from New Hampshire, lost, blinded, he said, by blazing headlights, who drove right over the traffic island, straddling it in his high 1939 Buick, shearing off the Stop sign and eviscerating his muffler on the stump. And lost in the snowy mists of time is the child who sledded down Reservoir Road and was crushed beneath a Studebaker, in the days before cars could be counted on to be everywhere. It is strange that more accidents do not occur. Everyone ignores the rusty Stop sign. Teen-agers begin drag races down by the wharf and use the traffic island as a finish post. Friday and Saturday nights, there is screeching and roaring until two and three in the morning. Trucks heave and shift gears, turning north. Summer weekends see a parade of motorboats on trailers. The housing development, Marshview, on the east end of town, adds dozens of cars to the daily traffic. The corner has already been widened—the Van Der Bijns' house once had a front yard. Old photographs exist, on sepia cardboard, that show fewer wires on the poles, a great beech where none now stands, a front yard at the house that was not then a store, the dark house painted white, no porch at the Blandys', no traffic island, and a soft, trodden, lanelike look to the surface of the street. When the Van Der Bijns move or die (the same thing to the Town Clerk), their house will be taken by eminent domain and the corner widened still further, enabling the cars to go still faster. Engineers' drawings are already on file at Town Hall.

Yet, though the inhabitants strain their ears at night waiting for the squeal of tires to mushroom into the crash of metal and the splintering of glass, nothing usually happens. The corner is one of those places where nothing much happens except traffic and weather. Even death, when it came for Miss Cogswell, came as a form of traffic, as an ambulance in the driveway, and a cluster of curious neighborhood children.

The weather happens mostly in the elm, a vast elm not yet felled by the blight. Its branches overarch the corner. Its drooping twigs brush the roofs of the dark house, the young couple's house, and the Latroys'. Shaped like a river system, meandering tributaries thickening and flowing into the trunk, but three-dimensional, a solid set of streets where pigeons strut, meet, and mate, the tree's pattern of limbs fills the Blandys' bedroom windows and their eyes on awaking in all weathers: glistening and sullen in November rain, so one feels the awful weight the tree upholds, like a cast-iron cloud; airy tracery after a snow, or in the froth of bloom; in summer a curtain of green, with a lemon-yellow leaf, turned early, here and there like a random stitch. Lying bedridden in fever or in despair, each of the Blandys has concluded, separately, that though there was nothing to life but lying here looking at the elm forever, it would suffice—it would be, though just barely, enough.

The elm's leaves in autumn blow by the bushel down Prudence Avenue into the Van Der Bijns' side yard, confirming the old man's contention that the weather is always

outrageous. He came to this country before the war, foreseeing it, and still finds the intemperances of the American
climate remarkable. The faithful gray damp of Holland is in
his bones. For months ahead of time, he foresees the troublesome wonder of snow, and gloats over his bizarre fate of
having to shovel it. Though weak from his long days of
sitting, he shovels compulsively, even during a blizzard trying
to keep his forty feet of sidewalk as clean as swept tiles.
Some ironical gallantry seems intended—a humorous grateful
willingness to have the land that gave him refuge take his life
with its barbaric weather. Our summer's extremes also as-
tonish him. Four sunny days become a drought in his eyes,
which are delft blue and perpetually wide open, within deep,
skeletal sockets. Each growing season, as he observes its effects
on Mrs. Hannaford's bushes and lawn, seems in some way
abnormal, unprecedented, weird. "Naaow, da forsydia last
yaar wasn't aaout yet vor two weeks!" "Naaow, I'fe nefer
once zeen her grass zo zoon brown!"

And Mrs. Hannaford, whose house of all the houses on the
corner is most distant from the elm, sees this tree as a benign
veil drawn across the tar-shingled roofs and ungainly dor-
mers of the neighborhood, as a sea fan superimposed on a
cockleshell sunset, as a living entity that has doubled its size
since as a girl she studied it from the same windows she now
sleeps behind, and thought she saw the robed shadow of Jesus
moving in its branches, and prayed that the end of the world
be not yet come.

The people on the corner do not know each other very
well. It is the houses who know each other, whose windows
watch. Mrs. Billy Hannaford goes to the Episcopal church
whenever Communion is offered; she dresses in purple and
walks with a cane, her cheeks painted salmon, her hair rinsed

blue. Some weekend nights, cars belonging to the Blandys' friends are parked in front of their house until hours after midnight. The young couple's baby cries. The man who lives in the dark house is off in his car from seven to seven, and his wife is indistinguishable among the two or three ginger-haired women who come and go. The Latroys have beautiful blond daughters, and much of the hot-rodding on the corner is for their benefit. This is what the houses know of each other's inner lives, what their windows can verify.

Rain made Ray Blandy romantic and he had hoped to make love, but his wife had fallen asleep in the middle of an embrace, and he had risen from the bed in anger. It was Saturday midnight. He stood by the window, wanting to be loved by the rain. There was a nearing roar of motors and a braking slither, and he saw (this is what he thought he saw) a speeding VW bus pursued by a black sedan. The bus disappeared behind the edge of the dark house. The sedan skidded on the smooth patch where just that April some frost-heaves had been re-tarred. The sedan's weight swung from side to side, like an accelerated dance step. Out of control, the car went up with one pair of tires onto the sidewalk, and also disappeared. Then, there was a thump, not deafening but definite, and deeply satisfying; and a silence. Then the high-pitched gear whine of a prolonged backing-up. The VW bus appeared, backward, from behind the dark house. Shouting voices dropped to a mutter. Mr. Latroy, wearing his auxiliary-policeman's badge, appeared in front of his house. The Van Der Bijns' lights went on.

June Blandy sat up in bed. "What was that?"

"You mean you weren't asleep, you were just faking?"

"I was sound asleep, but something thumped."

"Sonic boom," he told her. She missed the allusion. He told her, "A car lost control going around the corner and hit something up the street. I can't see what."

"Why are you just standing there? Let's *go*." Last year, when a dog had been hit on the corner and their neighbors from the curb idly watched it yelp and writhe, she had spontaneously run into the street and taken the broken animal into her arms. Now she put on her bathrobe and was past him, and down the stairs, and out of the door. He looked in two closets for a bathrobe or a raincoat and finally, afraid of missing everything, followed her into the drizzle in his pajamas.

The corner had cracked open like a piñata, spilling absurdly dressed people. Mr. Van Der Bijn wore a long nightcap, with a tassel—who would have imagined it? Mrs., her daytime braids undone, had gray hair down to her waist. The young mother, baby on hip, wore bell-bottom pants of crimson crushed velvet: her normal at-home costume? Why were so many people up and dressed after midnight? Did Mr. Latroy never sleep? His milk route began at four. From the dark house emerged two middle-aged women, ginger-haired and flirtatious, in house slippers. "That's a cute costume," one of them said to Ray. A tense, slight man with a rash of pimples on his forehead, he looked down and adjusted his pajama fly.

His wife told him, "About six people got out of the car into the bus and drove away. Shouldn't somebody have stopped them, or done *some*thing?" She had turned from him to address a larger audience, her voice lifted operatically.

The mother in red pants said, "One of them came into the house to call the police and another one came after her and said not to bother, they'd drive to the station, it'd be faster."

She had a narrow, impoverished face but an exotic broad accent, Midwestern or Western. As she spoke, she kept bouncing the baby on her hip.

A ginger-haired lady said, "One of them said it was all right, she was the wife of a fireman."

"Uh-ohh," the other said. "He's been going to too many fires." There was general laughter.

The drizzle was lifting, but they drew snugly closer beneath the sheltering elm, as if to consolidate their sudden conquest of the distance the houses had always imposed between them. "Naaow, isn't dis wedder somezing," Mr. Van Der Bijn said, and again they all laughed, having heard him say it so often before. The driver of the disabled car glanced toward them enviously. His sedan was up the street, sideways against a telephone pole; it had spun almost totally around. His gaze inhibited the carnival crowd on the corner. He smelled of recent danger, and was dangerous. The man who lived in the dark house emerged in pants and rumpled shirt and spectacles; his eyes looked rubbed, as after sleep or a long bout of television. His ladies grew animated; the more flirtatious one told Ray her version of the accident. The VW was coming down Prudence Street, and didn't stop at the Stop sign, they never do, and the black sedan, to avoid hitting it, swerved to the left, into the pole. Ray told her, No, he had happened to be at his window, and the VW was being chased by the other—a drag race, obviously. June asked, "Hasn't anybody called the police?"

Mrs. Van Der Bijn said, "Mr. Latroy has." But by this she meant, probably, that in a sense he *was* police; for he had not moved from the sidewalk. He stood there serenely, his face tilted upward, as if basking on a sunny day. The window above him lit up, and two of his beautiful daughters were framed in it, their blond hair incandescent. A carload of male teen-agers swung around the corner, abruptly braked, and eased by. The two daughters waved. Another car stopped, and asked the way to East Mather. Three voices at once—Ray, Mr. Latroy, and a ginger-haired lady—chorused the directions.

June was conferring with the girl in velvet pants. The girl agreed to go inside and call the police. Her husband was asleep. He was a very sound sleeper. "I can never get the lunk up, to take care of the brat. Every night, it's the same story."

"She has fear," Mrs. Van Der Bijn announced. "You must sing her to sleep."

The girl studied Mrs. Van Der Bijn and handed her the baby and went into her house. The baby began its feeble, well-practiced whimper, paced to last for hours. Mrs. Van Der Bijn began to sing, in a distant lost language, low in her throat.

The driver of the sedan came closer. He swaggered like a man with something to sell, his hands in his pockets. He was a young stocky man, with hair combed wet, so the tooth furrows showed. "It's all right," he told them. "I got everybody's number. Nothing to worry about," he said, and told them his story. There was a third car. A yellow convertible, a crazy man. Down by the wharf, it had cut right in front of him, right through that metal rail there, and tried to run him off the road. He had given chase, lost control at the corner, and had this accident. There was a VW bus right behind him. It had stopped, and the people in it had said they knew the driver of the convertible, and would catch him and bring him back. As some kind of insurance, the sedan's passengers had crowded into the bus, and off they had all gone. They should be back any minute. At any rate, it didn't matter, because he had the numbers.

It was a strange story, but he pulled from a pocket the little pad upon which he had firmly written down two long numbers. Ray wondered how the man had focussed his eyes on those speeding, shuttling vehicles, and why in his own memory the bus had been ahead of the sedan, and why he had not seen the third car, the convertible. The rest of the corner, too, distrusted the driver's story, and, amid polite comments and expressions of interest, slowly closed against him, isolating him again. Undiscouraged, like an encyclopedia salesman turned from the door, the driver walked briskly away, toward his crippled car and, farther down the street, an approaching blue twinkle.

The police car pulled up. They all knew the cops that emerged; one was a wife-beater, and the other had been a high-school football star. The baby's mother came out of her house and stood so close that Ray, looking down, saw beside his own knobby bare feet cerise satin slippers, with bunny-tail pompons. It was as when bombs fall, baring swaths of wallpaper, tasselled pull-cords, unexpected bathroom tiles, broken diagrams. The two policemen softly interviewed the driver, the people at the corner watched from a safe distance and kept their versions to themselves, the gentle event of the rain ceased, the law closed its notebook, the elm sighed, the little crowd reluctantly broke up and returned to their houses. Later, some heard, but only the street lamp saw, the tow truck come and take the sedan away. Overhead, the clouds paled and pulled apart, revealing stars.

The Corner

The driver's story had been strange, but no stranger, to the people who live here, than the truth that the corner is one among many on the map of the town, and the town is a dot on the map of the state, and the state a mere patch on the globe, and the globe insignificant from any of the stars overhead.

The Witnesses

FRED PROUTY, I was told yesterday, is dead—dead, as I imagine it, of cigarettes, confusion, and conscience, though none of these was the *c* my informant named. He died on the West Coast, thousands of miles from both his ex-wives and all his sad expensive children. I pictured him lying in a highly clean hospital bed, smothering in debt, interlaced with tubular machinery, overlooking a sprawling colorless spireless land-scape worlds removed from the green and pointed East that had formed him. Though we had come from the same town (New Haven) and the same schools (Hotchkiss, Yale) and the same background (our grandfathers had been ministers and our fathers lawyers), Fred and I never were very close. We belonged to a generation that expressed affection through shades of reticence. The war, perhaps, had made us conservative and cautious; our task had been to bring a soci-ety across a chasm and set it down safely on the other side, unchanged. That it changed later was not our affair. After the war Fred had gone into advertising, and I into securities. For a decade, we shared Manhattan and intermittent meals.

The Witnesses

The last time I had him in my home, there had been a strangeness and, worse, a tactlessness for which I suppose I never quite forgave him. It was the high noon of the Eisenhower era, just before Fred's first divorce. He called me at work and invited himself to our apartment for a drink, and asked, surprisingly, if he might bring a friend.

Jeanne and I had the West Thirteenth Street place then. Of our many apartments, I remember it most fondly. The front windows looked across the street into an elementary school, and the back windows, across some untended yards crammed with trees of heaven, into a mysterious factory. Whatever the factory made, the process entailed great shimmering ribbons and spinning reels of color being manipulated like giant harps by Negro men and Puerto Rican women. Rising in the morning, we could see them spinning and, eating breakfast in the kitchen, we saw into windows where children were snipping and pasting up, in season, Easter eggs and pumpkins, Christmas trees and hearts and hatchets and cherries. Almost always a breeze flowed through our two large rooms, now from bedroom to living room, from factory to school, and now the other way, bringing with it the sounds of street traffic, which included the drunks on the pavement outside the Original Mario's. Ours was the third floor—the lowest we have ever lived.

Fred came promptly at seven. As he climbed the stairs, I thought the woman behind him was his wife. Indeed, she resembled his wife—an inch taller, perhaps, and a bit more adventurously dressed, but the same physical type, heavy and rounded below the waist, ectomorphically slender above. The two women had the same kind of ears, cupped and protruding, which compelled the same cover-up hairdo and understated earrings. Fred introduced her to us as Priscilla

Evans. Jeanne had not known Marjorie Prouty well, yet to ask her to meet and entertain this other woman on no basis beyond the flat implication of her being Fred's mistress was, as perhaps Fred in his infatuation imperfectly understood, a *gaffe*. Jeanne's arm went forward stiffly to take the girl's hand.

A "girl" more by status than by age. Priscilla was, though unmarried and a year or two younger, one of us—I never knew where Fred met her, but it could have been at work or a party or a crew race, if he still went to them. She had the social grace to be embarrassed, and I wondered how Fred had persuaded her to come. He must have told her I was a very close friend, which perhaps, in his mind, I was. I was New Haven to him, distant and safe; touchingly, his heart had never left that middling town. I would like to reward the loyalty of a ghost by remembering that evening—hour, really, for we did not invite them for dinner—as other than dull. But, in part because Jeanne and I felt constrained from asking them any direct questions, in part because Priscilla put on a shy manner, and in part because Fred seemed sheepishly bewildered by this party he had arranged, our conversation was stilted. We discussed what was current in those departed days: McCarthy's fall, Kefauver's candidacy, Dulles' tactlessness. Dulles had recently called Goa a "Portuguese province," offending India, and given his "brinkmanship" interview, offending everyone. Priscilla said she thought Dulles deserved credit for at least his honesty, for saying out loud what everybody knew anyway. It is the one remark of hers that I remember, and it made me look at her again.

She was like Marjorie but with a difference. There was something twisted and wry about her face, some arresting trace of pain endured and wisdom reluctantly acquired. Her life, I felt, had been cracked and mended, and in this her form differed from that of Fred's wife or, for that matter, of my own. My attention, then, for an instant snagged on the irregularity where Fred's spirit had caught, taken root, and hastily flourished. I try to remember them sitting beside each other—he slumped in the canvas sling chair, she upright on the half of the Sheraton settee nearer him. He had bronze hair receding on a brow where the freckles advanced. His nose was thin and straight, his eyes pale blue and slightly bulged behind the silver-frame spectacles that, through some eccentricity of the nose pads, perched too far out from his face. Fred's mouth was one of those sharply cut sets of lips, virtually pretty, that frown down from portraits on bank walls. Something farmerish made his hands heavy; when he clasped his knee, the knuckles were squeezed white. In the awkward sling chair, he clasped his knee; his neck seemed red above the fresh white collar; he was anxious for her. He disagreed with her praise of Dulles, knowing we were liberals. She sat demure, yet with something gaudy and man-catching about her clothes, and there was—I imagine or remember—a static energy imposed on the space between her body and Fred's, as in that visual fooler which now seems two black profiles and now a single white vase, so that the arm of the settee, the mahogany end table inlaid with satinwood, the unlit lamp with the base of beaten copper, the ceramic ashtray full of unfiltered butts shaped like commas, the very shadows and blurs of refraction were charged with a mysterious content, the "relationship" of these two tense and unwelcome visitors.

I want to believe that Jeanne, however halfheartedly, invited them to dine with us; of course Fred refused, saying they must go, suddenly rising, apologetic, his big hands dangling, his lady looking up at him for leadership. They left before eight, and my embarrassed deafness lifts. I can hear Jeanne complaining distinctly, "Well, that was strange!"

"Very strange behavior, from Fred."

"Was he showing her that he has respectable friends, or what?"

"Surely that's a deduction she didn't need to have proved."

"She may have a mistrustful nature."

"What did you make of her?"

"I'm afraid I must say she struck me as very ordinary."

I said, "It's hilarious, how much of a copy she is of his wife."

"Yes, and not as finished as Marjorie. A poor copy."

"How far," I said, "people go out of their way to mess up their lives." I was trying to agree with some unstated assertion of hers.

"Yes," Jeanne said, straightening the bent cushions on the settee, "that was very dismal. Tell me. Are we going to have to see them again? Are we some sort of furniture so they can play house, or what?"

"No, I'm sure not. I'll tell Fred not, if I must."

"I don't care what people do, but I don't like being used."

I felt she expected me, though innocent, to apologize. I said, "I can't imagine what got into Fred. He's usually nothing if not correct."

For a moment, Jeanne may have considered letting me have the last word. Then she said firmly, "I found the whole thing extremely dreary."

. . .

: 74 :

The Witnesses

The next day, or the day after, Fred called me at the office, and thanked me. He said, with an off-putting trace of the stammering earnestness his clients must have found endearing, that it had meant more to him than I could know, and some day he would tell me why. I may have been incurious and cool. He did not call again. Then I heard he was divorced, and had left Madison Avenue for a consulting outfit starting up in Chicago. His new wife, I was told, came originally from Indianapolis. I tried to remember if Priscilla Evans had had a Midwestern accent and could not.

Years later, but some time ago, when Kennedy Airport was still called Idlewild, Fred and I accidentally met in the main terminal—those acres of white floor where the islands of white waiting chairs cast no shadows. He was on his way back to Los Angeles. He was doing publicity work for one of the studios that can television series. Although he did not tell me, he was on the verge of his second divorce. He seemed heavier, and his hands were puffy. His bronze hair was thinning now on the back of his skull; there were a few freckles in the bald spot. He was wearing horn-rimmed glasses, which did not make him look youthful. He kept taking them off, as if bothered by their fit, exposing, on the bridge of his nose, the red moccasin-shaped dents left by the pads of his old silver frames. He had somehow gone pasty, sheltered from the California sun, and I wondered if I looked equally tired and corrupt to him. Little in my life had changed. We had had one child, a daughter. We had moved uptown, to a bigger, higher, bleaker apartment. Kennedy's bear market had given me a dull spring.

Fred and I sought shelter in the curtained bar a world removed from the sun-stricken airfield and the glinting planes whose rows of rivets and portholes seemed to be spelling a

: 75 :

message in punched code. He told me about his life without complaint and let me guess that it was going bad. He had switched to filtered cigarettes but there was a new recklessness in his drinking. I watched his hands and suddenly remembered how those same hands looked squeezed around the handle of a lacrosse stick. He apologized for the night he had brought the girl to our apartment.

I said I had almost forgotten, but that at the time it had seemed out of character.

"How did we look?" he asked.

I didn't understand. "Worried," I said. "She seemed to us much like Marjorie."

He smiled and said, "That's how it turned out. Just like Marjorie." He had had three drinks and took off his glasses. His eyes were still a schoolboy's, but his mouth no longer would have looked well on a bank wall; the prim cut of it had been boozed and blurred away, and a dragging cynicism had done something ineradicable to the corners. His lips groped for precision. "I wanted you to see us," he said. "I wanted somebody to see us in love. I loved her so much," he said, "I loved her so much it makes me sick to remember it. Whenever I come back to the city, whenever I pass any place we went together when it was beginning, I fall, I kind of drop an inch or so inside my skin. Herbie, do you know what I'm talking about, have you ever had the feeling?"

I did not think it was a correct question or that I was expected to answer it. Perhaps my silence was construed as a rebuke.

Fred rubbed his forehead and closed his bulged blue eyes and said, "I knew it was wrong. I knew it was going to end in a mess, it had nowhere else to go. That's why I brought her over that time. She hated it, she didn't want to come. But I wanted it. I wanted somebody I knew to see us when it was good. No, I wanted somebody who knew me to see me happy. I had never known I could be that happy. God. I wanted you and Jeanne to see us together before it went bad." He opened his scared eyes and told me, "So it wouldn't be totally lost."

Solitaire

THE CHILDREN WERE ASLEEP, and his wife had gone out to a
meeting; she was like his father in caring about the community. He found the deck of cards in the back of a desk
drawer and sat down at the low round table. He had
reached a juncture in his life where there was nothing to do
but play solitaire. It was the perfect, final retreat—beyond
solitaire, he imagined, there was nothing but madness. Only
solitaire utterly eased the mind; only solitaire created that
blankness into which a saving decision might flow. Convivial-
ity demanded other people, with their fretful emanations of
desire; reading imposed the author's company; and one
emerged from the anesthetic of drunkenness to find that the
operation had not been performed. But in the rise and
collapse of the alternately colored ranks of cards, in the
grateful transpositions and orderly revelations and unexpected redemptions, the circuits of the mind found an
occupation exactly congruent with their own secret structure.
The mind was filled without being strained. The week after
he graduated from college—already married, his brain worn

to the point where a page of newspaper seemed a cruelly ramifying puzzle—he played solitaire night after night by the glow of a kerosene lamp on an old kitchen table in Vermont; and at the end of the week he had seen the way that his life must go in the appallingly wide world that had opened before him. He had drawn a straight line from that night to the night of his death, and began walking on it.

During that week he had remembered how in his childhood his mother would play solitaire by the light of the stained-glass chandelier in the dining room. His father would be out somewhere, doing good for the community, and he and his mother would be alone. He was an only child, and as such obscurely felt himself to be the center of the sadness that oppressed them. Frightened of her silence and of the slithering of the cards, he would beg her to stop. Tell me a story, come into the kitchen and make some toast, go to bed, anything; but stop.

"One more game," his mother said, her faced pitted and dragged by the shadows cast by the overhead chandelier. And then she slipped into one of the impersonations whereby she filled their empty house with phantoms, as if to make up to him for the brothers and sisters she had not, somehow, been permitted to give him. "The weary gambler stakes his all," she said in a soft but heavy monotone. "The night is late. The crowds have left the gaming tables. One lonely figure remains, his house, his car, his yacht, his jewels, his very life hinging on the last turn of the cards."

"Don't, Mother; *don't!*" He burst into tears, and she looked up and smiled, as if greeting a fond forgotten sight upon her return from a long journey. He felt her wonder, *Who is this child?* It was as if the roof of the house were torn off, displaying the depth of night sky.

He knew now that her mind had been burdened in that period. Everything was being weighed in it. He remembered very faintly—for he had tried to erase it immediately —her asking him if he would like to go alone with her far away, and live a new life. *No*, must have been his answer, *Mother, don't;* for he had loved his father, loved him out of the silence and blindness that wait at the bottom of our brains as the final possibility, the second baptism. The removal of his father plunged him toward that black pool prematurely. And she, too, must have felt a lack of ripeness, for in the end she merely moved them all a little distance, to a farm where he grew up in solitude and which at the first opportunity he left, a farm where now his father and mother still performed, with an intimate expertness that almost justified them, the half-comic routines of their incompatibility. In the shrill strength of his childish fear he had forced this on them; he was, in this sense, their creator, their father.

And now the father of others. Odd, he thought, setting a black nine below a red ten, how thoroughly our lives are devoted to doing the contrary of what our parents did. He had married early, to escape the farm, and had rapidly given his wife children, to make his escape irrevocable. Also he had wished to spare his children the responsibility and terror of solitude. He wondered if they loved him as he had loved his father, wondered what depth of night sky would be displayed to them by his removal. To some extent he was already removed. They formed a club from which he was excluded. Their corporate commotion denied him access. The traces of his own face in their faces troubled him with the suspicion that he had squandered his identity. Slowly he had come to see that children are not our creations but our guests, people who enter the world by our invitation but with their smiles and dispositions already prepared in some mysterious other room. Their predictable woe and fright and the crippled shapes they might take had imperceptibly joined the finances and the legalities as considerations that were finite, manageable. Problems to which there is any solution at all, no matter how difficult and complex, are not really problems. (*Red four on black five.*) Night by night, lying awake, he had digested the embarrassments, the displacements, the disappointments, the reprimands and lectures and appeals that were certain; one by one he had made impossibilities possible. At last he had stripped the problem to its two white poles, the two women.

His wife was fair, with pale eyelashes and hair containing, when freshly shampooed, reddish lights. His mistress was as black-and-white as a drawing in ink: her breasts always shocked him with their electric silken pallor, and the contrast with the dark nipples and aureoles. In the summer, she tanned; his wife freckled. His wife had the more delicate mind, but his mistress, having suffered more, knew more that he didn't know. Their opposition was not simple. His wife's handwriting, developed out of the printing she had been taught at a progressive school, looked regular but was often illegible; the other's, with its hurried stenographic slant, was always clear, even when phrasing panic. His wife, carnally entered, opened under him as an intimidating moist void; his mistress in contrast felt dry and tight, so tight the first thrusts quite hurt. His wife, now that she saw herself on the edge of an abyss, clung to him with an ardor that his mistress would have found immodest. He had come to feel a furtive relief when a day passed without love-making being thrust upon him; pinned between whirlpools, he was sated with the sound and sight of women crying. His mistress cried big: with thrilling swiftness her face dissolved and, her mouth smeared out of all shape, she lurched against him with an awkward bump and soaked his throat in abusive sobs. Whereas his wife wept like a miraculous icon, her face immobile while the tears ran, and so silently that as they lay together in bed at night he would have to ask her, "Are you crying?" Back and forth, back and forth like a sore fist his heart oscillated between them, and the oscillations grew in intensity as the two poles drew together and demanded that he choose one. He had allowed them to draw together, had allowed his wife to know, and allowed his mistress to know that she knew, in the hope that they would merge—would turn out to be, in fact, one woman, with no choice needed, or the decision settled between them. He had miscalculated. Though he had drawn them so close that one settling into his embrace could smell the other's perfume, each woman became more furiously herself.

(*A king uncovered, but nowhere to put him.*) How could he balance their claims and rights? The list was entirely one-sided. Prudence, decency, pity—not light things—all belonged to the guardian of his children and home; and these he would lose. He would lose the half-run-down neighborhood that he loved, the summer evenings spent scratching in his little garden of lettuce, the gritty adhesion of his elder daughter's hand to his as they walked to the popsicle store, the decade of books and prints and records and furniture that had accumulated, the cellar full of carpentry tools, the attic full of old magazines. And he would as well lose his own conception of himself, for to abandon his children and a woman who with scarcely a complaint or a quarrel had given him her youth was simply not what he would do. He was the son of parents who had stayed together for his sake. That straight line, once snapped, could not be set straight again.

While on the other side there was nothing, or next to nothing—merely a cry, a cry for him that he had never heard before. No doubt it was momentary; but so was life. She had nothing to give him but bereavement and a doubtless perishable sense of his existing purely as a man. Her presence made him happy and her near presence made him very happy. Yet even when they were so close together their very skins felt wished away, strange glass obstacles came between them, transparent elbows and icy hard surfaces that constituted, he supposed, the structure of what is called morality.

The weary gambler stakes his all. This game was clearly headed nowhere. An ominous unanimity of red had pretty well blocked the seven ranks. The kings had been buried for lack of space, one of the aces was not yet up, and the cards left in his hand were few. He fanned them and found that in fact there were three. He turned the top one up. The eight of spades. He put it below a red nine, but this unblocked nothing. Two cards left. He decided upon a gamble. A card for his wife, a card for *her*. His heart began to tremble at this boldness. In the months past, he had learned to listen to his heart; he had never noticed before what a positive will this supposedly oblivious organ possessed. On his way to a tryst it would press in his throat like a large bird trying to escape a trap, and at night when he lay down in the hope of sleeping it would churn and rattle on his ribs like the blade of a Waring Blender chopping ice.

He turned the first card and looked down at it from what felt like a great height. The ten of diamonds, for his wife. It was a strong card. He felt frightened, and looked down at the spiderweb back of the last card with a sensation of his vision being impaired by the roaring in his chest.

Instead of turning the last card over, he tore it across; the card was plastic-coated and tough, and crumpled before it tore. From a fragment he saw that it had been the missing ace. No matter. He was a modern man, not superstitious even alone with himself; his life must flow from within. He had made his decision, and sat inert, waiting for grief to be laid upon him.

The Orphaned
Swimming Pool

MARRIAGES, like chemical unions, release upon dissolution packets of the energy locked up in their bonding. There is the piano no one wants, the cocker spaniel no one can take care of. Shelves of books suddenly stand revealed as burdensomely dated and unlikely to be reread; indeed, it is difficult to remember who read them in the first place. And what of those old skis in the attic? Or the doll house waiting to be repaired in the basement? The piano goes out of tune, the dog goes mad. The summer that the Turners got their divorce, their swimming pool had neither a master nor a mistress, though the sun beat down day after day, and a state of drought was declared in Connecticut.

It was a young pool, only two years old, of the fragile type fashioned by laying a plastic liner within a carefully carved hole in the ground. The Turners' side yard looked infernal while it was being done; one bulldozer sank into the mud and had to be pulled free by another. But by mid-summer the new grass was sprouting, the encircling flagstones were in place, the blue plastic tinted the water a heavenly blue, and it had to be admitted that the Turners had scored again. They were always a little in advance of their friends. He was a tall, hairy-backed man with long arms, and a nose flattened by football, and a sullen look of too much blood; she was a fine-boned blonde with dry blue eyes and lips usually held parted and crinkled as if about to ask a worrisome, or whimsical, question. They never seemed happier, nor their marriage healthier, than those two summers. They grew brown and supple and smooth with swimming. Ted would begin his day with a swim, before dressing to catch the train, and Linda would hold court all day amid crowds of wet matrons and children, and Ted would return from work to find a poolside cocktail party in progress, and the couple would end their day at midnight, when their friends had finally left, by swimming nude, before bed. What ecstasy! In darkness the water felt mild as milk and buoyant as helium, and the swimmers became giants, gliding from side to side in a single languorous stroke.

The next May, the pool was filled as usual, and the usual after-school gangs of mothers and children gathered, but Linda, unlike her, stayed indoors. She could be heard within the house, moving from room to room, but she no longer emerged, as in the other summers, with a cheerful tray of ice and a brace of bottles, and Triscuits and lemonade for the children. Their friends felt less comfortable about appearing, towels in hand, at the Turners' on weekends. Though Linda had lost some weight and looked elegant, and Ted was cumbersomely jovial, they gave off the faint, sleepless, awkward-making aroma of a couple in trouble. Then, the day after school was out, Linda fled with the children to her parents in

Ohio. Ted stayed nights in the city, and the pool was deserted. Though the pump that ran the water through the filter continued to mutter in the lilacs, the cerulean pool grew cloudy. The bodies of dead horseflies and wasps dotted the still surface. A speckled plastic ball drifted into a corner beside the diving board and stayed there. The grass between the flagstones grew lank. On the glass-topped poolside table, a spray can of Off! had lost its pressure and a gin-and-tonic glass held a sere mint leaf. The pool looked desolate and haunted, like a stagnant jungle spring; it looked poisonous and ashamed. The postman, stuffing overdue notices and pornography solicitations into the mailbox, averted his eyes from the side yard politely.

Some June weekends, Ted sneaked out from the city. Families driving to church glimpsed him dolefully sprinkling chemical substances into the pool. He looked pale and thin. He instructed Roscoe Chace, his neighbor on the left, how to switch on the pump and change the filter, and how much chlorine and Algitrol should be added weekly. He explained he would not be able to make it out every weekend—as if the distance that for years he had travelled twice each day, gliding in and out of New York, had become an impossibly steep climb back into the past. Linda, he confided vaguely, had left her parents in Akron and was visiting her sister in Minneapolis. As the shock of the Turners' joint disappearance wore off, their pool seemed less haunted and forbidding. The Murtaugh children—the Murtaughs, a rowdy, numerous family, were the Turners' right-hand neighbors—began to use it, without supervision. So Linda's old friends, with their children, began to show up, "to keep the Murtaughs from drowning each other." For if anything were to happen to a Murtaugh, the poor Turners (the adjective had become automatic) would be sued for everything, right when they could least afford it. It became, then, a kind of duty, a test of loyalty, to use the pool.

July was the hottest in twenty-seven years. People brought their own lawn furniture over in station wagons and set it up. Teen-age offspring and Swiss *au-pair* girls were established as lifeguards. A nylon rope with flotation corks, meant to divide the wading end from the diving end of the pool, was found coiled in the garage and reinstalled. Agnes Klee-field contributed an old refrigerator, which was wired to an outlet above Ted's basement workbench and used to store ice, quinine water, and soft drinks. An honor-system shoebox containing change appeared beside it; a little lost-and-found —an array of forgotten sunglasses, flippers, towels, lotions, paperbacks, shirts, even underwear—materialized on the Turners' side steps. When people, that July, said, "Meet you at the pool," they did not mean the public pool past the shopping center, or the country-club pool beside the first tee. They meant the Turners'. Restrictions on admission were difficult to enforce tactfully. A visiting Methodist bishop, two Taiwanese economists, an entire girls' softball team from Darien, an eminent Canadian poet, the archery champion of Hartford, the six members of a black rock group called The Good Intentions, an ex-mistress of Aly Khan, the lavender-haired mother-in-law of a Nixon adviser not quite of Cabinet rank, an infant of six weeks, a man who was killed the next day on the Merritt Parkway, a Filipino who could stay on the pool bottom for eighty seconds, two Texans who kept cigars in their mouths and hats on their heads, three telephone linemen, four expatriate Czechs, a student Maoist from Wesleyan, and the postman all swam, as guests, in the Turners' pool, though not all at once. After the daytime crowd ebbed, and the shoebox was put back in the refrigerator, and the last *au-pair* girl took the last goosefleshed, wrinkled child shivering home to supper, there was a tide of evening activity, trysts (Mrs. Kleefield and the Nicholson boy, most notoriously) and what some called, overdramatically, orgies. True, late splashes and excited guffaws did often keep Mrs. Chace awake, and the Murtaugh children spent hours at their attic window with binoculars. And there was the evidence of the lost underwear.

One Saturday early in August, the morning arrivals found an unknown car with New York plates parked in the garage. But cars of all sorts were so common—the parking tangle frequently extended into the road—that nothing much was thought of it, even when someone noticed that the bedroom windows upstairs were open. And nothing came of it, except that around suppertime, in the lull before the evening crowd began to arrive in force, Ted and an unknown woman, of the same physical type as Linda but brunette, swiftly exited from the kitchen door, got into the car, and drove back to New York. The few lingering babysitters and beaux thus unwittingly glimpsed the root of the divorce. The two lovers had been trapped inside the house all day; Ted was fearful of the legal consequences of their being seen by anyone who might write and tell Linda. The settlement was at a ticklish stage; nothing less than terror of Linda's lawyers would have led Ted to suppress his indignation at seeing, from behind the window screen, his private pool turned public carnival. For long thereafter, though in the end he did not marry the woman, he remembered that day when they lived together like fugitives in a cave, feeding on love and ice water, tiptoeing barefoot to the depleted cupboards, which they, arriving late last night, had hoped to stock in the morning, not foreseeing the onslaught of interlopers that would pin them in. Her hair, he remembered, had tickled his shoulders as she crouched behind him at the window, and through the angry pounding of his own blood he had felt her slim body breathless with the attempt not to giggle.

August drew in, with cloudy days. Children grew bored with swimming. Roscoe Chace went on vacation to Italy; the pump broke down, and no one repaired it. Dead dragon-flies accumulated on the surface of the pool. Small deluded toads hopped in and swam around and around hopelessly. Linda at last returned. From Minneapolis she had gone on to Idaho for six weeks, to be divorced. She and the children had burnt faces from riding and hiking; her lips looked drier and more quizzical than ever, still seeking to frame that troubling question. She stood at the window, in the house that already seemed to lack its furniture, at the same side window where the lovers had crouched, and gazed at the deserted pool. The grass around it was green from splashing, save where a long-lying towel had smothered a rectangle and left it brown. Aluminum furniture she didn't recognize lay stewn and broken. She counted a dozen bottles beneath the glass-topped table. The nylon divider had parted, and its two halves floated independently. The blue plastic beneath the colorless water tried to make a cheerful, otherworldly statement, but Linda saw that the pool in truth had no bottom, it held bottomless loss, it was one huge blue tear. Thank God no one had drowned in it. Except her. She saw that she could never live here again. In September the place was sold, to a family with toddling infants, who for safety's sake have not only drained the pool but have sealed it over with iron pipes and a heavy mesh, and put warning signs around, as around a chained dog.

When Everyone Was Pregnant

I'M IN SECURITIES, but I read a lot, on the train. Read yesterday that the Fifties were coming back. All through the Sixties writers kept knocking them: Eisenhower, Lester Lanin, skirts below the knee, ho-hum. Well, turns out Eisenhower was a great non-war President. Rock is dead. Skirts have dropped to the ankle. But *my* Fifties won't come back.

Kind years to me. Entered them poor and left them comfortable. Entered them chaste and left them a father. Of four and a miscarriage. Those the years when everyone was pregnant. Not only kind but beautiful years.

How they would float across the sand like billowed sails. My wife and the wives of our friends. Shakespeare, Titania to Oberon: "laughed to see the sails conceive, And grow big-bellied with the wanton wind." In their sun-paled plaid maternity bathing suits, the pregnant young women. Tugging behind them the toddlers already born. Dinghies. Moved to a town with a beach in '54: my first promotion, Nancy's second child.

Coming along the water's edge, heads higher than the line of the sea. The horizon blue, sparkling, severe. Proust and the "little band" at Balbec. Yet more fully in flower than those, bellies swollen stately. Faces and limbs freckled in every hollow, burnished on the ball of the shoulder, the tip of the nose. Sunburned nostril-wings, peeling. The light in their eyes stealing sparkle from the far hard edge of the sea. Where a few sails showed, leaning, curling.

They would come up to us, join us. Laughter, aluminum chairs, towels, infant sun hats, baby-food jars, thermoses chuckling in the straw hampers. Above me, edge of maternity skirt lifted by touch of wind, curl of pubic hair high inside thigh showed. Sickening sensation of love. Sand-warmed wind blowing cool out of the future.

They would settle with us, forming a ring. Their heads inward with gossip, their bare legs spokes of a wheel. On the rim, children with sandpails each digging by the feet of his own mother. The shades of sand darkening as they dug. The milk smell of sun lotion. The way our words drifted up and out: sandwich wrappers blowing.

Katharine, Sarah, Liz, Peggy, Angela, June. Notes of a scale, colors of a rainbow. Nancy the seventh. Now in the Seventies two have moved. To Denver, to Birmingham. Two are divorced. Two still among us with their husbands. But all are gone, receding. Can never be revisited, that time when everyone was pregnant guiltlessly.

Guiltlessness. Our fat Fifties cars, how we loved them, revved them: no thought of pollution. Exhaust smoke, cigarette smoke, factory smoke, all romantic. Romance of consumption at its height. Shopping for baby food in the gaudy trash of the supermarkets. Purchasing power: young, newly powerful, born to consume. To procreate greedily. A smug conviction that the world was doomed. Beyond the sparkling horizon, an absolute enemy. Above us, bombs whose flash would fill the scene like a cup to overflowing.

Old slides. June's husband had a Kodak with a flash attachment (nobody owned Japanese cameras then). How young we were. The men scrawny as boys. Laughable military haircuts: the pea-brain look. The women with bangs and lipsticked smiles. We look drunk. Sometimes we were.

Jobs, houses, spouses of our own. Permission to drink and change diapers and operate power mowers and stay up past midnight. At college Nancy had not been allowed to smoke upstairs, made herself do it in our home. Like a sexual practice personally distasteful but recommended by Van der Velde. Dreadful freedom. Phrase fashionable then.

Had we expected to starve in the Depression? Be bayonetted by Japs when they invaded California? Korea seemed the best bargain we could strike: extremities of superpowers tactfully clashing in distant cold mud. The world's skin of fear shivered but held. Then came Eisenhower and gave us a precarious peace and a sluggishly rising market and a (revokable) license to have fun, to make babies. Viewed the world through two lenses since discarded: fear and gratitude. Young people now are many things but they aren't afraid, and aren't grateful.

Those summer parties. Should remember them better. Sunlight in the gin, the sprig of mint wilting. The smell of grass freshly mowed coming in through the evening screens. Children wandering in and out with complaints their mothers brushed away like cigarette smoke. What were we saying? The words we spoke were nonsense except the breath we took to speak them was life—us alive, able.

Katharine's husband Jerry had only one eye, the other frosted by childhood accident. No one felt sorry for him, too healthy, hearty. Born salesman. Him saying across to Sarah Harris, her pregnant in a big-flowered dress, sitting dreaming in a plush wing chair, "Sarah, sitting there you look just like a voluptuous big piece of wallpaper!" I thought, *has only one eye, everything looks flat to him.* Sickening sensation of love.

Years later I said to Sarah "You voluptuous piece of wallpaper you" but she had forgotten and I had to explain.

Another night, my flat tire in the Connellys' newly gravelled driveway. Sharp bluestones. Two in the morning. Ed came up out of his cellar holding high a cruciform lug wrench chanting Veni Creator Spiritus. Shocked me. My own footsteps on the gravel, *unch, unch.* A monster coming closer. Most of us at least sent the kids to Sunday school.

Dancing. Hand squeezes. Moonlight songs, smoke getting in your eyes. All innocent enough. The bump, bump of pregnant bellies against me. Seeing each other's names in the Birth column of the local paper a private joke. Hospital visits, wifeless nights. The time our fourth was born, night after the first storm of winter. Gynecologist swung by for her in his car on the way to the hospital. Just starting up practice, handsome man in ski hat. On the stark white empty street below our window looked like a lover tossing pebbles. Her contractions coming every three minutes, her little suitcase, hurrying from room to room kissing the children in their sleep. Gynecologist waiting, his face turned upward in the moonlight, in the silence. A lover howling.

Nervous of the creaking wind I slept one or two of those nights with a golf club in the bed. I think a seven iron. Figured I could get it around on a burglar quicker than a wood.

The time Sarah was with me. Nancy off in the hospital with varicose veins. Diagnosis: no more babies. Our last baby cried. Sarah rose and mothered it. Child went silent, laughed, knew something was funny, maybe thought Sarah was Nancy making a face, pretending something. Same smell, woman smell, same safety. Mullioned moonlight on Sarah's bare shoulders, bent over crib. Baby gurgled and laughed. "Crazy kid you have here." Too much love. Too many babies, breathing all over the dark house like searchlights that might switch on.

Sarah's lovely wide shoulders, big hips, breasts shallow and firm. First time I saw them it tore at me, exclaimed she had breasts like a Greek statue. She laughed and told me I read too much. But it had been torn out of me.

The ritual of taking out Nancy's hairpins one by one before making love. Rain on the roof. Fifties a house decade, never ventured into the streets. Cuba, Sputnik, Tibet. Rain on the roof.

The brown line on her belly a woman brings back from the hospital, after being pregnant. Nobody had ever told me that line existed. Why hadn't they?

The babies got bigger. The parties got wilder. Time at the beach, after Cancer dance, hot summer, might have been 1960. We took off our clothes and swam. Scary tide, strong moon, could see the women had aged. Slack bellies, knees and faces full of shadow. Used their long gauzy dance dresses as towels, wrapped around them as sarongs. Over the ocean, riots. Assassinations, protests, a decade's overdue bills heaped like surf thunder on the sand bar. We were no longer young. Embarrassed. Groped for our underclothes and shoes. Yet the warm kiss of wind off of sand, even at night.

I make some notes on the train. My hand shakes. My town slides by, the other comfortable small towns, the pastures and glimpses of sea, a single horse galloping, a golf course with a dawn foursome frozen on the green, dew-white, and then the lesser cities, the little one-hotel disgruntled cities, black walls hurled like fists at our windows, broken factory windows, a rusted drawbridge halted forever at almost-down, a gravel yard with bluestones pyramided by size, a dump smoldering, trash gaudy with all the colors of jewels; then the metropolis, the tracks multiplying in lightning calculations, the hazed skyscrapers changing relationship to one another like the steeples in Proust, the tunnels of billboards, the station, vast and derelict; the final stop. This evening, the same thing backwards.

But never get bored with how the train slices straight. Lightly rocking. Through intersections of warning bells tingling, past playgrounds and back yards, warehouses built on a bias to fit the right-of-way. Like time. Cuts sleepwalking through everything.

Notes not come to anything. Lives not come to anything. Life a common stock that fluctuates in value. But you cannot sell, you must hold, hold till it dips to nothing. The big boys sell you out.

Edgar to blinded Gloucester: Ripeness is all. Have never exactly understood. Ripeness is all that is left? Or, deeper and more hopeful, ripeness is all that matters? Encloses all, answers all, justifies all. Ripeness is God.

Now: our babies drive cars, push pot, shave, menstruate,

riot for peace, eat macrobiotic. Wonderful in many ways, but not ours, never ours, we see now. Now: we go to a party and see only enemies. Fifteen shared years have made us wary, survival-conscious. Sarah looks away. Spokes of the wheel are missing. Our babies accuse us.

Did the Fifties exist? Voluptuous wallpaper. Crazy kid. Sickening sensation of love. The train slides forward. The decades slide seaward, taking us along. I am still afraid. Still grateful.

Man and Daughter
in the Cold

"Look at that girl ski!" The exclamation arose at Ethan's side as if, in the disconnecting cold, a rib of his had cried out; but it was his friend, friend and fellow-teacher, an inferior teacher but superior skier, Matt Langley, admiring Becky, Ethan's own daughter. It took an effort, in this air like slices of transparent metal interposed everywhere, to make these connections and to relate the young girl, her round face red with windburn as she skimmed down the run-out slope, to himself. She was his daughter, age thirteen. Ethan had twin sons, two years younger, and his attention had always been focussed on their skiing, on the irksome comedy of their double needs—the four boots to lace, the four mittens to find—and then their cute yet grim competition as now one and now the other gained the edge in the expertise of geländesprungs and slalom form. On their trips north into the mountains, Becky had come along for the ride. "Look how solid she is," Matt went on. "She doesn't cheat on it like your boys—those feet are absolutely together." The girl, grinning as if she could hear herself praised, wiggle-waggled to a flashy stop that sprayed snow over the men's ski tips.

"Where's Mommy?" she asked.

Ethan answered, "She went with the boys into the lodge. They couldn't take it." Their sinewy little male bodies had no insulation; weeping and shivering, they had begged to go in after a single T-bar run.

"What sissies," Becky said.

Matt said, "This wind is wicked. And it's picking up. You should have been here at nine; Lord, it was lovely. All that fresh powder, and not a stir of wind."

Becky told him, "Dumb Tommy couldn't find his mittens, we spent an *hour* looking, and then Daddy got the Jeep stuck." Ethan, alerted now for signs of the wonderful in his daughter, was struck by the strange fact that she was making conversation. Unafraid, she was talking to Matt without her father's intercession.

"Mr. Langley was saying how nicely you were skiing."

"You're Olympic material, Becky."

The girl perhaps blushed; but her cheeks could get no redder. Her eyes, which, were she a child, she would have instantly averted, remained a second on Matt's face, as if to estimate how much he meant it. "It's easy down here," Becky said. "It's babyish."

Ethan asked, "Do you want to go up to the top?" He was freezing standing still, and the gondola would be sheltered from the wind.

Her eyes shifted to his, with another unconsciously thoughtful hesitation. "Sure. If you want to."

"Come along, Matt?"

"Thanks, no. It's too rough for me; I've had enough runs. This is the trouble with January—once it stops snowing, the wind comes up. I'll keep Elaine company in the lodge." Matt himself had no wife, no children. At thirty-eight, he was as free as his students, as light on his skis and as full of brave know-how. "In case of frostbite," he shouted after them, "rub snow on it."

Becky effortlessly skated ahead to the lift shed. The encumbered motion of walking on skis, not natural to him, made Ethan feel asthmatic: a fish out of water. He touched his parka pocket, to check that the inhalator was there. As a child he had imagined death as something attacking from outside, but now he saw that it was carried within; we nurse it for years, and it grows. The clock on the lodge wall said a quarter to noon. The giant thermometer read two degrees above zero. The racks outside were dense as hedges with idle skis. Crowds, any sensation of crowding or delay, quickened his asthma; as therapy he imagined the emptiness, the blue freedom, at the top of the mountain. The clatter of machinery inside the shed was comforting, and enough teen-age boys were boarding gondolas to make the ascent seem normal and safe. Ethan's breathing eased. Becky proficiently handed her poles to the loader points up; her father was always caught by surprise, and often as not fumbled the little maneuver of letting his skis be taken from him. Until, five years ago, he had become an assistant professor at a New Hampshire college an hour to the south, he had never skied; he had lived in those Middle Atlantic cities where snow, its moment of virgin beauty by, is only an encumbering nuisance, a threat of suffocation. Whereas his children had grown up on skis.

Alone with his daughter in the rumbling isolation of the

gondola, he wanted to explore her, and found her strange—
strange in her uninquisitive child's silence, her accustomed
poise in this ascending egg of metal. A dark figure with
spreading legs veered out of control beneath them, fell forward, and vanished. Ethan cried out, astonished, scandalized;
he imagined the man had buried himself alive. Becky was
barely amused, and looked away before the dark spots struggling in the drift were lost from sight. As if she might know,
Ethan asked, "Who was that?"

"Some kid." Kids, her tone suggested, were in plentiful
supply; one could be spared.

He offered to dramatize the adventure ahead of them: "Do
you think we'll freeze at the top?"

"Not exactly."

"What do you think it'll be like?"

"Miserable."

"Why are we doing this, do you think?"

"Because we paid the money for the all-day lift ticket."

"Becky, you think you're pretty smart, don't you?"

"Not really."

The gondola rumbled and lurched into the shed at the
top; an attendant opened the door, and there was a howling
mixed of wind and of boys whooping to keep warm. He
was roughly handed two pairs of skis, and the handler,
muffled to the eyes with a scarf, stared as if amazed that
Ethan was so old. All the others struggling into skis in the lee
of the shed were adolescent boys. Students: after fifteen years
of teaching, Ethan tended to flinch from youth—its harsh
noises, its cheerful rapacity, its cruel onward flow as one class
replaced another, ate a year of his life, and was replaced by
another.

Away from the shelter of the shed, the wind was a high

monotonous pitch of pain. His cheeks instantly ached, and the hinges linking the elements of his face seemed exposed. His septum tingled like glass—the rim of a glass being rubbed by a moist finger to produce a note. Drifts ribbed the trail, obscuring Becky's ski tracks seconds after she made them, and at each push through the heaped snow his scope of breathing narrowed. By the time he reached the first steep section, the left half of his back hurt as it did only in the panic of a full asthmatic attack, and his skis, ignored, too heavy to manage, spread and swept him toward a snowbank at the side of the trail. He was bent far forward but kept his balance; the snow kissed his face lightly, instantly, all over; he straightened up, refreshed by the shock, thankful not to have lost a ski. Down the slope Becky had halted and was staring upward at him, worried. A huge blowing feather, a partition of snow, came between them. The cold, unprecedented in his experience, shone through his clothes like furious light, and as he rummaged through his parka for the inhalator he seemed to be searching glass shelves backed by a black wall. He found it, its icy plastic the touch of life, a clumsy key to his insides. Gasping, he exhaled, put it into his mouth, and inhaled; the isoproterenol spray, chilled into drops, opened his lungs enough for him to call to his daughter, "Keep moving! I'll catch up!"

Solid on her skis, she swung down among the moguls and wind-bared ice, and became small, and again waited. The moderate slope seemed a cliff; if he fell and sprained anything, he would freeze. His entire body would become locked tight against air and light and thought. His legs trembled; his breath moved in and out of a narrow slot beneath the pain in his back. The cold and blowing snow all around him constituted an immense crowding, but there was no way out of this white cave but to slide downward toward the dark spot that was his daughter. He had forgotten all his lessons. Leaning backward in an infant's tense snowplow, he floundered through alternating powder and ice.

"You O.K., Daddy?" Her stare was wide, its fright underlined by a pale patch on her cheek.

He used the inhalator again and gave himself breath to tell her, "I'm fine. Let's get down."

In this way, in steps of her leading and waiting, they worked down the mountain, out of the worst wind, into the lower trail that ran between birches and hemlocks. The cold had the quality not of absence but of force: an inverted burning. The last time Becky stopped and waited, the colorless crescent on her scarlet cheek disturbed him, reminded him of some injunction, but he could find in his brain, whittled to a dim determination to persist, only the advice to keep going, toward shelter and warmth. She told him, at a division of trails, "This is the easier way."

"Let's go the quicker way," he said, and in this last descent recovered the rhythm—knees together, shoulders facing the valley, weight forward as if in the moment of release from a diving board—not a resistance but a joyous acceptance of falling. They reached the base lodge, and with unfeeling hands removed their skis. Pushing into the cafeteria, Ethan saw in the momentary mirror of the door window that his face was a spectre's; chin, nose, and eyebrows had retained the snow from that near-fall near the top. "Becky, look," he said, turning in the crowded warmth and clatter inside the door. "I'm a monster."

"I know, your face was absolutely white, I didn't know whether to tell you or not. I thought it might scare you."

He touched the pale patch on her cheek. "Feel anything?"

"No."

"Damn. I should have rubbed snow on it."

Matt and Elaine and the twins, flushed and stripped of their parkas, had eaten lunch; shouting and laughing with a strange guilty shrillness, they said that there had been repeated loud-speaker announcements not to go up to the top without face masks, because of frostbite. They had expected Ethan and Becky to come back down on the gondola, as others had, after tasting the top. "It never occurred to us," Ethan said. He took the blame upon himself by adding, "I wanted to see the girl ski."

Their common adventure, and the guilt of his having given her frostbite, bound Becky and Ethan together in complicity for the rest of the day. They arrived home as sun was leaving even the tips of the hills; Elaine had invited Matt to supper, and while the windows of the house burned golden Ethan shovelled out the Jeep. The house was a typical New Hampshire farmhouse, less than two miles from the college, on the side of a hill, overlooking what had been a pasture, with the usual capacious porch running around three sides, cluttered with cordwood and last summer's lawn furniture. The woodsy sheltered scent of these porches, the sense of rural waste space, never failed to please Ethan, who had been raised in a Newark half-house, then a West Side apartment, and just before college a row house in Baltimore, with his grandparents. The wind had been left behind in the mountains. The air was as still as the stars. Shovelling the light dry snow became a lazy dance. But when he bent suddenly, his knees creaked, and his breathing shortened so that he paused. A sudden rectangle of light was flung from the shadows of the porch. Becky came out into the cold with him. She was carrying a lawn rake.

He asked her, "Should you be out again? How's your frostbite?" Though she was a distance away, there was no need, in the immaculate air, to raise his voice.

"It's O.K. It kind of tingles. And under my chin. Mommy made me put on a scarf."

"What's the lawn rake for?"

"It's a way you can make a path. It really works."

"O.K., you make a path to the garage and after I get my breath I'll see if I can get the Jeep back in."

"Are you having asthma?"

"A little."

"We were reading about it in biology. Dad, see, it's kind of a tree inside you, and every branch has a little ring of muscle around it, and they tighten." From her gestures in the dark she was demonstrating, with mittens on.

What she described, of course, was classic unalloyed asthma, whereas his was shading into emphysema, which could only worsen. But he liked being lectured to—preferred it, indeed, to lecturing—and as the minutes of companionable silence with his daughter passed he took inward notes on the bright quick impressions flowing over him like a continuous voice. The silent cold. The stars. Orion behind an elm. Minute scintillae in the snow at his feet. His daughter's strange black bulk against the white; the solid grace that had stolen upon her. The conspiracy of love. His father and he shovelling the car free from a sudden unwelcome storm in Newark, instantly gray with soot, the undercurrent of desperation, his father a salesman and must get to Camden. Got to get to Camden, boy, get to Camden or bust. Dead of a heart attack at forty-seven. Ethan tossed a shovelful into the air so the scintillae flashed in the steady golden chord from the house windows. Elaine and Matt sitting flushed at the lodge table, parkas off, in deshabille, as if sitting up in bed. Matt's way of turning a half circle on the top of a mogul, light as a diver. The cancerous unwieldiness of Ethan's own skis. His jealousy of his students, the many-headed immortality of their annual renewal. The flawless tall cruelty of the stars. Orion intertwined with the silhouetted elm. A black tree inside him. His daughter, busily sweeping with the rake, childish yet lithe, so curiously demonstrating this preference for his company. Feminine of her to forgive him her frostbite. Perhaps, flattered on skis, felt the cold her element. Her womanhood soon enough to be smothered in warmth. A plow a mile away painstakingly scraped. He was missing the point of the lecture. The point was unstated: an absence. He was looking upon his daughter as a woman but without lust. The music around him was being produced, in the zero air, like a finger on crystal, by this hollowness, this generosity of negation. Without lust, without jealousy. Space seemed love, bestowed to be free in, and coldness the price. He felt joined to the great dead whose words it was his duty to teach.

The Jeep came up unprotestingly from the fluffy snow. It looked happy to be penned in the garage with Elaine's station wagon, and the skis, and the oiled chain saw, and the power mower dreamlessly waiting for spring. Ethan was happy, precariously so, so that rather than break he uttered a sound: "Becky?"

"Yeah?"

"You want to know what else Mr. Langley said?"

"What?" They trudged toward the porch, up the path the gentle rake had cleared.

"He said you ski better than the boys."

"I bet," she said, and raced to the porch, and in the precipitate way, evasive and female and pleased, that she flung herself to the top step he glimpsed something generic and joyous, a pageant that would leave him behind.

I Am Dying, Egypt, Dying

CLEM CAME FROM BUFFALO and spoke in the neutral American accent that sends dictionary makers there. His pronunciation was clear and colorless, his manners impeccable, his clothes freshly laundered and appropriate no matter where he was, however far from home. Rich and unmarried, he travelled a lot; he had been to Athens and Rio, Las Vegas and Hong Kong, Leningrad and Sydney and now Cairo. His posture was perfect, but he walked without swing; people at first liked him, because his apparent perfection reflected flatteringly upon them, and then distrusted him, because his perfection revealed no flaw. As he travelled, he studied the guidebooks conscientiously, picked up phrases of the local language, collected prints and artifacts. He was serious but not humorless; indeed, his smile, a creeping but finally complete revelation of utterly even and white front teeth, with a bit of tongue flirtatiously pinched between them, was one of the things that led people on, that led them to hope for the

flaw, the entering crack. There were hopeful signs. At the bar
he took one drink too many, the hurried last drink that robs
the dinner wine of taste. Though he enjoyed human society,
he couldn't dance. He had a fine fair square-shouldered body,
surely masculine and yet somehow neutral, which he so-
licitously covered with oil against the sun that, as they moved
up the Nile, grew sharper and more tropical. He fell asleep
in deck chairs, beautifully immobile, glistening, as the two
riverbanks at their safe distance glided by—date palms, taut
green fields irrigated by rotating donkeys, pyramids of
white round pots, trapezoidal houses of elephant-colored
mud, mud-colored children silently waving, and the roseate
desert cliffs beyond, massive parentheses. Glistening like a
mirror, he slept in this gliding parenthesis with a godlike calm
that possessed the landscape, transformed it into a steady
dreaming. Clem said of himself, awaking, apologizing, smiling
with that bit of pinched tongue, that he slept badly at night,
suffered from insomnia. This also was a hopeful sign. People
wanted to love him.

There were not many on the boat. The war discouraged
tourists. Indeed, at Nag Hammadi they did pass under a
bridge in which Israeli commandos had blasted three neat but
not very conclusive holes; a wooden ramp had been laid on
top and the traffic of carts and rickety lorries continued. And
at Aswan they saw anti-aircraft batteries defending the
High Dam. But for the cruise between, the war figured only
as a luxurious amount of space on deck and a pleasant dis-
proportion between the seventy crewmen and the twenty
paying passengers. These twenty were:

Three English couples, middle-aged but for one miniskirted
wife, who was thought for days to be a daughter.

Two German boys; they wore bathing trunks to all the

temples, yet seemed to know the gods by name and perhaps were future archaeologists.

A French couple, in their sixties. The man had been tortured in World War II; his spine had fused in a curve. He moved over the desert rubble and uneven stairways with tiny shuffling steps and studied the murals by means of a mirror hung around his neck. Yet he, too, knew the gods and would murmur worshipfully.

Three Egyptians, a man and two women, in their thirties, of a professional class, teachers or museum curators, cosmopolitan and handsome, given to laughter among themselves, even while the guide, a cherubic old Bedouin called Poppa Omar, was lecturing.

A fluffy and sweet, ample and perfumed American widow and her escort, a short bald native of New Jersey who for fifteen years had run tours in Africa, armed with a fancy fly whisk and an impenetrable rudeness toward natives of the continent.

An amateur travelogist from Green Bay working his way south to Cape Town with two hundred pounds of photographic equipment.

A stocky blond couple, fortyish, who kept to themselves, hired their own guides, and were presumed to be Russian.

A young Scandinavian woman, beautiful, alone.

Clem.

Clem had joined the cruise at the last minute; he had been in Amsterdam and become oppressed by the low sky and tight-packed houses, the cold canal touring boats and the bad Indonesian food and the prostitutes illuminated in their windows like garish great candy. He had flown to Cairo and not liked it better. A cheeseburger in the Hilton offended him by being gamy. In the plaza outside, a man rustled up to him and asked if he had had any love last night. The city, with its incessant twinkle of car horns and furtive-eyed men in pajamas, seemed unusable, remote. The museum was full of sandbags. The heart of King Tut's treasure had been hidden in case of invasion; but his gold sarcophagus, feathered in lapis lazuli and carnelian, did touch Clem, with a whisper of death, of flight, of floating. A pamphlet in the Hilton advertised a six-day trip on the Nile, Luxor north to Abydos, back to Luxor, and on south to Aswan, in a luxurious boat. It sounded passive and educational, which appealed to Clem; he had gone to college at the University of Rochester and felt a need to keep rounding off his education, to bring it up to Ivy League standards. Also, the tan would look great back in Buffalo.

Stepping from the old DC-3 at the Luxor airport, he was smitten by the beauty of the desert, roseate and motionless around him. His element, perhaps. What was his travelling, his bachelorhood, but a search for his element? He was thirty-four and still seemed to be merely visiting the world. Even in Buffalo, walking the straight shaded streets where he had played as a small boy, entering the homes and restaurants where he was greeted by name, sitting in the two-room office where he put in the few hours of telephoning that managed the parcel of securities and property fallen to him from his father's death, he felt somehow light, limited to forty-four pounds of luggage, dressed with the unnatural correctitude people assume at the outset of a trip. A puff of air off Lake Erie and he would be gone, and the city, with its savage blustery winters, its deep-set granite mansions, its factories, its iron bison in the railroad terminal, would not have noticed. He would leave only his name in gilt paint on a list of singles tennis champions above the bar of his country

club. But he knew he had been a methodical joyless player
to watch, too full of lessons to lose.

He knew a lot about himself: he knew that this lightness,
the brittle unmarred something he carried, was his treasure,
which his demon willed him to preserve. Stepping from the
airplane at Luxor, he had greeted his demon in the air—air
ideally clean, with the poise of a mirror. From the window
of his cabin he sensed again, in the glittering width of the
Nile—much bluer than he had expected—and in the unflecked
alkaline sky and in the tapestry strip of anciently worked
green between them, that he would be happy for this trip.
He liked sunning on the deck that first afternoon. Only the
Scandinavian girl, in an orange bikini, kept him company.
Both were silent. The boat was still tied up at the Luxor
dock, a flight of stone steps; a few yards away, across a gulf
of water and paved banking, a traffic of peddlers and cart
drivers stared across. Clem liked that gulf and liked it when
the boat cast loose and began gliding between the fields, the
villages, the desert. He liked the first temples: gargantuan
Karnak, its pillars upholding the bright blank sky; gentler
Luxor, with its built-in mosque and its little naked queen
touching her king's giant calf; Hollywoodish Dendera—its
restored roofs had brought in darkness and dampness and
bats that moved on the walls like intelligent black gloves.

Clem even, at first, liked the peddlers. Tourist-starved, they
touched him in their hunger, thrusting scarabs and old coins
and clay mummy dolls at him, moaning and grunting English:
"How much? How much you give me? Very fine. Fifty.
Both. Take both. Both for thirty-five." Clem peeked down,
caught his eye on a turquoise glint and wavered; his mother
liked keepsakes and he had friends in Buffalo who would be
amused. Into this flaw, this tentative crack of interest, they

stuffed more things, strange sullied objects salvaged from the desert, alabaster vases, necklaces of mummy heads. Their brown hands probed and rubbed; their faces looked stunned, unblinking, as if, under the glaring sun, they were conducting business in the dark. Indeed, some did have eyes whitened by trachoma. Hoping to placate them with a purchase, Clem bargained for the smallest thing he could see, a lapis-lazuli bug the size of a fingernail. "Ten, then," the old peddler said, irritably making the "give me" gesture with his palm. Holding his wallet high, away from their hands, Clem leafed through the big notes for the absurdly small five-piaster bills, tattered and silky with use. The purchase, amounting to little more than a dime, excited the peddlers; ignoring the other tourists, they multiplied and crowded against him. Something warm and hard was inserted into his hand, his other sleeve was plucked, his pockets were patted and he wheeled, his tongue pinched between his teeth flirtatiously, trapped. It was a nightmare; the dream thought crossed his mind that he might be scratched.

He broke away and rejoined the other tourists in the sanctum of a temple courtyard. One of the Egyptian women came up to him and said, "I do not mean to remonstrate, but you are torturing them by letting them see all those fifties and hundreds in your wallet."

"I'm sorry." He blushed like a scolded schoolboy. "I just didn't want to be rude."

"You must be. There is no question of hurt feelings. You are the man in the moon to them. They have no comprehension of your charm."

The strange phrasing of her last sentence, expressing not quite what she meant, restored his edge and dulled her rebuke. She was the shorter and the older of the two Egyptian women; her eyes were green and there was an earnest mischief, a slight pressure, in her upward glance. Clem relaxed, almost slouching. "The sad part is, some of their things, I'd rather like to buy."

"Then do," she said, and walked away, her hips swinging. So a move had been made. He had expected it to come from the Scandinavian girl.

That evening the Egyptian trio invited him to their table in the bar. The green-eyed woman said, "I hope I was not scolding. I did not mean to remonstrate, merely to inform."

"Of course," Clem said. "Listen. I was being plucked to death. I needed rescuing."

"Those men," the Egyptian man said, "are in a bad way. They say that around the hotels the shoeshine boys are starving." His face was triangular, pock-marked, saturnine. A heavy weary courtesy slowed his speech.

"What did you buy?" the other woman asked. She was sallower than the other, and softer. Her English was the most British-accented.

Clem showed them. "Ah," the man said, "a scarab."

"The incarnation of Khepri," the green-eyed woman said. "The symbol of immortality. You will live forever." She smiled at everything she said; he remembered her smiling with the word "remonstrate."

"They're jolly things," the other woman pronounced, in her stately way. "Dung beetles. They roll a ball of dung along ahead of them, which appealed to the ancient Egyptians. Reminded them of themselves, I suppose."

"Life is that," the man said. "A ball of dung we push along."

The waiter came and Clem said, "Another whiskey sour.

And another round of whatever they're having." Beer for the man, Scotch for the taller lady, lemonade for his first friend.

Having bought, he felt, the right to some education, Clem asked, "Seriously. Has the"—he couldn't bring himself to call it a war, and he had noticed that in Egypt the word Israeli was never pronounced—"trouble cut down on tourism?"

"Oh, immensely," the taller lady said. "Before the war, one had to book for this boat months ahead. Now, my husband was granted two weeks and we were able to come at the last moment. It is pathetic."

"What do you do?" Clem asked.

The man made a self-deprecatory and evasive gesture, as a deity might have, asked for employment papers.

"My brother," the green-eyed woman stated, smiling, "works for the government. In, what do you call it, planning?"

As if in apology for having been reticent, her brother abruptly said, "The shoeshine boys and the dragomen suffer for us all. In everyone in my country, you have now a deep distress."

"I noticed," Clem said, very carefully, "those holes in the bridge we passed under."

"They brought *Jeeps* in, Jeeps. By helicopter. The papers said bombs from a plane, but it was Jeeps by helicopters from the Red Sea. They drove onto the bridge, set the charges and drove away. We are not warriors. We are farmers. For thousands of years now, we have had others do our fighting for us—Sudanese, Libyans, Arabs. We are not Arabs. We are Egyptians. The Syrians and Jordanians, they are Arabs— crazy men. But we, we don't know who we are, except we are very old. The man who seeks to make warriors of us creates distress."

His wife put her hand on his to silence him while the waiter brought the drinks. His sister said to Clem, "Are you enjoying our temples?"

"Quite." But the temples within him, giant slices of lime-stone and sun, lay mute. "I also quite like," he went on, "our guide. I admire the way he says everything in English to some of us and then in French to the rest."

"Most Egyptians are trilingual," the wife stated. "Arabic, English, French."

"Which do you think in?" Clem was concerned, for he was conscious in himself of an absence of verbal thoughts; instead, there were merely glints and reflections.

The sister smiled. "In English, the thoughts are clearest. French is better for passion."

"And Arabic?"

"Also for passion. Is it not so, Amina?"

"What so, Leila?" She had been murmuring with her husband.

The question was restated in French.

"Oh, *c'est vrai, vrai.*"

"How strange," Clem said. "English doesn't seem precise to me; quite the contrary. It's a mess of synonyms and lazy grammar."

"No," the wife said firmly—she never, he suddenly noticed, smiled—"English is clear and cold, but not *nuancé* in the emotions, as is French."

"And is Arabic *nuancé* in the same way?"

The green-eyed sister considered. "More *angoisse.*"

Her brother said, "We have ninety-nine words for camel dung. All different states of camel dung. Camel dung, we understand."

"Of course," Leila said to Clem, "Arabic here is nothing

compared with the pure Arabic you would hear among the Saudis. The language of the Koran is so much more—can I say it?—gutsy. So guttural, nasal; strange, wonderful sounds. Amina, does it still affect you inwardly, to hear it chanted? The Koran."

Amina solemnly agreed, "It is terrible. It tears me all apart. It is too much passion."

Italian rock music had entered the bar via an unseen radio and one of the middle-aged English couples was trying to waltz to it. Noticing how intently Clem watched, the sister asked him, "Do you like to dance?"

He took it as an invitation; he blushed. "No, thanks, the fact is I can't."

"Can't dance? Not at all?"

"I've never been able to learn. My mother says I have Methodist feet."

"Your mother says that?" She laughed; a short shocking noise, the bark of a fox. She called to Amina, *"Sa mère dit que l'Américain a les pieds méthodistes!"*

"Les pieds méthodiques?"

"Non, non, aucune méthode, la secte chrétienne—méthodisme!"

Both barked, and the man grunted. Clem sat there rigidly, immaculate in his embarrassment. The girl's green eyes, curious, pressed on him like gems scratching glass. The three Egyptians became overanimated, beginning sentences in one language and ending in another, and Clem understood that he was being laughed at. Yet the sensation, like the blurred plucking of the scarab salesmen, was better than untouched emptiness. He had another drink before dinner, the drink that was one too many, and when he went in to his single table, everything—the tablecloths, the little red lamps, the waiting droves of waiters in blue, the black windows beyond which the Nile glided—looked triumphant and glazed.

He slept badly. There were bumps and scraping above him, footsteps in the hall, the rumble of the motors and, at four o'clock, the sounds of docking at another temple site. Once, he had found peace in hotel rooms, strange virgin corners where his mind could curl into itself, cut off from all nagging familiarities, and painlessly wink out. But he had known too many hotel rooms, so they had become themselves familiar, with their excessively crisp sheets and boastful plumbing and easy chairs one never sat in but used as clothes racks. Only the pillows varied—neck-cracking fat bolsters in Leningrad, in Amsterdam hard little wads the size of a lady's purse, and as lumpy. Here on the floating hotel Osiris, two bulky pillows were provided and, toward morning, Clem discovered it relaxed him to put his head on one and his arms around the other. Some other weight in the bed seemed to be the balance that his agitated body, oscillating with hieroglyphs and sharp remonstrative glances, was craving. In his dream, the Egyptian woman promised him something marvelous and showed him two tall limestone columns with blue sky between them. He awoke unrefreshed but conscious of having dreamed. On his ceiling there was a dance of light, puzzling in its telegraphic rapidity, more like electronic art than anything natural. He analyzed it as sunlight bouncing off the tremulous Nile through the slats of his Venetian blinds. He pulled the blinds and there it was again, stunning in its clarity: the blue river, the green strip, the pink cliffs, the unflecked sky. Only the village had changed. The other tourists—the Frenchman being slowly steered, like a fragile cart, by an Arab boy—were already heading up a flight of wooden stairs toward a bus. Clem ran after them, into the broad day, without shaving.

Their guide, Poppa Omar, sat them down in the sun in a temple courtyard and told them the story of Queen Hatshepsut. "Remember it like this," he said, touching his head and rubbing his chest. "Hat—cheap—suit. She was wonderful woman here. Always building the temples, always winning the war and getting the nigger to be slaves. She marry her brother Tuthmosis and he grow tired here of jealous and insultation. He say to her, 'OK, you done a lot for Egypt, take it more easy now.' She say to him, 'No, I think I just keep rolling along.' What happen? Tuthmosis die. The new king also Tuthmosis, her niece. He is a little boy. Hatshepsut show herself in all big statues wearing false beard and all flatness here." He rubbed his chest. "Tuthmosis get bigger and go say to her now, 'Too much jealous and insultation. Take it easy for Egypt now.' She say, 'No.' Then she die, and all over Egypt here, he take all her statue and smash, hit, hit, so not one face of Hatshepsut left and everywhere her name in all the walls here, become Tuthmosis!" Clem looked around, and the statues had, indeed, been mutilated, thousands of years ago. He touched his own face and the whiskers scratched.

On the way back in the bus, the Green Bay travelogist asked them to stop so he could photograph a water wheel with his movie camera. A tiny child met them, weeping, on the path, holding one arm as if crippled. "Baksheesh, baksheesh," he said. "Musha, musha." One of the British men flicked at him with a whisk. The bald American announced aloud that the child was faking. Clem reached into his pocket for a piaster coin, but then remembered himself as torturer. Seeing his gesture, the child, and six others, chased after him. First they shouted, then they tossed pebbles at his heels.

From within the haven of the bus, the tourists could all see
the child's arm unbend. But the weeping continued and was
evidently real. The travelogist was still doing the water
wheel and the peddlers began to pry open the windows and
thrust in scarabs, dolls, alabaster vases not without beauty.
The window beside Clem's face slid back and a brown
hand insinuated an irregular parcel about six inches long,
wrapped in brown cloth. "Feesh mummy," a disembodied
voice said, and to Clem it seemed hysterically funny. He
couldn't stop laughing; the tip of his tongue began to hurt
from being bitten. The Scandinavian girl, across the aisle,
glanced at him hopefully. Perhaps the crack in his surface
was appearing.

Back on the Osiris, they basked in deck chairs. The white
boat had detached itself from the brown land and men in
blue brought them lemonade, daiquiris, salty peanuts called
soudani. Though Clem, luminous with suntan oil, appeared to
be asleep, his lips moved in answer to Ingrid beside him. Her
bikini was chartreuse today. "In my country," she said, "the
summers are so short, naturally we take off our clothes. But
it is absurd, this myth other countries have of our paganism,
our happy sex. We are a harsh people. My father, he was like
a man in the Bergman films. I was forbidden everything
growing up—to play cards, lipstick, to dance."

"I never did learn to dance," Clem said, slightly shifting.

"Yes," she said, "I saw in you, too, a stern childhood. In a
place of harsh winters."

"We had two yards of snow the other year," Clem told
her. "In one storm. Two *yards*."

"And yet," Ingrid said, "I think the thaw, when at last it
comes in such places, is so dramatic, so intense." She glanced
toward him hopefully.

I Am Dying, Egypt, Dying

Clem appeared oblivious within his gleaming placenta of suntan oil.

The German boy who spoke a little English was on the other side of him. By now, the third day, the sun bathers had declared themselves: Clem, Ingrid, the two young Germans, the bald-headed American, the young English wife, whose skirted bathing suits were less immodest than her ordinary dresses. The rest of the British sat on the deck in the shade of the canopy and drank; the three Egyptians sat in the lounge and talked; the supposed Russians kept out of sight altogether. The travelogist was talking to the purser about the immense chain of tickets and reservations that would get him to Cape Town; the widow was in her cabin with Egyptian stomach and a burning passion to play bridge; the French couple sat by the rail, in the sun but fully dressed, reading guidebooks, his chair tipped back precariously, so he could see the gliding landscape.

The German boy asked Clem, "Haff you bot a caftan?"

He had been nearly asleep, beneath a light, transparent headache. He said, *"Bitte?"*

"Ein caftan. You shoot. In Luxor; ve go back tonight. He will measure you and haff it by morning ven ve go. Sey are good—wery cheap."

Hatcheapsuit, Clem thought, but grunted that he might do it. His frozen poise contended within him with something promiscuous and American, that must go forth and test, and purchase. He felt, having spurned so many scarabs and alabaster vases, that he owed Egypt some of the large-leafed money that fattened his wallet uncomfortably.

"It vood be wery handsome on you."

"Ravishing," the young English wife said behind them. She had been listening. Clem sometimes felt like a mirror

: 121 :

that everyone glanced into before moving on.

"You're all kidding me," he announced. "But I confess, I'm a sucker for costumes."

"Again," Ingrid said, "like a Bergman film." And languorously she shifted her long arms and legs; the impression of flesh in the side of his vision disturbingly merged, in his sleepless state, with a floating sensation of hollowness, of being in parentheses.

That afternoon they toured the necropolis in the Valley of the Kings. King Tut's small two-chambered tomb; how had they crammed so much treasure in? The immense tunnels of Ramses III; or was it Ramses IV? Passageways hollowed from the limestone chip by chip, lit by systems of tilted mirrors, painted with festive stiff figures banqueting, fishing, carrying offerings of fruit forward, which was always slightly down, down past pits dug to entrap grave robbers, past vast false chambers, toward the real and final one, a square room that would have made a nice night club. Its murals had been left unfinished, sketched in gray ink but uncolored. The tremors of the artist's hand, his nervous strokes, were still there. Abdul, the Egyptian planner, murmured to him, "Always they left something unfinished; it is a part of their religion no one understands. It is thought perhaps they dreaded finishing, as closing in the dead, limiting the life beyond." They climbed up the long slanting passageway, threaded with electric lights, past hundreds of immaculate bodies carried without swing. "The dead, you see, are not dead. In their language, the word for death and the word for life are the same. The death they feared was the second one, the one that would come if the tomb lacked provisions for life. In the tombs of the nobles, more than here, the scenes of life are all about, like a musical—you say score?—that only the dead have the instrument to play. These hieroglyphs are all instructions to the dead man, how to behave, how to make the safe journey."

"Good planning," Clem said, short of breath.

Abdul was slow to see the joke, since it was on himself.

"I mean the dead are much better planned for than the living."

"No," Abdul said flatly, perhaps misunderstanding. "It is the same."

Back in Luxor, Clem left the safe boat and walked toward the clothing shop, following the German boy's directions. He seemed to walk a long way. The narrowing streets grew shadowy. Pedestrians drifted by him in a steady procession, carrying offerings forward. No peddlers approached him; perhaps they all kept businessmen's hours, went home and totalled up the sold scarabs and fish mummies in double-entry ledgers. Radio Cairo blared and twanged from wooden balconies. Dusty intersections flooded with propaganda (or was it prayer?) faded behind him. The air was dark by the time he reached the shop. Within its little cavern of brightness, a young woman was helping a small child with homework, and a young man, the husband and father, lounged against some stacked bolts of cloth. All three persons were petite; Egyptian children, Clem had observed before, are proportioned like miniature adults, with somber staring dolls' heads. He felt oversize in this shop, whose reduced scale was here and there betrayed by a coarse object from the real world—a steam press, an inflated pastel of Nasser on the wall. Clem's voice, asking if they could make a caftan for him by morning, seemed to boom; as he tuned it down, it cracked and trembled. Measuring him, the small man touched him all over; and touches that at first had been excused as accidental declared themselves as purposeful, determined.

"Hey," Clem said, blushing.

Shielded from his wife by the rectangular bulk of Clem's body, the young man, undoing his own fly with a swift light tailor's gesture, exhibited himself. "I can make you very happy," he muttered.

"I'm leaving," Clem said.

He was at the doorway instantly, but the tailor had time to call, "Sir, when will you come back tomorrow?" Clem turned; the little man was zipped, the woman and child had their heads bent together over the homework. Nasser, a lurid ochre, scowled toward the future. Clem had intended to abandon the caftan but pictured himself back in Buffalo, wearing it to New Year's Eve at the country club, with sunglasses and sandals. The tailor looked frightened. His little mustache twitched uncertainly and his brown eyes had been worn soft by needlework.

Clem said he would be back no later than nine. The boat sailed south after breakfast. Outside, the dry air had chilled. From the tingling at the tip of his tongue, he realized he had been smiling hard.

Ingrid was sitting at the bar in a backwards silver dress, high in the front and buckled at the back. She invited herself to sit at his table during dinner; her white arms, pinched pink by the sun, shared in the triumphant glaze of the tablecloth, the glowing red lamp. They discussed religion. Clem had been raised as a Presbyterian, she as a Lutheran. In her father's house, north of Stockholm, there had been a guest room held ready against the arrival of Jesus Christ. Not quite seriously, it had been a custom, and yet . . . she supposed religion had bred into her a certain *expectancy*. Into him, he thought, groping, peering with difficulty into that glittering blank area which in other people, he imagined, was the cave of self, religion had bred a *dislike of litter*. It was a disappointing answer, even after he had explained the word "litter." He advanced in its place the theory that he was a royal tomb, once crammed with treasure, that had been robbed. Her white hand moved an inch toward him on the tablecloth, intelligent as a bat, and he began to cry. The tears felt genuine to him, but she said, "Stop acting."

He told her that a distressing thing had just happened to him.

She said, "That is your flaw; you are too self-conscious. You are always in costume, acting. You must always be beautiful." She was so intent on delivering this sermon that only as an afterthought did she ask him what had been the distressing thing.

He found he couldn't tell her; it was too intimate, and his own part in provoking it had been, he felt, unspeakably shameful. The tailor's homosexual advance had been, like the child's feigning a crippled arm, evoked by his money, his torturing innocence. He said, "Nothing. I've been sleeping badly and don't make sense. Ingrid: have some more wine." His palms were sweating from the effort of pronouncing her name.

After dinner, though fatigue was making his entire body shudder and itch, she asked him to take her into the lounge, where a three-piece band from Alexandria was playing dance music. The English couples waltzed and Gwenn, the young wife, frugged with one of the German boys. The green-eyed Egyptian woman danced with the purser. Egon, the German boy who knew some English, came and, with a curt bow and a curious hard stare at Clem, invited Ingrid. She danced,

Clem observed, very close, in the manner of one who, puritanically raised, thinks of it only as a substitute for intercourse. After many numbers, she was returned to him unmarred, still silver, cool, and faintly admonitory. Downstairs, in the corridor where their cabin doors were a few steps apart, she asked him, her expression watchful and stern, if he would sleep better tonight. Compared with her large eyes and long nose, her mouth was small; she pursed her lips in a thoughtful pout, holding as if in readiness a small slot of dark space between them.

He realized that her face was stern because he was a mirror in which she was gauging her beauty, her power. His smile sought to reassure her. "Yes," he said, "I'm sure I will, I'm dead."

And he did fall asleep quickly, but woke in the dark, to escape a dream in which the hieroglyphs and Pharaonic cartouches had left the incised walls and inverted and become stamps, sharp-edged stamps trying to indent themselves upon him. Awake, he identified the dream blows with the thumping of feet and furniture overhead. But he could not sink back into sleep; there was a scuttling, an occasional whispering in the corridor that he felt was coming toward him, toward his door. But once, when he opened his door, there was nothing in the corridor but bright light and several pairs of shoes. The problem of the morning prevented him from sinking back. If he went to pick up his caftan, it would seem to the tailor a submission. He would be misunderstood and vulnerable. Also, there was the danger of missing the boat. Yet the caftan would be lovely to have, a shimmering striped polished cotton, with a cartouche containing Clem's monogram in silver thread. In his agitation, his desire not to make a mistake, he could not achieve peace with his pillows; and then the telegraphic staccato of sunlight appeared on his ceiling and Egypt, that green thread through the desert, was taut and bright beyond his blinds. Leaving breakfast, light-headed, he impulsively approached the bald American on the stairs. "I beg your pardon; this is rather silly, but could you do me an immense favor?"

"Like what?"

"Just walk with me up to this shop where something I ordered should be waiting. Uh . . . it's embarrassing to explain."

"The boat's pulling out in half an hour."

"I know."

The man sized Clem up—his clean shirt, his square shoulders, his open hopeful face—and grunted, "O.K. I left my whisk in the cabin, I'll see you outside."

"Gee, I'm very grateful, uh——"

"Walt's the name."

Ingrid, coming up the stairs late to breakfast, had overheard. "May I come, too, on this expedition that is so dangerous?"

"No, it's stupid," Clem told her. "Please eat your breakfast. I'll see you on the deck afterward."

Her face attempted last night's sternness, but she was puffy beneath her eyes from sleep, and he revised upward his estimate of her age. Like him, she was over thirty. How many men had she passed through to get here, alone; how many self-forgetful nights, traumatic mornings of separation, hung-over heartbroken afternoons? It was epic to imagine, her history of love; she loomed immense in his mind, a monumental statue, forbidding and foreign, even while under his nose she blinked and puckered her lips, rejected. She went into breakfast alone.

On the walk to the shop, Clem tried to explain what had happened the evening before. Walt impatiently interrupted. "They're scum," he said. "They'll sell their mother for twenty piasters." His accent still had Newark gravel in it. A boy ran shyly beside them, offering them *soudani* from a bowl. "Amscray," Walt said, brandishing his whisk.

"Is very good," the boy said.

"You make me puke," Walt told him.

The woman and the boy doing homework were gone from the shop. Unlit, it looked dingy; Nasser's glass was cracked. The tailor sprang up when they entered, pleased and relieved. "I work all night," he said.

"Like hell you did," Walt said.

"Try on?" the tailor asked Clem.

In the flecked dim mirror, Clem saw himself gowned; a shock, because the effect was not incongruous. He looked like a husky woman, a big-boned square-faced woman, quick to blush and giggle, the kind of naïve healthy woman, with money and without many secrets, that he tended to be attracted to. He had once loved such a girl, and she had snubbed him to marry a Harvard man. "It feels tight under the armpits," he said.

The tailor rapidly caressed and patted his sides. "That is its cut," he said.

"And the cartouche was supposed to be in silver thread."

"You said gold."

"I said silver."

"Don't take it," Walt advised.

"I work all night," the tailor said.

"And here," Clem said. "This isn't a pocket, it's just a slit."

"No, no, no pocket. Supposed to let the hand through. Here, I show." He put his hand in the slit and touched Clem until Clem protested, "Hey."

"I can make you very happy," the tailor murmured.

"Throw it back in his face," Walt said. "Tell him it's a god-awful mess."

"No," Clem said. "I'll take it. The fabric is lovely. If it turns out to be too tight, I can give it to my mother." He was sweating so hard that the garment became stuck as he tried to pull it over his head, and the tailor, assisting him, was an enveloping blur of caresses.

From within the darkness of cloth, Clem heard a slap and Walt's voice snarl, "Hands off, sonny." The subdued tailor swiftly wrapped the caftan in brown paper. As Clem paid, Walt said, "I wouldn't buy that rag. Throw it back in his face." Outside, as they hurried back toward the boat, through crowded streets where women clad in black mantles stepped aside, guarding their faces against the evil eye, Walt said, "The little queer."

"I don't think it meant anything, it was just a nervous habit. But it scared me. Thanks a lot for coming along."

Walt asked him, "Ever try it with a man?"

"No. Good heavens."

Walt said, "It's not bad." He nudged Clem in walking and Clem shifted his parcel to that side, as a shield. All the way to the boat, Walt's conversation was anecdotal and obscene, describing a night he had had in Alexandria and another in Khartoum. Twice Clem had to halt and shift to Walt's other side, to keep from being nudged off the sidewalk. "It's not bad," Walt insisted. "It'd pleasantly surprise you, I guarantee it." Back on the Osiris, Clem locked the cabin door while changing into his bathing suit. The engines shivered; the boat glided away from the Luxor quay. On deck, Ingrid asked him if his dangerous expedition had been successful. She had reverted to the orange bikini.

"I got the silly thing, yes. I don't know if I'll ever wear it."

"You must model it tonight; we are having Egyptian Night."

Her intonation saying this was firm with reserve. Her air of pique cruelly pressed upon him in his sleepless, sensitive, brittle state. Ingrid's lower lip jutted in profile; her pale eyes bulged beneath the spears of her lashes. He tried to placate her by describing the tailor shop—its enchanted smallness, the woman and child bent over schoolwork.

"It is a farce," Ingrid said, with a bruising positiveness, "their schooling. They teach the poor children the language of the Koran, which is difficult and useless. The literacy statistics are nonsense."

Swirls of Arabic, dipping like bird flight from knot to knot, wound through Clem's brain and gently tugged him downward into a softness where Ingrid's tan body stretching beside him merged with the tawny strip of desert gliding beyond the ship's railing. Lemonade was being served to kings around him. On the ceiling of a temple chamber that he had seen, the goddess Nut was swallowing the sun in one corner and giving birth to it in another, all out of the same body. A body was above him and words were crashing into him like stones. He opened his eyes; it was the American widow, a broad cloud of cloth eclipsing the sun, a perfumed mass of sweet-voiced anxiety resurrected from her cabin, crying out to him, "Young man, you *look* like a bridge player. We're *des*perate for a fourth!"

. . .

The caftan pinched him under the arms; and then, later in Egyptian Night, after the meal, Ingrid danced with Egon and disappeared. To these discomforts the American widow and Walt added that of their company. Though Clem had declined her bridge invitation, his protective film had been broken and they had plunked themselves down around the little table where Clem and Ingrid were eating the buffet of *foule* and pilaf and *qualeema* and filafil and maamoule. To Clem's surprise, the food was to his taste—nutty, bland, dry. Then Ingrid was invited to dance and failed to return to the table, and the English couples, who had befriended the widow, descended in a cloud of conversation.

"This place was a hell of a lot more fun under Farouk," said the old man with a scoured red face.

"At least the poor *fellah*," a woman perhaps his wife agreed, "had a little glamour and excitement to look up to."

"Now what does the poor devil have? A war he can't fight and Soviet slogans."

"They *hate* the Russians, of course. The average Egyptian, he loves a show of style, and the Russians don't have any. Not a crumb."

"The poor dears."

And they passed on to ponder the inability, mysterious but proven a thousand times over, of Asiatics and Africans—excepting, of course, the Israelis and the Japanese—to govern themselves or, for that matter, to conduct the simplest business operation efficiently. Clem was too tired to talk and too preoccupied with the pressure chafing his armpits, but they all glanced into his face and found their opinions reflected there. In a sense, they deferred to him, for he was prosperous and young and as an American the inheritor of their colonial wisdom.

All had made attempts at native costume. Walt wore his pajamas, and the widow, in bed sheet and sunglasses and *kúfíyah*, did suggest a fat sheik, and Gwenn's husband had blacked his face with an ingenious paste of Bain de Soleil and instant coffee. Gwenn asked Clem to dance. Blushing, he declined, but she insisted. "There's nothing to it—you simply bash yourself about a bit," she said, and demonstrated.

She was dressed as a harem girl. For her top, she had torn the sleeves off one of her husband's shirts and left it unbuttoned, so that a strip of skin from the base of her throat to her navel was bare; she was not wearing a bra. Her pantaloons were less successful: yellow St.-Tropez slacks pinned in loosely below the knees. A blue-gauze scarf across her nose —setting her hectic English cheeks and Twiggy eyes eerily afloat—and gold chains around her ankles completed the costume. The band played "Delilah." As Clem watched Gwenn's feet, their shuffle, and the glitter of gold circlets, and the ten silver toenails, seemed to be rapidly writing something indecipherable. There was a quick half step she seemed unaware of, in counterpoint with her swaying head and snaking arms. "Why—oh—whyyy, De-liii-lah," the young Egyptian sang in a Liverpool whine. Clem braced his body, hoping the pumping music would possess it. His feet felt sculpturally one with the floor; it was like what stuttering must be for the tongue. The sweat of incapacity fanned outward from the pain under his arms, but Gwenn obviously rolled on, her pantaloons coming unpinned, her shirt loosening so that as she swung from side to side, one shadowy breast, and now the other, was entirely revealed. She had shut her eyes, and in the haven of her blindness Clem did manage to dance a little, to shift his weight and jerk his arms, though he was able to do it only by forgetting the music. The band changed songs and rhythms without his noticing; he was conscious mostly of the skirt of his caftan swinging around him, of Gwenn's rosy cheeks burning and turning below sealed slashes of mascara, and of her husband's stained face. He had come onto the dance floor with the American widow; as the Bain de Soleil had sunk into his skin, the instant coffee had powdered his *gallabíyah*. At last the band took a break. Gwenn's husband claimed her, and the green-eyed Egyptian woman, as Clem passed her table, said remonstratingly, "You can dance."

"He is a dervish," Amina stated.

"All Americans are dervishes," Abdul sighed. "Their energy menaces the world."

"I am the world's worst dancer; I'm hopeless," Clem said.

"Then you should sit," Leila said. All three Egyptians were dressed, with disdainful chic, in Western dress. Clem ordered a renewal of their drinks and a brandy for himself.

"Tell me," he begged Abdul. "Do you think the Russians have no style?"

"It is true," Abdul said. "They are a very ugly people. Their clothes are very baggy. They are like us, Asiatic. They are not yet convinced that this world absolutely matters."

"*Mon mari veut être un mystique*," Amina said to Clem.

Clem persisted. Fatigue made him desperate and dogged. "But," he said, "I was surprised, in Cairo, even now, with our ambassador kicked out, how many Americans were standing around the lobby of the Hilton. And all the American movies."

"For a time," Amina said, "they tried films only from the Soviet Union and China, about farming progressively. The theatre managers handed their keys in to the government and said, 'Here, you run them.' No one would come. So the Westerns came back."

"And this music," Clem said, "and your clothes."

"Oh, we love you," Abdul said, "but with our brains. You are like the stars, like the language of the Koran. We know we cannot be like that. There is a sullen place"—he moved his hand from his head to his stomach—"where the Russians make themselves at home. I speak in hope. There must be some compensation."

The waiter brought the drinks and Amina said "Shh" to her husband.

Leila said to Clem, "You have changed girl friends tonight. You have many girl friends."

He blushed. "None."

Leila said, "The big Swede, she danced very close with the German boy. Now they have both gone off."

"Into the Nile?" Amina asked. "Into the desert? How jolly romantic."

Abdul said slowly, as if bestowing comfort, "They are both Nordic. They are at home within each other. Like us and the Russians."

Leila seemed angry. Her green eyes flashed and Clem feared they would seek to scratch his face. Instead, her ankle touched his beneath the table; he flinched. "They are both," she said, "ice—ize—? They hang down in winter."

"Icicles?" Clem offered.

She curtly nodded, annoyed at needing rescue. "I have never seen one," she said in self-defense.

"Your friends the British," Abdul said, indicating the noisy table where they were finger-painting on Gwenn's husband's face, "understood us in their fashion. They had read Shakespeare. It is very good, that play. How we turned our sails and ran. Our cleverness and courage are all female."

"I'm sure that's not so," Clem said, to rescue him.

Leila snapped, "Why should it not be so? All countries are women, except horrid Uncle Sam." And though he sat at their table another hour, her ankle did not touch his again.

Floating on three brandies, Clem at last left the lounge, his robe of polished cotton swinging around him. The Frenchman was tipped back precariously in a corner, watching the dancers. He lifted his mirror in salute as Clem passed. Though even the Frenchman's wife was dancing, Ingrid had not returned, and this added to Clem's lightness, his freedom from litter. Surely he would sleep. But when he lay down on his bed, it was trembling and jerking. His cabin adjoined that of the unsociable plump couple thought to be Russian. Clem's bed and one of theirs were separated by a thin partition. His shuddered as theirs heaved with a playful, erratic violence; there was a bump, a giggle, a hoarse male sibilance. Then the agitation settled toward silence and a distinct rhythm, a steady, mounting beat that put a pulsing into the bed taut under Clem. Two or three minutes of this. Then: "Oh." The woman's exclamation was middle-pitched, totally curved, languageless; a man's guttural grunt came right on top of it. Clem's bed, in its abrupt stillness, seemed to float and spin under him. Then from beyond the partition some murmurs, a sprinkling of laughter and a resonant heave as one body left the bed. Soon, faint snoring. Clem had been robbed of the gift of sleep.

After shapeless hours of pillow wrestling, he went to the window and viewed the Nile gliding by, the constellations of village lights, the desert stars, smaller than he had expected. He wanted to open the window to smell the river and the desert, but it was sealed shut, in deference to the air conditioning. Clem remembered Ingrid and a cold silver rage, dense as an ingot, upright as an obelisk, filled his body. "You bitch," he said aloud and, by repeating those two words, over and over, leaving his mind no space to entertain any other images, he managed to wedge himself into a few hours' sleep, despite the tempting, problematical scuttle of presences in the hall, who now and then brushed his door with their fingernails. *You bitch, you bitch, you* . . . He remembered nothing about his dreams, except that they all took place back in Buffalo, amid aunts and uncles he had thought he had forgotten.

Temples. Dour dirty heavy Isna sunk in its great pit beside a city market where Clem, pestered by flies and peddlers, nearly vomited at the sight of ox palates, complete with arcs of teeth, hung up for sale. Vast sun-struck Idfu, an endless square spiral climb up steps worn into troughs toward a dizzying view, the amateur travelogist calmly grinding away on the unparapeted edge. Cheery little Kom Ombo, right by the Nile, whiter and later than the others. In one of them, dead Osiris was resurrected by a hawk alighting on his phallus; in another, Nut the sky god flowed above them nude, swimming amid gilt stars. A god was having a baby, baby Horus. Poppa Omar bent over and tenderly patted the limestone relief pitted and defaced by Coptic Christians. "See now here," he said, "the lady squat, and the other ladies hold her by the arms so, here, and the baby Horus, out he comes here. In villages all over Egypt now, the ladies there still have the babies in such manner, so we have too many the babies here." He looked up at them and smiled with unflecked benevolence. His eyes, surprisingly, were pale blue.

I Am Dying, Egypt, Dying

The man from Wisconsin was grinding away, the man from New Jersey was switching his whisk, the widow was fainting in the shade, beside a sphinx. Clem helped the Frenchman inch his feet across some age-worn steps; he was like one of those toys that walks down an inclined ramp but easily topples. The English and Egyptians were bored; too many temples, too much Ramses. Ingrid detached herself from the German boys and came to Clem. "How did you sleep?"

"Horribly. And you?"

"Well. I thought," she added, "you would be soothed by my no longer trying to rape you."

At noon, in the sun, as the Osiris glided toward Aswan, she took her accustomed chair beside Clem. When Egon left the chair on the other side of him and clamorously swam in the pool, Clem asked her, "How is he?"

"He is very nice," she said, holding her bronze face immobile in the sun. "Very earnest, very naïve. He is a revolutionary."

"I'm glad," he said, "you've found someone congenial."

"Have I? He is very young. Perhaps I went with him to make another jealous." She added, expressionless, "Did it?"

"Yes."

"I am pleased to hear it."

In the evening, she was at the bar when he went up from an unsuccessful attempt at a nap. They had docked for the last time; the boat had ceased trembling. She had reverted to the silver dress that looked put on backwards. He asked, "Where are the Germans?"

"They are with the Egyptians in the lounge. Shall we join them?"

"No," Clem said. Instead, they talked with the lanky man from Green Bay, who had ten months of advance tickets and reservations to Cape Town and back, including a homeward cabin on the Queen Elizabeth II. He spoke mostly to women's groups and high schools, and he detested the Packers. He said to Clem, "I take pride in being an eccentric, don't you?" and Clem was frightened to think that he appeared eccentric, he who had always been praised, even teased, by his mother as typically American, as even *too* normal and dependable. She sometimes implied that he had disappointed her by not defying her, by always returning from his trips.

After dinner, he and Ingrid walked in Aswan: a receding quay of benches, open shops burning a single light bulb, a swish of vehicles, mostly military. A true city, where the appetites did not beg. He had bought some postcards and let a boy shine his shoes. He paid the boy ten piasters, shielding his potent wallet with his body. They returned to the Osiris and sat in the lounge watching the others dance. A chaste circle around them forbade intrusion; or perhaps the others, having tried to enter Clem and failed, had turned away. Clem imagined them in the eyes of the others, both so composed and now so tan, two stately cool children of harsh winters. Apologizing, smiling, after three iced arracks, he bit his tongue and rose. "Forgive me, I'm dead. I must hit the hay. You stay and dance."

She shook her head, with a preoccupied stern gesture, gathered her dress tight about her hips and went with him. In the hall before his door, she stood and asked, "Don't you want me?"

A sudden numbness lifted from his stomach and made him feel unreally tall. "Yes," he said.

"Then why not take me?"

Clem looked within himself for the answer, saw only glints

refracted and distorted by a deep fatigue. "I'm frightened to," he told her. "I have no faith in my right to take things."

Ingrid listened intently, as if his words were continuing, clarifying themselves; she looked at his face and nodded. Now that they had come so far together and were here, her gaze seemed soft, as soft and weary as the tailor's. "Go to your room," she said. "If you like, then, I will come to you."

"Please do." It was as simple as dancing—you simply bash yourself about a bit.

"Would you like me to?" She was stern now, could afford to be guarded.

"Yes. *Please* do."

He left the latch off, undressed, washed, brushed his teeth, shaved the second time that day, left the bathroom light on. The bed seemed immensely clean and taut, like a sail. Strange stripes, nonsense patterns, crossed his mind. The sail held taut, permitting a gliding, but with a tipping. The light in the cabin changed. The door had been opened and shut. She was still wearing the silver dress; Clem had imagined she would change. She sat on his bed; her weight was the counterweight he had been missing. He curled tighter, as if around a pillow, and an irresistible peace descended, distinctly, from the four corners of space, along forty-five-degree angles marked in charcoal. He opened his eyes, discovering thereby that they had been shut, and the sight of her back—the belling solidity of her bottom, the buckle of the backward belt, the scoop of cloth exposing the nape of blond neck and the strong crescent of shoulder waiting to be touched—covered his eyes with silver scales. On one of the temple walls, one of the earlier ones, Poppa Omar had read off the hieroglyphs that spelled WOMAN IS PARADISE. The ship and its fittings were still and, confident she would not move, he postponed the beginning for one more second.

He awoke feeling rich, full of sleep. At breakfast, he met Ingrid by the glass dining-room doors and apologetically smiled, blushing and biting his tongue. "God, I'm sorry," he said. He added in self defense, "I told you I was dead."

"It was charming," she said. "You gave yourself to me that way."

"How long did you sit there?"

"Perhaps an hour. I tried to insert myself into your dreams. Did you dream of me?" She was a shade shy, asking.

He remembered no dreams but did not say so. Her eyes were permanently soft now toward him; they had become windows through which he could admire himself. It did not occur to him that he might admire her in the same fashion: in the morning light, he saw clearly the traces of age on her face and throat, the little scars left by time and a presumed promiscuity, for which he, though not heavily, did blame her. His defect was that, though accustomed to reflect love, he could not originate light within himself; he was as blind as the silvered side of a mirror to the possibility that he, too, might impose a disproportionate glory upon the form of another. The world was his but slid through him.

In the morning, they went by felucca to Lord Kitchener's gardens, and the Aga Khan's tomb, where a single rose was fresh in a vase. The afternoon expedition, and their last, was to the Aswan High Dam. Cameras were forbidden. They saw the anti-aircraft batteries and the worried brown soldiers in their little wooden cartoon guardhouses. The desert became very ugly: no longer the rose shimmer that had surrounded him at the airport in Luxor, it was a merciless gray that had never entertained a hope of life, not even fine in texture but littered to the horizon with black flint. And the makeshift pitted roads were ugly, and the graceless Russian machinery clanking and sitting stalled, and the styleless, already squalid propaganda pavilion containing a model of the dam. The dam itself, after the straight, elegantly arched dam the British had built upriver, seemed a mere mountain of heaped rubble, hardly distinguishable from the inchoate desert itself. Yet at its heart, where the turbines had been set, a plume like a cloud of horses leaped upward in an inverted Niagara that dissolved, horse after horse, into mist before becoming the Nile again and flowing on. Startled greenery flourished on the gray cliffs that contained the giant plume. The stocky couple who had been impassive and furtive for six days now beamed and crowed aloud; the man roughly nudged Clem to wake him to the wonder of what they were seeing. Clem agreed: "*Khorosho.*" He waited but was not nudged again. Gazing into the abyss of the trip that was over, he saw that he had been happy.

The Carol Sing

SURELY ONE OF THE NATURAL WONDERS OF TARBOX was Mr.
Burley at the Town Hall carol sing. How he would jubilate,
how he would God-rest those merry gentlemen, how he
would boom out when the male voices became Good King
Wenceslas:

> "Mark my footsteps, good my page;
> Tread thou in them boldly:
> Thou shalt find the winter's rage
> Freeze thy blood less co-*oh*-ldly."

When he hit a good "oh," standing beside him was like being
inside a great transparent Christmas ball. He had what you'd
have to call a God-given bass. This year, we other male
voices just peck at the tunes: Wendell Huddlestone, whose
hardware store has become the pizza place where the drop-
outs collect after dark; Squire Wentworth, who is still getting
up petitions to protect the marsh birds from the atomic
power plant; Lionel Merson, lighter this year by about three
pounds of gallstones; and that selectman whose freckled bald
head looks like the belly of a trout; and that fireman whose

face is bright brown all the year round from clamming; and the widow Covode's bearded son, who went into divinity school to avoid the draft; and the Bisbee boy, who no sooner was back from Vietnam than he grew a beard and painted his car every color of the rainbow; and the husband of the new couple that moved this September into the Whitman place on the beach road. He wears thick glasses above a little mumble of a mouth tight as a keyhole, but his wife appears perky enough.

> The-ey lo-okèd up and sa-haw a star,
> Shining in the east, beyond them far;
> And to the earth it ga-ave great light,
> And so it continued both da-hay and night.

She is wearing a flouncy little Christmassy number, red with white polka dots, one of those dresses so short that when she sits down on the old plush deacon's bench she has to help it with her hand to tuck under her bottom, otherwise it wouldn't. A lively bit of a girl with long thighs glossy as pond ice. She smiles nervously up over her cup of cinnamon-stick punch, wondering why she is here, in this dusty drafty public place. We must look monstrous to her, we Tarbox old-timers. And she has never heard Mr. Burley sing, but she knows something is missing this year; there is something failed, something hollow. Hester Hartner sweeps wrong notes into every chord: arthritis—arthritis and indifference.

> The first good joy that Mary had,
>   It was the joy of one;
> To see the blessèd Jesus Christ
>   When he was first her son.

The old upright, a Pickering, for most of the year has its keyboard turned to the wall, beneath the town zoning map,

its top piled high with rolled-up plot plans filing for
variances. The Town Hall was built, strange to say, as a Uni-
tarian church, around 1830, but it didn't take around here,
Unitarianism; the sea air killed it. You need big trees for a
shady mystic mood, or at least a lake to see yourself in like
they have over to Concord. So the town bought up the shell
and ran a second floor through the air of the sanctuary, between the balconies: offices and the courtroom below, more
offices and this hall above. You can still see the Doric pilasters
along the walls, the top halves. They used to use it more;
there were the Tarbox Theatricals twice a year, and political
rallies with placards and straw hats and tambourines, and get-
togethers under this or that local auspice, and town meetings
until we went representative. But now not even the holly
the ladies of the Grange have hung around can cheer it up,
can chase away the smell of dust and must, of cobwebs too
high to reach and rats' nests in the hot-air ducts and, if you
stand close to the piano, that faint sour tang of blueprints.
And Hester lately has taken to chewing eucalyptus drops.

> And him to serve God give us grace,
> *O lux beata Trinitas.*

The little wife in polka dots is laughing now: maybe the
punch is getting to her, maybe she's getting used to the look
of us. Strange people look ugly only for a while, until you
begin to fill in those tufty monkey features with a little
history and stop seeing their faces and start seeing their lives.
Regardless, it does us good, to see her here, to see young
people at the carol sing. We need new blood.

> This time of the year is spent in good cheer,
>   And neighbors together do meet,
> To sit by the fire, with friendly desire,

The Carol Sing

Each other in love to greet.
Old grudges forgot are put in the pot,
  All sorrows aside they lay;
The old and the young doth carol this song,
  To drive the cold winter away.

At bottom it's a woman's affair, a chance in the darkest of
months to iron some man-fetching clothes and get out of the
house. Those old holidays weren't scattered around the calen-
dar by chance. Harvest and seedtime, seedtime and harvest,
the elbows of the year. The women do enjoy it; they enjoy
jostle of most any kind, in my limited experience. The widow
Covode as full of rouge and purple as an old-time Scollay
Square tart, when her best hope is burial on a sunny day,
with no frost in the ground. Mrs. Hortense broad as a barn
door, yet her hands putting on a duchess's airs. Mamie Nevins
sporting a sprig of mistletoe in her neck brace. They miss
Mr. Burley. He never married and was everybody's gallant
for this occasion. He was the one to spike the punch and this
year they let young Covode do it, maybe that's why Little
Polka Dots can't keep a straight face and giggles across the
music like a pruning saw.

> *Adeste, fideles,*
> *Laeti triumphantes;*
> *Venite, venite*
> *In Bethlehem.*

Still that old tussle, "v" versus "wenite," the "th" as hard or
soft. Education is what divides us. People used to actually
resent it, the way Burley, with his education, didn't go to
some city, didn't get out. Exeter, Dartmouth, a year at the
Sorbonne, then thirty years of Tarbox. By the time he hit

: 145 :

fifty he was fat and fussy. Arrogant, too. Last sing, he two or three times told Hester to pick up her tempo. "Presto, Hester, not andante!" Never married, and never really worked. Burley Hosiery, that his grandfather had founded, was shut down and the machines sold South before Burley got his manhood. He built himself a laboratory instead and was always about to come up with something perfect: the perfect synthetic substitute for leather, the harmless insecticide, the beer can that turned itself into mulch. Some said at the end he was looking for a way to turn lead into gold. That was just malice. Anything high attracts lightning, anybody with a name attracts malice. When it happened, the papers in Boston gave him six inches and a photograph ten years old. "After a long illness." It wasn't a long illness, it was cyanide, the Friday after Thanksgiving.

> The holly bears a prickle,
> As sharp as any thorn,
> And Mary bore sweet Jesus Christ
> On Christmas day in the morn.

They said the cyanide ate out his throat worse than a blowtorch. Such a detail is satisfying but doesn't clear up the mystery. Why? Health, money, hobbies, that voice. Not having that voice makes a big hole here. Without his lead, no man dares take the lower parts; we just wheeze away at the melody with the women. It's as if the floor they put in has been taken away and we're standing in air, halfway up that old sanctuary. We peek around guiltily, missing Burley's voice. The absent seem to outnumber the present. We feel insulted, slighted. The dead turn their backs. The older you get, the more of them snub you. He was rude enough last year, Burley, correcting Hester's tempo. At one point, he even reached over, his face black with impatience, and slapped her hands that were still trying to make sense of the keys.

> Rise, and bake your Christmas bread:
> Christians, rise! The world is bare,
> And blank, and dark with want and care,
> Yet Christmas comes in the morning.

Well, why anything? Why do *we?* Come every year sure as the solstice to carol these antiquities that if you listened to the words would break your heart. Silence, darkness, Jesus, angels. Better, I suppose, to sing than to listen.

Plumbing

THE OLD PLUMBER bends forward tenderly, in the dusk of the cellar of my new house, to show me a precious, antique joint. "They haven't done them like this for thirty years," he tells me. His thin voice is like a trickle squeezed through rust. "Thirty, forty years. When I began with my father, we did them like this. It's an old lead joint. You wiped it on. You poured it hot with a ladle and held a wet rag in the other hand. There were sixteen motions you had to make before it cooled. Sixteen distinct motions. Otherwise you lost it and ruined the joint. You had to chip it away and begin again. That's how we had to do it when I started out. A boy of maybe fifteen, sixteen. This joint here could be fifty years old."

He knows my plumbing; I merely own it. He has known it through many owners. We think we are what we think and see when in truth we are upright bags of tripe. We think we have bought living space and a view when in truth we have bought a maze, a history, an archeology of pipes and cut-ins and traps and valves. The plumber shows me some stout dark

: 148 :

pipe that follows a diagonal course into the foundation wall. "See that line along the bottom there?" A line of white, a whisper of frosting on the dark pipe's underside—pallid oxidation. "Don't touch it. It'll start to bleed. See, they cast this old soil pipe in two halves. They were supposed to mount them so the seams were on the sides. But sometimes they mounted them so the seam is on the bottom." He demonstrates with cupped hands; his hands part so the crack between them widens. I strain to see between his dark palms and become by his metaphor water seeking the light. "Eventually, see, it leaks."

With his flashlight beam he follows the telltale pale line backward. "Four, five new sections should do it." He sighs, wheezes; his eyes open wider than other men's, from a life spent in the dusk. He is a poet. Where I see only a flaw, a vexing imperfection that will cost me money, he gazes fondly, musing upon the eternal presences of corrosion and flow. He sends me magnificent ironical bills, wherein catalogues of tiny parts—

1	1¼ × 1″ galv bushing	58¢
1	⅜″ brass pet cock	90¢
3	½″ blk nipple	23¢

—itemized with an accountancy so painstaking as to seem mad are in the end offset and swallowed by a torrential round figure attributed merely to "Labor":

Labor $550.

I suppose that his tender meditations with me now, even the long pauses when his large eyes blink, are Labor.

The old house, the house we left, a mile away, seems relieved to be rid of our furniture. The rooms where we lived, where we staged our meals and ceremonies and self-dramatizations and where some of us went from infancy to adolescence, rooms and stairways so imbued with our daily motions that their irregularities were bred into our bones and could be traversed in the dark, do not seem to mourn, as I had thought they would. The house exults in its sudden size, in the reach of its empty corners. Floor boards long muffled by carpets shine as if freshly varnished. Sun pours unobstructed through the curtainless windows. The house is young again. It, too, had a self, a life, which for a time was eclipsed by our lives; now, before its new owners come to burden it, it is free. Now only moonlight makes the floor creak. When, some mornings, I return, to retrieve a few final oddments—andirons, picture frames—the space of the house greets me with virginal impudence. Opening the front door is like opening the door to the cat who comes in with the morning milk, who mews in passing on his way to the beds still warm with our night's sleep, his routine so tenuously attached to ours, by a single mew and a shared roof. Nature is tougher than ecologists admit. Our house forgot us in a day.

I feel guilty that we occupied it so thinly, that a trio of movers and a day's breezes could so completely clean us out. When we moved in, a dozen years ago, I was surprised that the house, though its beams and fireplaces were three hundred years old, was not haunted. I had thought, it being so old, it would be. But an amateur witch my wife had known at college tapped the bedroom walls, sniffed the attic, and assured us—like my plumber, come to think of it, she had unnaturally distended eyes—that the place was clean. Puritan hay-farmers had built it. In the nineteenth century, it may have served as a tavern; the pike to Newburyport ran right by. In the nineteen-thirties, it had been a tenement, the rooms now so exultantly large then subdivided by plasterboard partitions that holes were poked through, so the tenants could trade sugar and flour. Rural days, poor days. Chickens had been kept upstairs for a time; my children at first said that when it rained they could smell feathers, but I took this to be the power of suggestion, a myth. Digging in the back yard, we did unearth some pewter spoons and chunks of glass bottles from a lost era of packaging. Of ourselves, a few plastic practice golf balls in the iris and a few dusty little Superballs beneath the radiators will be all for others to find. The ghosts we have left only we can see.

I see a man in a tuxedo and a woman in a long white dress stepping around the back yard, in a cold drizzle that makes them laugh, at two o'clock on Easter morning. They are hiding chocolate eggs in tinfoil and are drunk. In the morning, they will have sickly-sweet headaches, and children will wake them with the shrieks and quarrels of the hunt, and come to their parents' bed with chocolate-smeared mouths and sickening sweet breaths; but it is the apparition of early morning I see, from the perspective of a sober conscience standing in the kitchen, these two partygoers tiptoeing in the muddy yard, around the forsythia bush, up to the swing set and back. Easter bunnies.

A man bends above a child's bed; his voice and a child's voice murmur prayers in unison. They have trouble with "trespasses" versus "debts," having attended different Sunday schools. Weary, slightly asthmatic (the ghost of chicken feathers?), anxious to return downstairs to a book and a drink, he passes into the next room. The child there, a bigger child, when he offers to bow his head with her, cries softly, "Daddy, no, don't!" The round white face, dim in the dusk of the evening, seems to glow with tension, embarrassment, appeal. Embarrassed himself, too easily embarrassed, he gives her a kiss, backs off, closes her bedroom door, leaves her to the darkness.

In the largest room, its walls now bare but for phantasmal rectangles where bookcases stood and pictures hung, people are talking, gesturing dramatically. The woman, the wife, throws something—it had been about to be an ashtray, but even in her fury, which makes her face rose-red, she prudently switched to a book. She bursts into tears, perhaps at her Puritan inability to throw the ashtray, and runs into another room, not forgetting to hop over the little raised threshold where strangers to the house often trip. Children sneak quietly up and down the stairs, pale, guilty, blaming themselves, in the vaults of their innocent hearts, for this disruption. Even the dog curls her tail under, ashamed. The man sits slumped on a sofa that is no longer there. His ankles are together, his head is bowed, as if shackles restrict him. He is dramatizing his conception of himself, as a prisoner. It seems to be summer, for a little cabbage butterfly irrelevantly alights on the window screen, where hollyhocks rub and tap. The woman returns, pink in the face instead of red, and states matters in a formal, deliberated way; the man stands and shouts. She hits him; he knocks her arm away and punches her side, startled by how pleasant, how spongy, the sensation is. A sack of guts. They flounce among the furniture, which gets in their way, releasing whiffs of dust. The children edge one step higher on the stairs. The dog, hunched as if being whipped, goes to the screen door and begs to be let out. The man embraces the woman and murmurs. She is pink and warm with tears. He discovers himself weeping; what a good feeling it is!—like vomiting, like sweat. What are they saying, what are these violent, frightened people discussing? They are discussing change, natural process, the passage of time, death.

Feeble ghosts. They fade like breath on glass. In contrast I remember the potent, powerful, numinous Easter eggs of my childhood, filled solid with moist coconut, heavy as ingots, or else capacious like theatres, populated by paper silhouettes—miniature worlds generating their own sunlight. These eggs arose, in their nest of purple excelsior, that certain Sunday morning, from the same impossible-to-plumb well of mystery where the stars swam, and old photographs predating my birth were snapped, and God listened. At night, praying, I lay like a needle on the surface of this abyss, in a house haunted to the shadowy corners by Disneyesque menaces with clutching fingernails, in a town that boasted a funeral parlor at its main intersection and that was ringed all around its outskirts by barns blazoned with hex signs. On the front-parlor rug was a continent-shaped stain where as a baby I had vomited. Myth upon myth: now I am three or four, a hungry soul, eating dirt from one of the large parlor pots that hold strange ferns—feathery, cloudy, tropical presences. One of my grandmother's superstitions is that a child must eat a pound of dirt a year to grow strong. And then later, at nine or ten, I am lying on my belly, in the same spot, reading the newspaper to my blind grandfather—first the obituaries, then the rural news, and lastly the front-page headlines about Japs and Roosevelt. The paper has a deep smell, not dank like the smell of comic books but fresher, less sweet than doughnut bags but spicy, an exciting smell that has the future in it, a smell of things stacked and crisp and faintly warm, the smell of the *new*. Each day, I realize, this smell arrives and fades. And then I am thirteen and saying goodbye to the front parlor. We are moving. Beside the continent-shaped

stain on the carpet are the round stains of the fern flower-
pots. The uncurtained sunlight on these stains is a revelation.
They are stamped deep, like dinosaur footprints.

Did my children sense the frivolity of our Easter priest-
hoods? The youngest used to lie in her bed in the smallest of
the upstairs rooms and suck her thumb and stare past me at
something in the dark. Our house, in her, did surely possess
the dimension of dread that imprints every surface on the
memory, that makes each scar on the paint a clue to some
terrible depth. She was the only child who would talk about
death. Tomorrow was her birthday. "I don't want to have a
birthday. I don't want to be nine."

"But you must grow. Everybody grows. The trees grow."

"I don't want to."

"Don't you want to be a big girl like Judith?"

"No."

"Then you can wear lipstick, and a bra, and ride your
bicycle even on Central Street."

"I don't want to ride on Central Street."

"Why not?"

"Because then I will get to be an old old lady and die."

And her tears well up, and the man with her is dumb, as
all the men ever with her will be on this point dumb, in this
little room where nothing remains of us but scuffmarks and
a half-scraped Snoopy decal on the window frame. If we still
lived here, it would be time to put the screens in the windows.

Crocuses are up at the old house; daffodils bloom at the
new. The children who lived here before us left Superballs
under the radiators for us to find. In the days of appraisal and
purchase, we used to glimpse these children skulking around their
house, behind bushes and bannisters, gazing at us, the usurpers

of their future. In the days after they moved out but before our furniture moved in, we played hilarious games in the empty rooms—huge comic ricochets and bounces. Soon the balls became lost again. The rooms became crowded.

Tenderly, musingly, the plumber shows me a sawed-off section of the pipe that leads from the well to our pressure tank. The inside diameter of the pipe is reduced to the size of his finger by mineral accretions—a circle of stony layers thin as paper. It suggests a book seen endwise, but one of those books not meant to be opened, that priests wisely kept locked. "See," he says, "this has built up over forty, fifty years. I remember my dad and me putting in the pump, but this pipe was here then. Nothing you can do about it, minerals in the water. Nothing you can do about it but dig it up and replace it with inch-and-a-quarter, inch-and-a-half new."

I imagine my lawn torn up, the great golden backhoe trampling my daffodils, my dollars flooding away. Ineffectually, I protest.

The plumber sighs, as poets do, with an eye on the audience. "See, keep on with it like this, you'll burn out your new pump. It has to work too hard to draw the water. Replace it now, you'll never have to worry with it again. It'll outlast your time here."

My time, his time. His eyes open wide in the unspeaking presences of corrosion and flow. We push out through the bulkhead; a blinding piece of sky slides into place above us, fitted with temporary, timeless clouds. All around us, we are outlasted.

OTHER MODES

The Sea's Green Sameness

I WRITE THIS on the beach. Let us say, then, that I am a writer on the beach. It was once considered bad manners to admit anything of the sort, just as people walking to and from the bathroom were supposed to be invisible; but this is a rude age. Nothing is hidden. Yet everything is. In a sense a person *observed* walking to a closed door is *less* "there" than someone being forcibly imagined to be invisible.

I sit opposite the sea.[1] Its receding green surface is marked everywhere by millions of depressions, or nicks, of an uncertain color: much as this page is marked. But this page yields a meaning, however slowly, whereas the marks on the sea are everywhere the same. That is the difference between Art and Nature.

But the marks on the sea move, which is somehow portentous. And large distinctions in tone are perceptible: the purple shadows of clouds from above, of coral reefs from below; and the horizon is darker than the middle distance

---

1. The Caribbean—hence its idyllic aspect.

—almost black—and the water near me is tinted with the white of the sand underneath, so that its clear deep-throated green is made delicate, acidulous, artificial. And I seem to see, now and then, running vertically with no regard for perspective, veins of a metallic color; filaments of silver or gold —it is difficult to be certain which—waver elusively, but valuably, at an indeterminate distance below the skin of the massive, flat, monotonous volume.

Enough, surely. It is a chronic question, whether to say simply "the sea" and trust to people's imaginations, or whether to put in the adjectives. I have had only fair luck with people's imaginations; hence tend to trust adjectives. But are they to be trusted? Are they—words—anything substantial upon which we can rest our weight? The best writers say so. Sometimes I believe it. But the illogic of the belief bothers me: From whence did words gather this intrinsic potency? The source of language, the spring from which all these shadows (tinted, alliterative, shapely, but still shadows) flow, is itself in shadow.

But what, then, am I to do? Here am I, a writer, and there is the sea, a subject. For mathematical purity, let us exclude everything else—the sky, the clouds, the sand on my elbows, the threat of my children coming down the beach to join me. Let us posit a world of two halves: the ego and the external object. I think it is a fair representation of the world, a kind of biform Parliament, where two members sit, and speak for all parties. Tell me what I must do. Or rather, give me my excuse; for my vote is foreordained, it must be in opposition, and our Parliament will be stalemated until one of us dies.

The incantor of tales about the cave fire was excused by

the hungry glitter[2] of eyes. Homer swung his tides on this momentum. Aeschylus felt excused; Sophocles heroically bluffed out any doubt; with Euripides we definitely arrive at the sudden blankness, the embarrassed slapping of the pockets, the stammer, the flustered prolixity. But then a splendid excuse appeared, it seemed eternally. Dante had it. Milton. Tolstoy, Dickens, Balzac picked its bones. It was a huge creature and still gives some nourishment. Shakespeare and Dr. Johnson lived on money; it was a hearty diet, but is no longer considered hygienic. Beauty, said Keats. A trick of optics. Self, said Wordsworth and Goethe. A tautology. Reality, said the Realists, and the Opposition swamped them with pamphlets. I bore you. Even this raises an issue. Is it my duty not to bore you; my excuse, that I do not? This would bring me safely into the cozy hotel of pornographers, dinner guests, and television personalities. But you would be truly amazed, how indignantly I, the peer of the immense sea, reject such shelter. Forgive me; I know you made the offer with warm hearts. To continue my story—Conrad and James offer Groping As An End In Itself, and Proust and Joyce round out the tale with a magnificent cacophony of superb effects. I may, in this summation, have left out a few names, which you yourself can supply. The remaining question of interest: were Proust and Joyce an ending or a beginning? They seemed, from their newness, a beginning, but as time passes does not their continued newness make it clear that they are the opposite, that everything since comprises a vacuum in which the surfaces of these old works, that

---

2. Why were they hungry? Is there a narrative appetite as profound as the sexual? Why would Nature put it there? But then, why does Nature do half the things she does?

should be cracked and sunken, are preserved like fresh pigment?

How tired I am! All my intricate maneuvers, my loudly applauded and widely reprinted perorations, my passionate lobbying—all my stratagems are exhausted. I am near death. And the Opposition seems as young as ever. You see, he never exerts himself. The clerks—all the quick clerks have gone over to his side; I am left with but a few ancient men, hanging on for the pension—elicit his answers to prepared questionnaires, which he gives very reluctantly, with much coaxing. He never gets up on his feet and says a word the gallery can hear. Yet more and more his influence spreads among them. Oh, they still muster a few handclaps for my most gallant efforts, bent and breathless as I am; but it is his power they respect. Out with this metaphor—take away these congressional trappings! There. I still have some power of my own. His silence can still be twisted to my advantage.

I am writing this in the sun, which is difficult; perhaps here is a clue. You cannot write in the sun, or in perfect health. I must make myself sick with cigarettes before I can perform. Some writers use alcohol. Some read copiously. Some are gifted with infirmities. Health, sanity, and sunshine have deserted us. Even the clergy—as we labor to save them —despise us. Sitting on this beach, I wonder if I am one of those large crabs whom the operator of the Time Machine discovers at the extreme limit of the earth's senility scrabbling across a beach, stiffly waving their tentacles at a distended, dim, and oblate sun. Perhaps I am the last writer in the world. Perhaps, coming from a backward region of the country, to which news travels slow, I arrived in the capital a moment before the gates were locked forever. Perhaps all of us latter-day writers are like the priests that the peasantry continued to supply to the Church long after the aristocracy acknowledged that the jig was up.

For I look at the sea, my topic, and it seems null. No longer am I permitted to conceive charming legends about how it came to be salt, for this is known. Its chemistry, its weight, its depth, its age, its creatures so disturbingly suggestive of our own mortality—what is not known of these things, will be known. The veins of silver (or gold) in it are all mapped and will be mined tomorrow. This leaves, you say, its essence, its *ens*. Yes, but what, really, can we hope for in this line, after Plato, after Aquinas, after Einstein? Have not their brave fancies already gone the way of Poseidon?

Yet, surprisingly, I do have something new to contribute to human knowledge of the sea. It has just come to me. A revelation. If you lie down, put your head in the sand, and close one eye, the sea loses one dimension and becomes a wall. The black rim of the perfectly smooth top seems as close to me as the pale, acidulous bottom. A curious sideways tugging in the center of the wall, a freedom of motion inexplicable in a wall whose outlines are so inflexibly fixed, makes the vision strange. But it does not lead me to imagine that the wall is a fragile cloth which a blow of my hands will pierce. No, my fists and forehead are too sore for me to entertain such an illusion. But I do feel—and feel, as it were, from the outside, as if I were being beckoned—that if I were to run quickly to it, and press my naked chest against its vibrating perpendicular surface, and strain my body against it from my head to my toes, I should feel upon the beating of my heart the answer of another heart beating. I sit up, excited, foul with sand, and open both eyes, and the ocean withdraws again into its vast distances. Yet I seem to hear in the sigh of its surf encouragement from the other side of the wall of its appearance—sullen, muffled encouragement, the best it can do, trapped as it is also—encouragement for me to repeat the attempt, to rush forward in my mind again and again.

I have reverted, in my art (which I gaily admit I have not mastered [3]), to the first enchanters, who expected their nets of words to imprison the weather, to induce the trees to bear and the clouds to weep, and to drag down advice from the stars. I expect less. I do not expect the waves to obey my wand, or support my weight. I am too tired; my modesty, perhaps, damns me. All I expect is that once into my blindly spun web of words the thing itself will break: make an entry and an account of itself. Not declare what it will do. This is no mystery; we are old friends. I can observe. Not cast its vote with mine, and make a decree: I have no hope of this. The session has lasted too long. I wish it to yield only on the point of its identity. What is it? Its breadth, its glitter, its greenness and sameness balk me. *What is it?* If I knew, I could say.

---

3. As who has? Is not the Muse a mermaid whose slippery-scaled body pops from our arms the moment we try to tighten our embrace?

The Slump

THEY SAY REFLEXES, the coach says reflexes, even the papers
now are saying reflexes, but I don't think it's the reflexes so
much—last night, as a gag to cheer me up, the wife walks
into the bedroom wearing one of the kids' rubber gorilla
masks and I was under the bed in six-tenths of a second, she
had the stopwatch on me. It's that I can't see the ball the way
I used to. It used to come floating up with all seven continents showing, and the pitcher's thumbprint, and a grass
smooch or two, and the Spalding guarantee in ten-point sans-
serif, and *whop!* I could feel the sweet wood with the bat
still cocked. Now, I don't know, there's like a cloud around
it, a sort of spiral vagueness, maybe the Van Allen belt, or
maybe I lift my eye in the last second, planning how I'll
round second base, or worrying which I do first, tip my cap
or slap the third-base coach's hand. You can't see a blind spot,
Kierkegaard says, but in there now, between when the ball
leaves the bleacher background and I can hear it plop all fat
and satisfied in the catcher's mitt, there's somehow just nothing, where there used to be a lot, everything in fact, because

they're not keeping me around for my fielding, and already I see the afternoon tabloid has me down as trade bait.

The flutters don't come when they used to. It used to be, I'd back the convertible out of the garage and watch the electric eye put the door down again and drive in to the stadium, and at about the bridge turnoff I'd ease off grooving with the radio rock, and then on the lot there'd be the kids waiting to get a look and that would start the big butterflies, and when the attendant would take my car I'd want to shout *Stop, thief,* and walking down that long cement corridor I'd fantasize like I was going to the electric chair and the locker room was some dream after death, and I'd wonder why the suit fit, and how these really immortal guys, that I recognized from the bubble-gum cards I used to collect, knew my name. *They* knew *me.* And I'd go out and the stadium mumble would scoop at me and the grass seemed too precious to walk on, like emeralds, and by the time I got into the cage I couldn't remember if I batted left or right.

Now, hell, I move over the bridge singing along with the radio, and brush through the kids at just the right speed, not so fast I knock any of them down, and the attendant knows his Labor Day tip is coming, and we wink, and in the batting cage I own the place, and take my cuts, and pop five or six into the bullpen as easy as dropping dimes down a sewer. But when the scoreboard lights up, and I take those two steps up from the dugout, the biggest two steps in a ballplayer's life, and kneel in the circle, giving the crowd the old hawk profile, where once the flutters would ease off, now they dig down and begin.

They say I'm not hungry, but I still feel hungry, only now it's a kind of panic hungry, and that's not the right kind. Ever watch one of your little kids try to catch a ball? He gets so excited with the idea he's going to catch it he shuts his eyes. That's me now. I walk up to the plate, having come all this way—a lot of hotels, a lot of shagging—and my eyes feel shut. And I stand up there trying to push my eyeballs through my eyelids, and my retinas register maybe a little green, and the black patch of some nuns in far left field. That's panic hungry.

Kierkegaard called it dread. It queers the works. My wife comes at me without the gorilla mask and when in the old days, *whop!*, now she slides by with a hurt expression and a flicker of gray above her temple. I go out and ride the power mower and I've already done it so often the lawn is brown. The kids get me out of bed for a little fungo and it scares me to see them trying, busting their lungs, all that shagging ahead of them. In Florida—we used to love it in Florida, the smell of citrus and marlin, the flat pink sections where the old people drift around smiling with transistor plugs in their ears—we lie on the beach after a workout and the sun seems a high fly I'm going to lose and the waves keep coming like they've been doing for a billion years, up to the plate, up to the plate. Kierkegaard probably has the clue, somewhere in there, but I picked up *Concluding Unscientific Postscript* the other day and I couldn't see the print, that is, I could see the lines, but there wasn't anything on them, like the rows of deep seats in the shade of the second deck on a Thursday afternoon, just a single ice-cream vendor sitting there, nobody around to sell to, a speck of white in all that shade, old Søren Sock himself, keeping his goods cool.

I think maybe if I got beaned. That's probably what the wife is hinting at with the gorilla mask. A change of pace, like the time DiMaggio broke his slump by Topping's telling him to go to a night club and get plastered. I've stopped ducking, but the trouble is, if you're not hitting, they don't brush you back. On me, they've stopped trying for even the corners; they put it right down the pike. I can see it in his evil eye as he takes the sign and rears back, I can hear the catcher snicker, and for a second of reflex there I can see it like it used to be, continents and cities and every green tree distinct as a stitch, and the hickory sweetens in my hands, and I feel the good old sure hunger. Then something happens. It blurs, skips, fades, I don't know. It's not caring enough, is what it probably is, it's knowing that none of it—the stadium, the averages—is really there, just *you* are there, and it's not enough.

The Pro

I AM on my four-hundred-and-twelfth golf lesson, and my drives still have that pushed little tail, and my irons still take the divot on the wrong side of the ball. My pro is a big gloomy sun-browned man—age about thirty-eight, weight around 195. When he holds a club in his gloved hand and swishes it nervously (the nervousness comes over him after the first twenty minutes of our lesson), he makes it look light as a feather, a straw, a baton. Once I sneaked his 3-wood from his bag, and the head weighed more than a cannonball. "Easy does it, Mr. Wallace," he says to me. My name is not Wallace, but he smooths his clients toward one generic, acceptable name. I call him Dave.

"Easy does it, Mr. Wallace," he says. "That ball is not going anywhere by itself, so what's your hurry?"

"I want to clobber the bastard," I say. It took me two hundred lessons to attain this pitch of frankness.

"You dipped again," he tells me, without passion. "That right shoulder of yours dipped, and your knees locked, you were so anxious. Ride those knees, Mr. Wallace."

"I can't. I keep thinking about my wrists. I'm afraid I won't pronate them."

This is meant to be a joke, but he doesn't smile. "Ride those knees, Mr. Wallace. Forget your wrists. Look." He takes my 5-iron into his hands, a sight so thrilling it knocks the breath out of me. It is like, in the movies we all saw as children (oh, blessed childhood!), the instant when King Kong, or the gigantic Cyclops, lifts the beautiful blonde, who has blessedly fainted, over his head, and she becomes utterly weightless, a thing of sheer air and vision and pathos. I love it, I feel half sick with pleasure, when he lifts my club, and want to tell him so, but I can't. After four hundred and eleven lessons, I still repress.

"The hands can't *help* but be right," he says, "if the *knees* are right." He twitches the club, so casually I think he is brushing a bee from the ball's surface. There is an innocent click; the ball whizzes into the air and rises along a line as straight as the edge of a steel ruler, hangs at its remote apogee for a moment of meditation, and settles like a snowflake twenty yards beyond the shagging caddie.

"Gorgeous, Dave," I say, with an affectation of camaraderie, though my stomach is a sour churning of adoration and dread.

He says, "A little fat, but that's the idea. Did you see me grunt and strain?"

"No, Dave." This is our litany.

"Did you see me jerk my head, or freeze at the top of the backswing, or rock forward on my toes?"

"No, Dave, no."

"Well then, what's the problem? Step up and show me how."

I assume my stance, and take back the club, low, slowly; at

the top, my eyes fog over, and my joints dip and swirl like
barn swallows. I swing. There is a fruitless commotion of
dust and rubber at my feet. "Smothered it," I say promptly.
After enough lessons, the terminology becomes second nature.
The whole process, as I understand it, is essentially one of
self-analysis. The pro is merely a catalyst, a random sample,
I have read somewhere, from the grab bag of humanity.

He insists on wearing a droll porkpie hat from which his
heavy brown figure somehow downflows; his sloping shoulders, his hanging arms, his faintly pendulous belly, and his
bent knees all tend toward his shoes, which are ideally natty
—solid as bricks, black and white, with baroque stitching,
frilled kilties, and spikes as neat as alligator teeth. He looks at
me almost with interest. His grass-green irises are tiny,
whittled by years of concentrating on the ball. "Loosen up,"
he tells me. I love it, I clench with gratitude, when he deigns
to be directive. "Take a few practice swings, Mr. Wallace.
You looked like a rusty mechanical man on that one. Listen.
Golf is an effortless game."

"Maybe I have no aptitude," I say, giggling, blushing,
hoping to deflect him with the humility bit.

He is not deflected. Stolidly he says, "Your swing is sweet.
When it's there." Thus he uplifts me and crushes me from
phrase to phrase. "You're blocking yourself out," he goes on.
"You're not open to your own potential. You're not, as we
say, *free*."

"I know, I know. That's why I'm taking all these expensive
lessons."

"Swing, Mr. Wallace. Show me your swing."

I swing, and feel the impurities like bubbles and warps in
glass: hurried backswing, too much right hand at impact,
failure to finish high.

. . .

The pro strips off his glove. "Come over to the eighteenth green." I think we are going to practice chipping (a restricted but relaxed pendulum motion) for the fiftieth time, but he says, "Lie down."

The green is firm yet springy. The grounds crew has done a fine job watering this summer, through that long dry spell. Not since childhood have I lain this way, on sweet flat grass, looking up into a tree, branch above branch, each leaf distinct in its generic shape, as when, in elementary school, we used to press them between wax paper. The tree is a sugar maple. For all the times I have tried to hit around it, I never noticed its species before. In the fall, its dried-up leaves have to be brushed from the line of every putt. This spring, when the branches were tracery dusted with a golden budding, I punched a 9-iron right through the crown and salvaged a double bogey.

Behind and above me, the pro's voice is mellower than I remember it, with a lulling grittiness, like undissolved sugar in tea. He says, "Mr. Wallace, tell me what you're thinking about when you freeze at the top of your backswing."

"I'm thinking about my shot. I see it sailing dead on the pin, hitting six feet short, taking a bite with lots of backspin, and dribbling into the cup. The crowd goes *ooh* and cheers."

"Who's in the crowd? Anybody you know personally?"

"No . . . wait. There is somebody. My mother. She has one of those cardboard periscope things and shouts out, 'Gorgeous, Billy!' "

"She calls you Billy."

"That's my name, Dave. William, Willy, Billy, Bill. Let's cut out this Mr. Wallace routine. You call me Bill, I'll call you Dave." He is much easier to talk to, the pro, without the sight of his powerful passionless gloom, his hands (one bare, one gloved) making a mockery of the club's weight.

"Anybody else you know? Wife? Kids?"

"No, my wife's had to take the babysitter home. Most of the kids are at camp."

"What else do you see up there at the top of the back-swing?"

"I see myself quitting lessons." It was out, *whiz*, before I had time to censor. Silence reigns in the leafy dome above me. A sparrow is hopping from branch to branch, like a pencil point going from number to number in those children's puzzles we all used to do.

At last the pro grunts, which, as we said, he never does. "The last time you were out, Mr. Wallace, what did you shoot?"

"You mean the last time I kept count?"

"Mm."

"A hundred eight. But that was with some lucky putts."

"Mm. Better stand up. Any prolonged pressure, the green may get a fungus. This bent grass is hell to maintain." When I stand, he studies me, chuckles, and says to an invisible attendant, "A hundred eight, with a hot putter yet, and he wants to quit lessons."

I beg, "Not quit forever—just for a vacation. Let me play a few different courses. You know, get out into the world. Maybe even try a public course. Hell, or go to a driving range and whack out a bucket of balls. You know, learn to live with the game I've got. Enjoy life."

His noble impassivity is invested with a shimmering, twinkling humorousness; his leathery face softens toward a smile, and the trace of a dimple is discovered in his cheek. "Golf is life," he says softly, and his green eyes expand, "and life is lessons," and the humps of his brown muscles merge with the hillocks and swales of the course, whose red flags prick the farthest horizon, and whose dimmest sand traps are indistinguishable from galaxies. I see that he is right, as always, absolutely; there is no life, no world, beyond the golf course—just an infinite and terrible falling-off. "If I don't give *you* lessons," he is going on, "how will I pay for *my* lessons?"

"*You* take lessons?"

"Sure. I hook under pressure. Like Palmer. I'm too strong. Any rough on the left, there I am. You don't have that problem, with your nice pushy slice."

"You mean there's a sense," I ask, scarcely daring, "in which *you* need *me?*"

He puts his hand on my shoulder, the hand pale from wearing the glove, and I become a feather at the touch, all air and ease. "Mr. Wallace," he says, "I've learned a lot from your sweet swing. I hate it when, like now, the half hour's up."

"Next Tuesday, eleven-thirty?"

Solemnly my pro nods. "We'll smooth out your chipping. Here in the shade."

One of My Generation

SOMETIMES, to test my courage, I face students; they gaze at me with those drug-begentled eyes that have seen Krishna and the connection between a baby-pink dean and a canister of napalm, and their polite (more or less) silence poses the question "And what of *your* generation?" In search of an answer, I see myself climbing, nearly twenty Septembers ago, the five flights to my college room and finding, bent-necked and narrow-shouldered in an island of light, in a chamber bare but for the bleakest sticks of institutional furniture, my new roommate writing a poem. I tiptoe closer and peek over his shoulder. He writes with a tensely gripped pencil very tiny letters with long, gouging descenders. Now, as then, I cannot make out the poem, but it had a rose in it, and a cross, and a mother, and a lot of compacted backward phrasing. His poems, of which I was to read many, usually struck me as instances of misapplied force, like screws hammered into wood. However, through the mist of years certain images still wink: a father's arm outflung like a lighthouse beam, a ferret suddenly twisting in a nest of religious imagery, an orchidaceous canopy dappling the water ("lizarding / the glissant scum") during an imaginary trip down the Amazon. Writing on with his strange neat vehemence, my new room-mate completed the stanza before rising to shake my hand. His name was Ed Popper and he came from Nebraska. He had been raised a Baptist but had become an Anglo-Catholic. He was a disciple of Robert Lowell—the early, Boston Lowell, the Lowell of *Lord Weary's Castle* and "The Quaker Graveyard in Nantucket." I learned all this later; as he rose to shake my hand I knew only that his shoulders were narrow for the width of his hips and that, though alone in a drab dormitory room on the day before registration, he wore a rose-colored shirt with a tight starched collar and a silver collar pin beneath the tiniest, driest, most intense necktie knot I had ever seen. His glasses were so thick the flesh of his sockets formed concentric circles around blue bull's-eyes. His domination of me began at once: he was composed and intense and I panting and weak-kneed, for in those days I made it a point of honor always to run up the five flights two steps at a time, without stopping.

He had read everything, it seemed. His father was a grain farmer, and Ed's companions in his rural isolation had been Eliot and Lowell, Valéry and Pound, Ford Madox Ford and Anaïs Nin. I pictured him carrying the books down the aisles of cornfields and settling to read in the shade of a creekside willow. As an adolescent he had written letters East to great men (signed answers had come from John Dos Passos and William Carlos Williams) and to Manhattan booksellers. He owned Knopf's lovely first edition, bound in pastel clown stripes, of Wallace Stevens' *Harmonium;* the war-time pamphlets, in four different dusty colors, whereby Faber had issued the *Four Quartets* one by one; the dove-gray booklet, printed in Dijon in 1923, containing three stories and ten poems by Ernest Hemingway; and a polychrome row, from *To the Lighthouse* to *Between the Acts,* of Hogarth Press's delicately designed Virginia Woolfs. The acquisition, physical and mental, of these works belonged to Ed's past. Literature had ceased to be his study and had become his essence, an atmosphere he effortlessly breathed. In the year we lived together I never saw him read a book or heard him say a respectful word about any author save Lowell and, once, Lord Byron. We were building—Ed was building in my presence—a ladder of the English poets, ranking them by excellence. Tennyson? "Altogether soft," Ed said—"a Victorian moonbeam manufacturer," and placed him on the rung below Cowper. Browning, then? "A rhyming O. Henry," Ed pronounced, and banished him to the nether region below Cowley. I timidly offered him Pope. "Twaddle, and his only saving grace was that he knew it. A notch above Wordsworth and no higher." Hopkins received Ed's favorite verdict: "Minor. Except for two or three stanzas of the 'Deutschland,' a thoroughly unmajor poet. Better than Longfellow, worse than Sidney." Sidney in turn was better than Shelley, worse than Keats. Keats weighed in under Donne, who was inferior to Milton (on the sole strength of "On the Morning of Christ's Nativity"; Ed detested *Paradise Lost* and thought "Lycidas" unpleasantly homosexual), who, if we followed the guidelines of Eliot's rather overrated essay on the breakup of sensibility, was less worthy than Dryden, who could not in good conscience be ranked above Thomas Traherne. At the session's end, through the pewter haze of cigarette smoke, George Gordon, Lord Byron, emerged by negative deduction as the greatest of all English poets. Ed considered this unexpected result and thoughtfully nodded assent. "He has the necessary hardness," he said, adding, "We're speaking pre-Lowell, of course."

Could I explain, to a crowd of riot-minded guitarists, how real, if imperfectly read, these great names were to us? Or with what zest we executed the academic exercise, by now perhaps as obsolete as diagrammatic parsing, called *explication?* To train one's mind to climb, like a vine on a sunny wall, across the surface of a poem by George Herbert, seeking the handhold crannies of pun, ambiguity, and buried allusion; to bring forth from the surface sense of the poem an altogether other, hidden poem of consistent metaphor and, as it were, verbal subversion; to feel, in Eliot's phrase, a thought like an emotion; to *explicate*—this was life lived on the nerve ends. Ed was a master of explication; whatever on exams he lost on the facts he made up on the set passages. Once, for my amusement, he explicated a column of names in the Boston Telephone Directory and proved it to be really about night journeys, seed-planting rites, and the Eternal Return. Less playfully, beneath the surface text of history he spied the Christian counterpoint of Fall and Redemption, the radiant skeleton wrapped in earth's distasteful flesh. Ed was a master, too, of literary gossip, an unprinted Lives of the Poets; he would tell me, with the deadpan rattle of a secret agent, how one night in Paris Pound saved Eliot from suicide, or what Wallace Stevens said to Marianne Moore before disappearing forever into the disguise of a Hartford insurance executive. On an occasion of rare excitement, fresh from a festive night in the offices of the literary magazine of which he was an editor, he brought back to our room a holy relic, a blank piece of paper upon which had been impressed the wet ring, now dried to near-invisibility, of a Martini glass set down by Conrad Aiken.

Ed's devotion eventually earned him a martyrdom. At his oral exams, with a *summa* in the balance, he declined to discuss, on the ground that they were minor, a number of poets including Tennyson, Wordsworth, and Pope; he was knocked down to a *cum*. Out of college, his talents for explication and passionate discrimination lacked a ready market. For a time, I would see him in New York, where he was always about to be interviewed for a job with some textbook publisher or news magazine. But even when he kept the appointment, he must have betrayed his opinion that the organization, let alone his prospective function within it, was impossibly minor, for he was never hired. He grew eccentric and fat. His striped shirts were worn dirty; his tiny tie knots looked pained. My wife and I had him several times to dinner. The last time, we discussed Proust, whom I, in my plodding way, had just begun to read. "Charlus," Ed said. "What a horrible man! What a loathsome, incredible individual! Oh!" And, to our consternation, he couldn't stop ranting; he drank all our brandy, smashed a lampshade, and left at two in the morning, still spewing abhorrence of Charlus. I walked him to the corner, where he embraced me. He would have kissed me, had I not ducked my head. Roommates make such gauche hellos and goodbyes. A few months later, I heard that Ed had found a job, and a year later that he was very good at it, and rising rapidly. His employer was the C.I.A.

So, students, when you revile the "power structure" and storm the Pentagon, you are disturbing a haven of old English majors. It is only Ed Popper in there, with his narrow shoulders, his nicotine-orange fingers, his first editions (worth hundreds now), his farmboy twang, his crucifix, and his eyes like blind blue targets. He was an Arabist first, and spent years in Beirut, Istanbul, and Damascus. In the middle sixties he was taught Lao and sent to Southeast Asia. Now, I believe, he is in South America, perhaps seeing with more than a poet's inner eye the orchidaceous canopies that dapple the Amazon's gliding scum. Neither of us, surely, is capable of a "political" act; we rang doorbells for Stevenson, as I recall, because he seemed a poet *manqué*. When we met accidentally a year ago, before Ed disappeared into the "southern continent" that he refused to identify by name, and lunched in a Chinese restaurant, where he one-upped me by ordering in Chinese, I timidly asked about Vietnam. There must be, I suggested, some secret strategic reason, some resource worth fighting for. "Nonsense," Ed said, "there's nothing. Nobody wants it. We don't want it, Ho Chi Minh doesn't want it; it's simply a question of annoying the other side. Vietnam, I'm afraid, is thoroughly minor." Ed was impeccably dressed and slimmer—he had developed, I thought, the necessary hardness. He also told me, of my own poems, which had slowly begun to leak into print, that though I handled stanzaic patterns well I quite lacked resonance—which seemed true enough to be a reason not to see Ed soon again. I would rather look at a map, all those flat warring colors, and imagine him in it, a hidden allusion in the poem of the world.

God Speaks

THE WORLD IS MOCKED—belittled, perforated—by the success
of our contemporaries in it. The realm of deeds and wealth,
which to a child appears a gaudy heaven staffed with invin-
cible powers, is revealed as a tattered heirloom limply de-
scending from one generation of caretakers to the next. In
the ten years since our graduation, one of my Harvard classmates has become a Congressman; another a bit movie actor,
whose specialty is playing the "goofy" guy in those beach-
party movies that co-star Fred MacMurray and Elvis Presley;
a third a professor of Celtic languages at Brandeis. Three others
have annual incomes of over a hundred thousand a year.
Which these three are, the class report (a fat red paperback)
does not say. Nor does it say anything, beyond a curt forwarding address in Kabul, of my old tennis opponent Gish
Imra, whose fate has been the noblest and strangest of all;
for, if I read the newspapers right, he has become not merely
important but divine.

The numinous rumor haloing his slight and sallow person
—with his slicked-down hair the no-color of cardboard and

his lavender little lips like the lips of a sarcastic prepubescent girl—seemed, when I knew him, a kind of undergraduate joke. I understood only that his father was the "profoundly venerated" chieftain of the Shīgar tribe of Nuristan. Two years ago (that is, in 1962) when his father died, in an assassination so ambiguous in its effects that both the Russians and the C.I.A. were rumored to be responsible, the newspapers printed some helpful, if not entirely enlightening, background material. I synopsize briefly:

The region of Central Asia now called (though not by its own inhabitants) Afghanistan has been overswept by many political and religious tides—Greek and Arab from the west, Mongol from the north, Buddhist and Hindu from the east. The old Afghan chroniclers, surprisingly, call themselves the Children of Israel and claim descent from King Saul. Under the Kushan dynasty, derived from the Yue-chi tribe that expelled the Parthians in the first century A.D., the Buddhist religion was established. Huns ousted the Buddhists; Turkish adventurers brought Islam; Genghis Khan devastated the dynasty of Ghor. Aloof from these conversions and counter-conversions stood the mysteriously fair-skinned people of the Hindu Kush, a mountain range in the region north of Kabul traditionally known as Kafiristan, "The Country of Unbelievers." The region is impenetrably wild. The mountains are so steep some valleys are in shadow for six months of the year. Landslides of loose scree occur. Mulberries grow, and the ibex flourishes. A legend traces the human inhabitants back to stragglers from the army of Alexander the Great, who crossed the Hindu Kush on his way to the Indus in 327 B.C. But Alexander did battle in the Kunar Valley with a blond and warlike race called, then, the Aspasians. The Kafirs worshiped a pantheon of gods that included Imra the Creator and Gish the God of War, drank gross amounts of wine, kept slaves, robbed strangers, lived in tall wooden houses, and spoke, valley by valley, mutually unintelligible dialects of Dardic. Their women were, and are, renowned for handsomeness.

In 1895 the amir Abdur Rahman, with British complicity, on the provocation that the Russians might annex the area, sent his gigantic commander Ghulam Haider Khan on a campaign to convert the Kafirs by the sword—the last such conversion in history. The Kafirs succumbed, and the region was christened Nuristan, "The Country of Light." However, one pocket of resistance remained, in the remote valley inhabited by the Shīgar tribe. Winter snows sealed the valley off, and the legions of Ghulam Haider Khan turned back. In celebration, the Shīgars, who numbered not more than twelve thousand, gave their chief, my tennis friend's great-grandfather, the name Gish Imra—as if we were to call a President Thor Jehovah. Probably the Shīgar chieftains were already semi-deified. The ancient ceremony, for instance, whereby on the day of the vernal equinox the chief would take for himself as much treasure (lapis lazuli from Badakhshan, rubies from the famous mine in the Jagdalak Pass, and, in recent times, wristwatches from Switzerland) as he could hoist with a straight right arm onto an altar five feet high has many analogues in Frazer.

While the religious antecedents of this throne are obscure, its modern political career is a matter of record. The first Gish Imra was a prodigious brute who maintained his tribe, of necessity, in a state of impregnable ferocity. No European traveller or Moslem emissary is known to have returned from an audience with him, and in Nuristani art he is always represented simply as the sun—with blank features, circular face, and stylized radii. His son, who succeeded him in 1915, travelled with a bodyguard of two thousand men to Kabul to exchange rugs, pledges, and mulberry butter with the amir Habibullah, who had recently extended leniency to the Ghilzais and Mangals of Khost. Thus begins the recognized autonomy of the Shīgars under the amir. Shīgar tribesmen fought beside Amanullah in his war with the British in the summer of 1919, but remained aloof when, ten years later, his excessively progressive regime collapsed under pressure from the fanatical south. The second Gish Imra died, at the age of ninety-three, in 1946, whereupon his son, who in the nineteen-thirties had enjoyed a position in the League of Nations and in café society, succeeded him. An unhappy and thoroughly Europeanized man, the third Gish Imra, when he was not wintering in Cannes or Menton, fortified himself against the tireless machinations of the amirate with perhaps excessive helpings of American advice and French cuisine. Our mission in his court, headed by the shadowy "Major Damon," was never officially acknowledged, and Congressional investigations ran dry in the sands of obfuscation. The French foodstuffs, including truffles and goose livers, were imported into the fastnesses of the Hindu Kush on the backs of goats organized into fragrant caravans.

My friend had been tutored at home, schooled in Bern, and sent to Harvard as a political gesture, much as his father had gone to Oxford. His tennis, learned in Switzerland, was stronger from the backcourt than at the net. His backhand was slightly wristy, his serve loopy and fat; but his forehand, administered with a powerful straight right arm, came off the bounce with a pace that constantly surprised me, for Gish Imra could not have weighed more than one hundred and fifteen pounds. He drove a little red MG with numerous gears, and it was in this car that we went, on one occasion, into Boston, still in our tennis whites, to have dinner together. It was late in the spring, and perhaps the approaching end of our senior year had prompted his unexpected invitation. Gish kept habitually aloof, and after his sophomore year did not have roommates. I had met him when we were both freshmen, working off our physical-education requirements with tennis, which I had learned on some pitted public courts in Pennsylvania. My game, then as now, in I suppose the American style, disdained solid ground strokes for a hopeful mishmash of reckless, glamorous "gets" and satisfying overhead smashes. Despite his smaller size and soft serve, he beat me as often as I beat him. We were well matched, and each spring, until we graduated, on one of those sudden soft days when the classroom window is thrown open above the bust of Emerson and the Radcliffe girls venture down to the Charles with books and blankets, he would call me up and in his formal, faintly mischievous voice offer to renew our competition. I was pleased to accept. After a winter of sitting I needed the exercise, and I suppose, having this dim sense of his "divinity," I was flattered.

I recall our dinner imperfectly. I remember that it was still daylight outside, that the restaurant was the old Nile, long since vanished, and that the manager had frowned at our bare legs as we walked in. I remember the glow of the jukebox selector on my left, and the thoughtful pallor of my companion's face, and the startling ease with which he downed two very dry gimlets. But I do not remember the conversation that led up to the brief exchange I will never forget. It must have been by way of "Cross-currents." Though he was a

Government major and I in Mathematics, we were, that year, taking one course in common—a popular Comp. Lit. concoction designated "Cross-Currents in Nineteenth-Century Thought." The course, taught by a beetle-browed ironist from the University of Chicago, dealt with four thinkers— Nietzsche, Marx, Kierkegaard, and Dostoevski—who with their different strokes had paddled against the liberal, progressivist mainstream of their century. I dimly recall expressing to Gish my enthusiasm for Kierkegaard, and perhaps I confessed, in passing, the fact that I, like Kierkegaard, was a Lutheran.

He looked at me sharply; there was not much amiability in his face. Though his skin was as fair as mine, there was something taut and flattened underlying his fine features. "Do you believe in it?"

"I don't know. Part of it, I suppose."

"Which of it?"

I began to blush. I realized that in a primitive by-way of my being I had "revered" my slight friend and had regarded him, for all the times I had victimized his backhand, with what used to be called "superstitious awe"; so that I felt unworthy and embarrassed in the face of his questioning.

He insisted, "Do you believe in personal immortality?"

I assumed that, being a god, he was certainly pious. I said, "Why not? It can't be disproved."

"I can't see it," Gish said.

Though the remark seemed addressed, calmly, more to himself than to me, my heart sank, and kept sinking, through the depths of this somehow authoritative denial.

"But it's not supposed to be *seen*," I pleaded. "It must be be*lieved*. Belief is the option we've been given."

He shook his head, regretfully, inexorably. His voice was small and high-pitched, yet his enunciation was firm. "I agree with Marx," he said. "It's a hoax. It's a method whereby the powerful keep the ignorant from rebelling."

I was shocked; the ground lurched under me. Not until then—could it be?—did I realize by how much some of my classmates were older in spirit than I. Out of the blankness of my fright arose the sword-thin laugh of this other, and his voice saying to me, "Do you want to hear a Kafir legend? This is how the belly of the ibex became white. When God made the Great Flood, when you say Noah built his ark, the ibex ran into the mountains. The waters kept rising, and the ibex went from mountain to mountain, until at last he came to the highest of all, to Tirich Mir, and there he stood, waiting. The water rose to his feet, to his knees, to his belly; and then it subsided." Gish showed me, with slender hands and wrists flat like female wrists, the soft motion of the subsiding. "And that," he said, "is why the belly of the ibex is white. That is why you think you believe. The waters have not yet closed over you." His voice was gentle and bitter and the light in his gray eyes was, yes, gay.

Though the class report, for all its crimson bulk, has nothing in it but a Kabul forwarding address, the newspapers have printed a little about Gish's postgraduate career. Becoming king (if that is what it is) upon his father's violent death, the fourth Gish Imra has reversed all liberal trends in the Shīgar state. Contact with the south and the Kabul administration has dwindled; radios were destroyed by tribal decree; strangers venture into the region at their own risk and may expect to be robbed. Certain brutal aspects of the cult of worship, which had fallen into disuse, have been revived, in the name of cultural autonomy. My friend, seeking a policy, "can't see" the reign of his unhappy father and looks toward his grandfather, who left the mountains amid two thousand bodyguards, and even beyond, toward his great-grandfather, the inexorable sun.

Under the Microscope

IT WAS NOT HIS KIND OF POND; the water tasted slightly acid. He was a Cyclops, the commonest of copepods, and this crowd seemed exotically cladoceran—stylish water-fleas with transparent carapaces, all shimmer and bubbles and twitch. His hostess, a magnificent  Daphnia fully an eighth of an inch tall, her heart and cephalic ganglion visibly pulsing, welcomed him with a lavish gesture of her ciliate, branching antennae; for a moment he feared she would eat him. Instead she offered him a platter of living desmids. They were  bright green in color and shaped like crescents, hourglasses, omens. "Who do you know here?" Her voice was a distinct constant above the din. "Everybody knows *you*, of course. They've read your books." His books, taken all together, with generous margins, would easily have fitted on the period that ends this sentence.

The Cyclops modestly grimaced, answered "No one," and

 turned to a young specimen of water-mite, probably *Hydrachna geographica,* still bearing ruddy traces of the larval stage. "Have you been here long?" he asked, meaning less the party than the pond.

"Long enough." Her answer came as swiftly as a reflex. "I go back to the surface now and then; we breathe air, you know."

"Oh I know. I envy you." He noticed she had only six legs. She was newly hatched, then. Between her eyes, arranged in two pairs, he counted a fifth, in the middle, and wondered if in her he might find his own central single optic amplified and confirmed. His antennules yearned to touch her red spots; he wanted to ask her, *What do you see?* Young as she was, partially formed, she appeared, alerted by his abrupt confession of envy, ready to respond to any question, however presuming.

But at that moment a monstrous fairy shrimp, an inch in length and extravagantly tinted blue, green, and bronze, swam by on its back, and the water shuddered. Furious, the Cyclops asked the water-mite, "Who invites *them?* They're not even in our scale."

She shrugged permissively, showing that indeed she had been here long enough. "They're entomostracans," she said, "just like Daphnia. They amuse her."

"They're going to eat her up," the Cyclops predicted.

Though she laughed, her fifth eye gazed steadily into his wide lone one. "But isn't that what we all want? Subconsciously, of course."

"Of course."

An elegant, melancholy flatworm was passing *hors d'œuvres*. The Cyclops took some diatoms, cracked their delicate shells of sil-

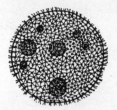

ica, and ate them. They tasted golden brown. Growing hungrier, he pushed through to the serving table and had a Volvox in algae dip. A shrill little rotifer, his head cilia whirling, his three-toothed mastax chattering, leaped up before him, saying, with the mixture of put-on and pleading characteristic of this pond, "I wead all your wunnaful books, and I have a wittle bag of pomes I wote myself, and I would wove it, *wove* it if you would wead them and wecommend them to a big bad pubwisher!" At a loss for a civil answer, the Cyclops consid-

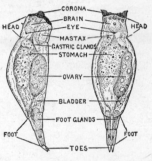

ered the rotifer silently, then ate him. He tasted slightly acid.

The party was thickening. A host of protozoans drifted in on a raft of sphagnum moss: a trumpet-shaped Stentor, apparently famous and interlocked with a lanky, bleached Spirostomum; a claque of paramœcia, swishing back and forth tickling the crustacea on the backs of their knees; an old Vorti-cella, a plantlike animalcule as dreary, the Cyclops thought, as the batch of puffs rooted to the flap of last year's *succès d'estime*.

The kitchen was crammed
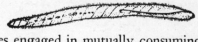
with ostracods and flagellates engaged in mutually consuming

conversation, and over in a corner, beneath an African mask, a great brown hydra, the real thing, attached by its sticky

foot to the hissing steam radiator, rhythmically swung its tentacles here and there until one of them touched, in the circle of admirers, something appetizing; then the poison sacs exploded, the other tentacles contracted, and the prey was stuffed into the hydra's swollen coelenteron, which gluttony had stretched to a transparency that veiled the preceding meals like polyethylene film protecting a rack of dry-cleaned suits. Hairy with bacteria, a Simocephalus was munching a rapt nematode. The fairy shrimps, having multiplied, their crimson tails glowing with hæmoglobin, came cruising in from the empty bedrooms. The party was thinning.

Suddenly fearful, fearing he had lost her forever, the Cyclops searched for the water-mite, and found her miserably crouching in a corner, quite drunk, her seventh and eighth legs almost sprouted. "What do you see?" he now dared ask.

"Too much," she answered swiftly. "Everything. Oh, it's horrible, horrible."

Out of mercy as much as appetite, he ate her. She felt prickly inside him. Hurriedly—the rooms were almost depleted, it was late—he sought his hostess. She was by the doorway, her antennae frazzled from waving goodbye, but still magnificent, Daphnia, her carapace a liquid shimmer of psychedelic pastel. "Don't go," she commanded, expanding, "I have a *minus*cule favor to ask. Now that my children, all thirteen billion of them, thank God, are off at school, I've taken a part-time editing job, and my first real break is this manuscript I'd be *so* grateful to have you read and comment on, whatever comes into your head, I admit it's a little long, maybe you can skim the part where Napoleon invades Russia, but it's the first *eff*ort by a perfectly delightful midge larva I know you'd enjoy meeting—"

"I'd adore to, but I can't," he said, explaining, "my eye. I can't afford to strain it, I have only this one . . ." He trailed off, he felt, feebly. He was beginning to feel permeable, acidic.

"You poor dear," Daphnia solemnly pronounced, and ate him.

And the next instant, a fairy shrimp, oaring by inverted, casually gathered her into the trough between his eleven pairs of undulating gill-feet and passed her toward his brazen mouth. Her scream, tinier than even the dot on this "i," was unobserved.

During the Jurassic

During the Jurassic

Waiting for the first guests, the iguanodon gazed along the path and beyond, toward the monotonous cycad forests and the low volcanic hills. The landscape was everywhere interpenetrated by the sea, a kind of metallic blue rottenness that daily breathed in and out. Behind him, his wife was assembling the *hors d'œuvres*. As he watched her, something unintended, something grossly solemn, in his expression made her laugh, displaying the leaf-shaped teeth lining her cheeks. Like him, she was an ornithischian, but much smaller—a compsognathus. He wondered, watching her race bipedally back and forth among the scraps of food (dragonflies wrapped in ferns, cephalopods on toast), how he had ever found her beautiful. His eyes hungered for size; he experienced a rage for sheer blind size.

The stegosauri, of course, were the first to appear. Among their many stupid friends these were the most stupid, and the most punctual. Their front legs bent out-ward and their little filmy-eyed faces virtually skimmed the  ground; the upward sweep of their backs was gigantic, and the double rows of giant bone plates along the spine clicked together in the sway of their cumbersome gait. With hardly a greeting, they dragged their tails, quadruply spiked, across the threshold and maneuvered themselves toward the bar, which was tended by a minute and shapeless mammal hired for the evening.

Next came the allosaurus, a carnivorous bachelor whose dangerous aura and needled grin excited the female herbivores; then Rhamphorhynchus, a pterosaur whose much admired "flight" was in reality a clumsy brittle glide ending

in an embarrassed bump and trot. The iguanodon despised
these pterosaurs' pretensions, thought grotesque the precarious
elongation of the single finger from which their levitating
membranes were stretched, and privately believed that the
less handsomely underwritten archaeopteryx, though sneered
at as unstable and feathered, had more of a future. The hypsi-
lophodon, with her graceful hands and branch-gripping feet,
arrived escorted by the timeless crocodile—an incongruous
pair, but both were recently divorced. Still the iguanodon
gazed down the path.

Behind him, the conversation gnashed on a thousand things
—houses, mortgages, lawns, fertilizers, erosion, boats, winds,
annuities, capital gains, recipes, education, the day's tennis,
last night's party. Each party was consumed by discussion of
the previous one. Their lives were subject to constant cross-
check. When did you leave? When did *you* leave? We'd been
out every night this week. We had an amphibious babysitter
who had to be back in the water by one. Gregor had to meet
a client in town, and now they've reduced the Saturday
schedule, it means the 7:43 or nothing. Trains? I thought
they were totally extinct. Not at all. They're coming back, it's
just a matter of time until the government . . . In the long
range of evolution, they are still the most efficient . . . Taking into account the heat-loss/weight ratio and assuming
there's no more glaciation . . . Did you know—I think this is
fascinating—did you know that in the financing of those great
ornate stations of the eighties and nineties, those real monsters,
there was no provision for amortization? They weren't amor-
tized at all, they were financed on the basis of eternity! The
railroad was conceived of as the end of Progress! *I* think—
though not an expert—that the key word in this over-all
industrio-socio-what-have-you-oh nexus or syndrome or bag

or whatever is *overextended*. Any competitorless object *bloats*. Personally, I miss the trolley cars. Now don't tell me I'm the only creature in the room old enough to remember the trolley cars!

The iguanodon's high pulpy heart jerked and seemed to split; the brontosaurus was coming up the path.

Her husband, the diplodocus, was with her. They moved together, rhythmic twins, buoyed by the hollow assurance of the huge. She paused to tear with her lips a clump of leaf from an overhanging paleocycas. From her deliberate grace the iguanodon received the impression that she knew he was watching her. Indeed, she had long guessed his love, as had her husband. The two saurischians entered his party with the languid confidence of the specially cherished. In the teeth of the iguanodon's ironic stance, her bulk, her gorgeous size, enraptured him, swelled to fill the massive ache he carried when she was not there. She rolled outward across his senses—the dawn-pale underparts, the reticulate skin, the vast bluish muscles whose management required a second brain at the base of her spine.

Her husband, though even longer, was more slenderly built, and perhaps weighed less than twenty-five tons. His very manner was attenuated and tabescent. He had recently abandoned an orthodox business career to enter an Episcopalian seminary. This regression—as the iguanodon felt it—seemed to make his wife more prominent, less supported, more accessible.

How splendid she was! For all the lavish solidity of her hips and legs, the modelling of her little flat diapsid skull was delicate. Her facial essence appeared to narrow, along the diagram-

matic points of her auricles and eyes and nostrils, toward a
single point, located in the air, of impermutable refinement
and calm. This irreducible point was, he realized, in some
sense her mind: the focus of the minimal interest she brought
to play upon the inchoate and edible green world flowing all
about her, buoying her, bathing her. The iguanodon felt himself as an upright speckled stain in this world. He felt himself,
under her distant dim smile, impossibly ugly: his mouth a
sardonic chasm, his throat a pulsing curtain of scaly folds, his
body a blotched bulb. His feet were heavy and horny and
three-toed and his thumbs—strange adaptation!—were erect
rigidities of pointed bone. Wounded by her presence, he
savagely turned on her husband.

"*Comment va le bon Dieu?*"

"Ah?" The diplodocus was maddeningly good-humored.
Minutes elapsed as stimuli and reactions travelled back and
forth across his length.

The iguanodon insisted. "How are things in the supernatural?"

"The supernatural? I don't think that category exists in the
new theology."

"*N'est-ce pas?* What *does* exist in the new theology?"

"Love. Immanence as opposed to transcendence. Works as
opposed to faith."

"Work? I had thought you had quit work."

"That's an unkind way of putting it. I prefer to think that
I've changed employers."

The iguanodon felt in the other's politeness a detestable
aristocracy, the unappealable oppression of superior size. He
said gnashingly, "The Void pays wages?"

"Ah?"

"You mean there's a living in nonsense? I said nonsense. Dead, fetid nonsense."

"Call it that if it makes it easier for you. Myself, I'm not a fast learner. Intellectual humility came rather natural to me. In the seminary, for the first time in my life, I feel on the verge of finding myself."

"Yourself? That little thing? *Cette petite chose?* That's all you're looking for? Have you tried pain? Myself, I have found pain to be a great illuminator. *Permettez-moi.*" The iguanodon essayed to bite the veined base of the serpentine throat lazily upheld before him; but his teeth were too specialized and could not tear flesh. He abraded his lips and tasted his own salt blood. Disoriented, crazed, he thrust one thumb deep into a yielding gray flank that hove through the smoke and chatter of the party like a dull wave. But the nerves of his victim lagged in reporting the pain, and by the time the distant head of the diplodocus was notified, the wound would have healed.

The drinks were flowing freely. The mammal crept up to him and murmured that the dry vermouth was running out. The iguanodon told him to use the sweet. Behind the sofa the stegosauri were Indian-wrestling; each time one went over, his spinal plates raked the recently papered wall. The hypsilophoden, tipsy, perched on a bannister; the allosaurus darted forward suddenly and ceremoniously nibbled her tail. On the far side of the room, by the great slack-stringed harp, the compsognathus and the brontosaurus were talking. He was drawn to them, amazed that his wife would presume to delay the much larger creature and to insert herself, with her scrabbling nervous motions and chattering leaf-shaped teeth, into the crevices of that queenly presence. As he drew closer to them, music began. His wife confided to him, "The salad is running out." He murmured to the brontosaurus, "*Chère madame, voulez-vous danser avec moi?*"

Her dancing was awkward, but even in this awkwardness, this ponderous stiffness, he felt the charm of her abundance. "I've been talking to your husband about religion," he told her, as they settled into the steps they could do.

"I've given up," she said. "It's such a deprivation for me and the children."

"He says he's looking for himself."

"It's so selfish," she blurted. "The children are teased at school."

"Come live with me."

"Can you support me?"

"No, but I would gladly sink under you."

"You're sweet."

"*Je t'aime.*"

"Don't. Not here."

"Somewhere, then?"

"No. Nowhere. Never." With what delightful precision did her miniature mouth encompass these infinitesimal concepts!

"But I," he said, "but I lo—"

"Stop it. You embarrass me. Deliberately."

"You know what I wish? I wish all these beasts would disappear. What do we see in each other? Why do we keep getting together?"

She shrugged. "If they disappear, we will too."

"I'm not so sure. There's something about us that would survive. It's not in you and not in me but between us, where we almost meet. Some vibration, some enduring cosmic factor. Don't you feel it?"

"Let's stop. It's too painful."

"Stop dancing?"

"Stop being."

"That is a beautiful idea. *Une belle idée.* I will if you will."

"In time," she said, and her fine little face precisely fitted this laconic promise; and as the summer night yielded warmth to the multiplying stars, he felt his blood sympathetically cool, and grow thunderously, fruitfully slow.

The Baluchitherium

In 1911, C. Forster-Cooper of the British Museum unearthed in Baluchistan some extraordinary foot bones and a single provocative neck vertebra. Thus the Baluchitherium first intruded upon modern consciousness. Eleven years later, in Mongolia,

an almost complete skull of the creature was uncovered, and in 1925 the four legs and feet of another individual, evidently trapped and preserved in quicksand, came to light. From these unhappy fragments an image of the living Baluchitherium was assembled. His skull was five feet long, his body twenty-seven. He stood eighteen feet high at the shoulders (where the North American titanothere measured a mere eight feet, the bull African elephant eleven). Though of the family Rhinocerotidae, the Baluchitherium's face was innocent of any horn; his neck was long and his upper lip prehensile, for seizing leaves twenty-two feet above the ground. He was the largest mammal that ever lived on land.

Recently, I had the pleasure of an interview with the Baluchitherium. The technical process would be tedious to describe; briefly, it involved feeding my body into a computer (each cell translates into approximately 120,000,000 electronic "bits") and then transecting the tape with data on the object and moment in time-space to be "met." The process proved painless; a sustained, rather dental humming tingled in every nerve, and a strange, unpopulous vista opened up around me. I knew I was in Asia, since the baluchitheres in the millions of years of their thriving never ventured off this most amorphous of continents. The landscape was typical Oligocene: a glossy green mush of subtropical vegetation—palms, fig trees, ferns—yielded, on the distant pink hillsides of aeolian shale, to a scattering of conifers and deciduous hardwoods. Underfoot, the spread of the grasses was beginning.

 Venturing forward, I found the Baluchitherium embowered in a grove of giant extinct cycads. He was reading a document or missive printed on a huge sheet of what appeared to be rough-textured cardboard. When I expressed surprise at this, the Baluchitherium laughed genially and explained, "We pulp it by mastication and then stamp it flat with our feet." He held up for my admiration one of his extraordinary feet—columnar, ungulate, odd-toed. What I had also not been led by the fossil record to expect, his foot, leg, and entire body as far as my eye could reach were covered by a lovely fur, bristly yet lustrous, of an

elusive color I can only call reddish-blue, with decklings of white in the underparts. Such are the soft surprises with which reality pads the skeleton of hard facts.

"How curious it is," the Baluchitherium said, "that you primates should blunder upon my five-foot skull without deducing my hundred-kilogram brain. True, our technology, foreseeing the horrors of industrialism, abjured the cruel minerals and concerned itself purely with vegetable artifacts— and these solely for our amusement and comfort." He benignly indicated the immense chaise longue, carved from a single ginkgo trunk, that he reposed upon; the rug beside it, artfully braided of wisteria vines; the hardwood sculptures about him, most of them glorifying, more or less abstractly, the form of the female Baluchitherium. "All, of course," he said, "by your time sense, fallen into dust aeons ago."

By now, I had adjusted my tape recorder to the immense volume and curious woofing timbre of his voice, so his remaining statements are not at the mercy of my memory. His accent, I should say, was Oxonian, though his specialized upper lip and modified incisors played havoc with some of our labials and fricatives, and he quaintly pronounced all silent consonants and even the terminal "e" of words. To my natural query as to his own time sense, he replied, with a blithe wave, "If you are able from a few crusty chips of calcium to posit an entire phylum of creature, why should not I, with a brain so much greater, be able, by a glance at my surroundings, to reconstruct, as it were, the future? The formation of your pelvis, the manner of your speech, even the moment of your visit are transparent in the anatomy of yon single scuttling insectivore." He indicated—what my lower perspective would have missed—a tiny gray plesiadipid miserably cowering high in one of the cycads.

The Baluchitherium

The Baluchitherium brandished the printed sheet in his hand; it rattled like thunder. "In here, for instance," he said, "one may read of numerous future events—the mammoth's epic circumambulation of the globe, the drastic shrinkage of the Tethys Sea, the impudent and hapless attempt of the bird kingdom, in the person of the running giant Diatryma, to forsake the air and compete on land. Hah! One may even find"—he turned the sheet, to what seemed to be its lesser side—"news of *Homo sapiens*. I see here, for example, that your wheat-growing cultures will make war upon your rice-growers, having earlier destroyed the maize-growers. And one also finds," he continued, "horoscopes and comic strips and lively correspondent discussions as to whether God is, as I firmly believe, odd-toed or, as the artiodactyls vainly hold, even-toed."

"B-but," I said, stammering in my anxiety to utter this, the crucial question, "given, then, such a height of prescience and civilized feeling, why did you make the evolutionary error—the gross, if I may so put it, miscalculation—of brute size? That is, with the catastrophic example of the dinosaurs still echoing down the silted corridors of geologic time—"

Imperiously he cut me short. "The past," he said, "is bunk. The future"—and he trumpeted—"is our element."

"But," I protested, "the very grasses under my feet spell doom for large leaf-browsers, presaging an epoch of mobile plains-grazers." As if to illustrate my point, a rabbit darted from the underbrush, chased by a dainty eohippus. "As you must know," I said, "the artiodactyls, in the form of swine, camels, deer, cattle, sheep, goats, and hippopotami, will flourish, whereas the perissodactyls, dwindled to a few tapirs and myopic rhinoceri in my own era, will meet extinct—"

"Size," he bellowed, pronouncing it "siz-eh," "is not a matter of choice but of destiny. Largeness was thrust upon us. We bear it—bore it, bear it, will bear it—as our share of the universal heaviness. We bear it gratefully, and gratefully will restore it to the heaviness of the Earth." And he fixed me with a squint so rhinoceroid I involuntarily backed a step, tripping the computer's reverse mechanism. All my nerves began humming. The Baluchitherium, as he faded, stretched himself toward the leaf-clouded sky; the reddish-blue fur on his throat shimmered white. Ravenously he resumed what I saw to be, under one form or another, an endless, unthinkable meal.

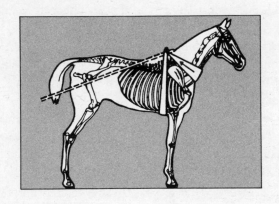

The Invention of the
Horse Collar

IN THE DARKEST DARK AGES, the horse collar appeared. A Frankish manuscript of the tenth century first depicts it, along with the concomitantly epochal shafts and traces *attached to the middle of the collar*. In antiquity, from primitive Egypt to decadent Rome, horse-harness consisted of a yoke *attached at the withers* by a double girth passing under the chest and

around the throat of the animal. When the horse pulled at his load, the throat-girth rode up, cutting into his windpipe, compressing his vein-walls, and slow-

ing his heart-beat. The loss of tractive power was three- or four-fold. Yet antiquity, which sentimental humanism so much encourages us to admire, did little to remedy this stran-  gling, but for in- effectual measures like passing a strap between the fore- legs to keep the throat-band low (observable on a Greek vase *c.* 500 B.C.) or tying the two bands at the horse's sides, as illustrated in a bone-carving of a war chariot on the Byzantine casket.

No, it fell to some obscure fellow in the Dark Ages, a *villein* no doubt, to invent the horse collar. His name, I imagine, was Canus—an odd name, meaning gray, though our hero is young; but name-giving, like everything else in this ill-lit and anarchic period, is in a muddled, transitive condition. Canus sits in his thatched hut pondering. Beside him, on a bench of hewn planks and dowels, lies a sheaf of sketches, an array of crude tools both blunt and sharp, an ox-yoke for purposes of comparison, and a whitened fragment of equine scapula with the stress-lines marked in charcoal. Outside, darkness reigns unrelieved; even noon, in this year of (say) 906, has about it something murky, something slanting and askew. Roman ruins insanely dot the landscape. Blind eyes gaze from the gargantuan heads of marble emperors half-buried in the earth. Aqueducts begin and halt in mid-air. Forested valleys seclude mazelike monasteries where feeble-minded clerics miscopy Vergil over and over, having mistaken him for a magician. Slit-windowed castles perch fantastically on unscalable outcroppings and lift villages upward toward themselves like ladies gathering their skirts while crossing a stretch of mud. In the spaces between these tentative islands of order, guttural chieftains, thugs not yet knights, thunder back and forth, bellowing in a corrupt Latin not yet French, trampling underfoot the delicate stripwork of a creeping agriculture. Canus is one of those who work these precarious fields, urging forward the gagging, staggering plowhorse. He has been troubled, piqued. There must be . . . something better . . . Now, under his hands, the mock-up of the first horse collar, executed in straw and flour paste, has taken shape!

The door of the hut wrenches open. Enter Ablatus, Canus's brother. Though they are twins, born in the last year of the non-existent reign of Charles the Fat, they are not identical. Canus in his eyes and hair shows the scaly brilliance of burnished metal and of the hardened peat called coal; Ablatus, the more elusive lambency of clouds, of water running over quartz, of fire sinking in the hearth. Canus tends toward swarthy, Ablatus toward fair. Both are clad in the era's style of shapelessness, between toga and cloak, bunches of colorless cloth such as a poor child would use to wrap a doll of sticks. On his head Ablatus wears a hat like a beanbag. He takes it off. He stares at the bright hoop of straw. "What is that?" he asks, in a language whose archaic music is forever lost to ears.

Triumphantly Canus explains his invention. He describes new worlds: the four-fold tractive increase, the improved

deep plowing, the more rapid transportation, the ever more tightly knit and well-fed Christendom. Cathedrals will arise; the Viking and the Mohammedan shall be repulsed. Crusades can be financed. Out of prosperity will arise city-states, usury, and a middle class—all these blessings pouring from this coarse circlet of glued straw. "The real collars, of course, will be leather, padded, with increasing ingenuity, to eliminate chafing and to render the horse's pulling all the more pleasurable."

Toward the end of his twin's long recital, Ablatus betrays agitation. He flings down his scythe, scarcely changed in design since the Egyptians first lopped maize. His pallid eyes throw sparks. "My own brother," he utters at last, "a devil!"

"Nay," says Canus, rising from his bench in surprise, "an angel, rather, to relieve both beasts and men by the means of an insensate and efficient"—and here, groping for the Latin "*mechina*," he slurs into creation a new word—"machine. I have created"—and again he must coin the word—"horse-power."

"You would bind up the anarchy that has set us free," Ablatus pursues, pacing the rectangle of dirt floor in his visionary distress. "You would bring back the ponderous order of Rome, that crazed even emperors, ere the sea of slaves dried and like a galleon of millstones the Empire sank. Oh, *Canus frater meus*, reflect! With the great flail of bishops and barbarians God broke Rome into a thousand fragments so that men might breathe. In the subsequent darkness, in this our confusion, men have found their souls, have fallen into right relation with one another—the lords protecting the vassals, the vassals supporting the lord, on all sides love and enlightened self-interest. True, there is brutality and waste, but it stems from our natures, it is true to our image, which is God's. The seal of the divine sits upon the organic. Out of Eden, Adam groaned at toil and Eve screamed in the travail of birth so that men might know their sin. Wisely the ancients consecrated the first poor tools and disdained to improve them. You would presume to forge a second Nature —better the hellish blackness of midnight than a blasphemous Paradise! Better impede the windpipes of beasts than strangle the souls of men! From this impudent seed of invention, what iron vines will flourish! With interconnection comes restriction; with organization, oppression. This device of yours, so beneficent in its apparent effects, is Satan's stalking-horse, wherewith to conquer again the kingdom so dearly redeemed by Christ's blood! You call it a blessing, I call it a curse! I call it a—*pollution!*" And, inspired, fair Ablatus scizes one of the candles that in this dark age burn even at mid-day, and hurls it upon the artifact of straw, and it becomes a hoop of flame.

Canus, inspired in his swarthier fashion, takes up one of the blunt tools from his bench and strikes his brother a firm blow.

"Devil!" exclaims Ablatus, sinking.

"Fool," replies Canus and, with one of the sharp tools from the same set, deftly finishes his brother off.

Ablatus abolitus est. It does not arouse remorse in us when we slay a twin; it is too much like suppressing an aspect of ourselves. Serenely Canus carries off the body (*Ablatus*

ablatus est) and digs the grave. The earth is heavy, northern soil—more resistant and more rewarding than the earth the ancients scratched. In the distance, a scrimmage of nobility reverberates. A monastery bell—a silver thread thrown across a chasm—sounds from a muffling valley. The Dark Ages begin to decline. As Canus leans on the shovel, a breeze of evening caresses his face, and he idly reflects that here is power too, to be harnessed. He imagines sails, gears, drive-shafts. Inside the hut, he composes himself for sleep. His muscles agreeably ache from useful labor performed. The prototypical horse collar lies consumed beside the bench, but the ashes preserve the design. Tomorrow he will recon-struct it. The slippery little half-dreams that augur sleep begin to visit him. And tomorrow, he thinks, he will invent the horizontal-shafted windmill . . . and the next day, *Deus volens* . . . the wheelbarrow . . .

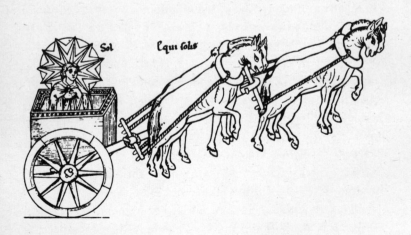

Jesus on Honshu

Japanese Legend Says
Jesus Escaped to Orient

—Headline, and passages in
italics below, from the Times.

TOKYO—*A Japanese legend has excited some curiosity here,*
that Jesus did not die on the cross outside Jerusalem, but lived
in a remote village on the northern part of the Japanese island
of Honshu until his death at 106 years of age.

The distances within His blue eyes used to frighten the
children. Though toward the end, when His age had passed
eighty, His stoop and brittle movements within the kimono
approximated the manner of an elderly Japanese, His face,
up close, never conformed—the olive skin, the tilted nostrils
sprouting hair, the lips excessive in flesh and snarling humor,
the eyelids very strange, purplish and wrinkled like the
armpits of a salamander. There was never much doubt in the
village that He was some sort of god. Even had His eyes
given on less immensity, had their blue been flawed by one

fleck of amber or one weak ray of pearl, He would have
been revered and abhorred by the children. His skin was
abnormally porous, His voice came from too deep in His
body.

*Jesus, so the legend runs, first arrived in Japan at the age
of 21 during the reign of the emperor Suinin in what would
have been the year 27 B.C. He remained for 11 years under
the tutorship of a sage of Etchu Province, the modern
Toyama prefecture, from whom he learned much about the
country and its customs.*

Strangely the distances had melted within Him, leaving
little more trace than the ice cakes along the shore leave in
spring. What a man does when young becomes a legend to
himself when he is old. The straight roads through orange
deserts, the goat paths winding through mauve mountains,
the silver rivers whose surfaces He discovered He could
walk, the distant herds like wandering lakes, the clouds of
birds darkening the sun, the delegations of brown people,
of yellow people, the green forests where sunlight fell in
tiger stripes, the brown forests (tree trunks shaggy as bears,
star-blue butterflies fluttering in glades no man had haunted
before), unexpected emerald meadows, sheets of snow a
month of walking did not dismiss, and in the distance always
more mountains, more deserts, the whole world then tasting
of vastness as of nectar, glistening, men huddling in mud
nests like wasps, the spaces innocent. He had walked because,
obscurely, His Father had told Him to. His Father was an
imperious restlessness within Him. At last He came to the
land of Wa, beyond which was only an enamelled sea without a nether edge. The sage of Etchu took Him in and taught
Him many things. He taught the young Jesus that dual consciousness was not to be avoided but desired: only duality

reflected the universe. That the eight hundred myriads of daemons (*yao-yorodzu-no-kami*) are false save in that they stand guard against an even more false monism. That the huntsman must bend his thought upon the prey and not upon the bow. That a faith containing fear is an imperfect faith. That the mountains wait to be moved by the touch of a child. That the motions of the mind are full of *Kami* (holy force). That the ways of the gods (*shintō*) are the ways of plants. That a seed must die to live. That the weak are the strong. And many more such things He later preached, and forgot, as the ice cake deposits pebbles and straw in melting. After eleven years, the restlessness seized Him again, and He returned. The trip returning, strangely, was the more difficult of the two; He kept searching for familiar landmarks, and there were none.

Jesus returned to Jerusalem, passing through Monaco on the way, to tell his own people of his experiences in the Orient, it is said. It was his younger brother, known in Japanese as Isukiri, who was later crucified, according to the legend.

No one ever got it quite right, and He Himself ceased trying to understand. Judas (Isukiri) had not been His brother; he had been the troublesomely sensitive disciple, the cloying adorer. Selecting the twelve, Jesus had chosen solid men, to whom a miracle was a way of affecting matter, a species of work. Judas, with his adoration and high hopes and theoretical demands on the Absolute, had attached himself hysterically. The kiss in the garden was typical—all showmanship and symbolism. Then, the priesthood proving obdurate (and why not? any Messiah at all would put them out of a job), Judas had offered to be crucified instead, as if we were dealing with some Moloch that had a simple body quota to meet. The poor Romans were out of their depth; eventually they hanged Judas, as they generally hanged informers—a straightforward policy of prudence. For Him, there had been nails in the palms, and a crying-out, and then dark coolness, a scuffle in which He overheard women's voices, and a scarlet dawn near the borders of Palestine. For the first days eastward, until the wounds in His feet healed, He had had an escort, He dimly remembered. Gruff men, officials of some sort.

Jesus is said to have escaped and come back to Japan after wandering through the wastes of Siberia. The legend has it that he landed at Hachinoe in Aomori, and settled in Herai, whose name, it has been suggested, derives from the Japanese for Hebrew (Heburai). He married and became the father of three daughters, according to the legend.

Asagao was the oldest, Oigimi the youngest; both married before the age of fifteen, and in them and their children He saw no trace of Himself, only of His wife and the smooth race that had taken Him in as a pond swallows a stone. Ukifune, the middle daughter, called Dragonfly, was tall like Him, with His wrinkled lids and big-knuckled hands and surges of restlessness and mockery. She never married; her scandals affronted the village until she was found dead in her hut, black-lipped, cold. He would have called her back to life, but her face had been monstrously slashed. Poisoned and disfigured by a lover or the wife of a lover. She left a fatherless male infant, Kaoru. Shared between the households of his aunts, the infant grew to be a man, living always in the village, as a mender of nets and thatching. Conscious of himself only as Japanese, Kaoru grew old, with white hair and warts, and Jesus, now over a hundred, would suddenly, senselessly, weep to see in this venerable grandson—

hook-nosed profile bent above a chisel, his forearms as gnarled as grapevines—the very image of old Joseph of Bethlehem, seen upwards through the eyes of a child. Things return, form in circles, unravel and reravel, the sage had insisted, crouching with the young traveller on a ledge in the mauve mountains of Etchu, in view of the enamelled sea. Jesus had argued, insisting that there was also a vertical principle in the world, something thrusting, which did not repeat. Now, Himself ancient, He had come to live the sage's scorned truth. He lived in the village as a healer, and the healed kept coming back to Him, their health unravelled, and again He would lay on His hands, and the devils would flee, and the healed would depart upright and rejoicing; only to unravel again, and at last to die, even as He must. A soft heaviness sweetened His veins; His naps lengthened unaccountably. As death neared, His birth and travail far ago, in that minor desert place, among Rome's centurions, seemed more and more miraculous: a seed He had left behind, and that had died, engendering a growth perhaps as great as a mustard tree. Or perhaps His incarnation there, those youthful events, were lost in the scuffle of history, dust amid dust. Whatever the case, He never doubted that He was unique, the only son of God. In this, at least, He resembled all men.

One family in the village says it is descended from Jesus. Many of the children have the star of David sewn on their clothes, and parents sometimes mark the sign of the cross in ink on the foreheads of children to exorcise evil spirits. . . . An annual "Christ festival," held on June 10, attracts many visitors.

THE MAPLES

Marching Through Boston

THE CIVIL RIGHTS MOVEMENT had a salubrious effect on Joan Maple. A suburban mother of four, she would return late at night from a non-violence class in Roxbury with rosy cheeks and shining eyes, eager to describe, while sipping Benedictine, her indoctrination. "This huge man in overalls—"

"A Negro?" her husband asked.

"Of course. This huge man, with a *very* refined vocabulary, told us if we march anywhere, especially in the South, to let the Negro men march on the outside, because it's important for their self-esteem to be able to protect us. He told us about a New York fashion designer who went down to Selma and said she could take care of herself. Furthermore she flirted with the State troopers. They finally asked her to come home."

"I thought you were supposed to love the troopers," Richard said.

"Only abstractly. Not on your own. You mustn't do *any*thing within the movement as an individual. By flirting, she gave the trooper an opportunity to feel contempt."

"She blocked his transference, as it were."

"Don't laugh. It's all very psychological. The man told us, those who want to go, to face our ego-gratificational motives no matter how irrelevant they are and then put them behind us. Once you're in a march, you have no identity. It's elegant. It's beautiful."

He had never known her like this. It seemed to Richard that her posture was improving, her figure filling out, her skin growing lustrous, her very hair gaining body and sheen. Though he had resigned himself, through twelve years of marriage, to a rhythm of apathy and renewal, he distrusted this raw burst of beauty.

The night she returned from Alabama, it was three o'clock in the morning. He woke and heard the front door close behind her. He had been dreaming of a parallelogram in the sky that was also somehow a meteor, and the darkened house seemed quadrisected by the four sleeping children he had, with more than paternal tenderness, put to bed. He had caught himself speaking to them of Mommy as a distant departed spirit, gone to live, invisible, in the newspapers and the television set. The little girl, Bean, had burst into tears. Now the ghost closed the door and walked up the stairs, and came into his bedroom, and fell on the bed.

He switched on the light and saw her sunburned face, her blistered feet. Her ballet slippers were caked with orange mud. She had lived for three days on Coke and dried apricots; she had not gone to the bathroom for sixteen hours. The Montgomery airport had been a madhouse—nuns, social workers, divinity students fighting for space on the northbound planes. They had been in the air when they heard about Mrs. Liuzzo.

He accused her: "It could have been you."

She said, "I was always in a group." But she added guiltily, "How were the children?"

"Fine. Bean cried because she thought you were inside the television set."

"Did you see me?"

"Your parents called long distance to say they thought they did. I didn't. All I saw was Abernathy and King and their henchmen saying, 'Thass right. Say it, man. Thass sayin' it.'"

"Aren't you mean? It was very moving, except that we were all so tired. These teen-age Negro girls kept fainting; a psychiatrist explained to me that they were having psychotic breaks."

"What psychiatrist?"

"Actually, there were three of them, and they were studying to be psychiatrists in Philadelphia. They kind of took me in tow."

"I bet they did. Please come to bed. I'm very tired from being a mother."

She visited the four corners of the upstairs to inspect each sleeping child and, returning, undressed in the dark. She removed underwear she had worn for seventy hours and stood there shining; to the sleepy man in the bed it seemed a visitation, and he felt as people of old must have felt when greeted by an angel—adoring yet resentful, at this flamboyant proof of better things.

She spoke on the radio; she addressed local groups. In garages and supermarkets he heard himself being pointed out as her husband. She helped organize meetings at which dapper young Negroes ridiculed and abused the applauding suburban audience. Richard marvelled at Joan's public composure. Her shyness stayed with her, but it had become a kind of weapon, as if the doctrine of non-violence had given it point. Her voice, as she phoned evasive local realtors in the campaign for fair housing, grew curiously firm and rather obstinately melodious—a note her husband had never heard in her voice before. He grew jealous and irritable. He found himself insisting, at parties, on the Constitutional case for states' rights, on the misfortunes of African independence, on the tangled history of the Reconstruction. Yet she had little trouble persuading him to march with her in Boston.

He promised, though he could not quite grasp the object of the march. Indeed, his brain, as if surgically deprived, quite lacked the faculty of believing in people considered generically. All movements, of masses or of ideas supposedly embodied in masses, he secretly felt to be phantasmal. Whereas his wife, a minister's daughter, lived by abstractions; her blood returned to her heart enriched and vivified by the passage through some capillarious figment. He was struck, and subtly wounded, by the ardor with which she rewarded his promise; under his hands her body felt baroque and her skin smooth as night.

The march was in April. Richard awoke that morning with a fever. He had taken something foreign into himself and his body was making resistance. Joan offered to go alone; as if something fundamental to his dignity, to their marriage, were at stake, he refused the offer. The day, dawning cloudy, had been forecast as sunny, and he wore a summer suit that enclosed his hot skin in a slipping, weightless unreality. At a highway drugstore they bought some pills designed to detonate inside him through a twelve-hour period. They parked near her aunt's house in Louisburg Square and took a taxi

toward the headwaters of the march, a playground in Roxbury. The Irish driver's impassive back radiated disapproval.
The cab was turned aside by a policeman; the Maples got
out and walked down a broad brown boulevard lined with
barbershops, shoe repair nooks, pizzerias, and friendliness as-
sociations. On stoops and stairways male Negroes loitered,
blinking and muttering toward one another as if a vast, decrepit
conspiracy had assigned them their positions and then collapsed.

"Lovely architecture," Joan said, pointing toward a curving side street, a neo-Georgian arc suspended in the large
urban sadness.

Though she pretended to know where she was, Richard
doubted that they were going the right way. But then
he saw ahead of them, scattered like the anomalous objects
with which Dali punctuates his perspectives, receding black
groups of white clergymen. In the distance, the hot lights of
police cars wheeled within a twinkling mob. As they drew
nearer, colored girls made into giantesses by bouffant hairdos
materialized beside them. One wore cerise stretch pants and
the golden sandals of a heavenly cupbearer, and held pressed
against her ear a transistor radio tuned to WMEX. On this
thin stream of music they all together poured into a playground surrounded by a link fence.

A loose crowd of thousands swarmed on the crushed grass.
Bobbing placards advertised churches, brotherhoods, schools,
towns. Popsicle venders lent an unexpected touch of carnival.
Suddenly at home, Richard bought a bag of peanuts and
looked around—as if this were the playground of his childhood—for friends.

But it was Joan who found some. "My God," she said.
"There's my old analyst." At the fringe of some Unitarians

stood a plump, doughy man with the troubled squint of a baker who has looked into too many ovens. Joan turned to go the other way.

"Don't suppress," Richard told her. "Let's go and be friendly and normal."

"It's too embarrassing."

"But it's been years since you went. You're cured."

"You don't understand. You're never cured. You just stop going."

"O.K., come this way. I think I see my Harvard section man in Plato to Dante."

But, even while arguing against it, she had been drifting them toward her psychiatrist, and now they were caught in the pull of his gaze. He scowled and came toward them, flat-footedly. Richard had never met him and, shaking hands, felt himself as a putrid heap of anecdotes, of detailed lusts and abuses. "I think I need a doctor," he madly blurted.

The other man produced, like a stiletto from his sleeve, a nimble smile. "How so?" Each word seemed precious.

"I have a fever."

"Ah." The psychiatrist turned sympathetically to Joan, and his face issued a clear commiseration: *So he is still punishing you.*

Joan said loyally, "He really does. I saw the thermometer."

"Would you like a peanut?" Richard asked. The offer felt so symbolic, so transparent, that he was shocked when the other man took one, cracked it harshly, and substantially chewed.

Joan asked, "Are you with anybody? I feel a need for group security."

"Come meet my sister." The command sounded strange

to Richard; "sister" seemed a piece of psychological slang, a euphemism for "mistress."

But again things were simpler than they seemed. His sister was plainly from the same batter. Ruddy and yeasty, she seemed to have been enlarged by the exercise of good will and wore a saucer-sized S.C.L.C. button in the lapel of a coarse green suit. Richard coveted the suit; it looked warm. The day was continuing overcast and chilly. Something odd, perhaps the successive explosions of the antihistamine pill, was happening inside him, making him feel elegantly elongated; the illusion crossed his mind that he was destined to seduce this woman. She beamed and said, "My daughter Trudy and her *best* friend, Carol."

They were girls of sixteen or so, one size smaller in their bones than women. Trudy had the family pastry texture and a darting frown. Carol was homely, fragile, and touching; her upper teeth were a gray blur of braces and her arms were protectively folded across her skimpy bosom. Over a white blouse she wore only a thin blue sweater, unbuttoned. Richard told her, "You're freezing."

"I'm freezing," she said, and a small love was established between them on the basis of this demure repetition. She added, "I came along because I'm writing a term paper."

Trudy said, "She's doing a history of the labor unions," and laughed unpleasantly.

The girl shivered. "I thought they might be the same. Didn't the unions use to march?" Her voice, moistened by the obtrusion of her braces, had a sprayey faintness in the raw gray air.

The psychiatrist's sister said, "The *way* they *make* these poor children *study* nowadays! The *books* they have them

: **227** :

read! Their *English* teacher *assigned* them 'Tropic of *Can-cer*'! I picked it *up* and read *one page*, and Trudy reassured me, 'It's all *right*, Mother, the teacher says he's a Transcen-*dent*alist!' "

It felt to Richard less likely that he would seduce her. His sense of reality was expanding in the nest of warmth these people provided. He offered to buy them all popsicles. His consciousness ventured outward and tasted the joy of so many Negro presences, the luxury of immersion in the polished shadows of their skins. He drifted happily through the crosshatch of their oblique sardonic hooting and blurred voices, searching for the popsicle vender. The girls and Trudy's mother had said they would take one; the psychiatrist and Joan had refused. The crowd was formed of jiggling fragments. Richard waved at the rector of a church whose nursery school his children had attended; winked at a folk singer he had seen on television and who looked lost and wan in depth; assumed a stony face in passing a long-haired youth guarded by police and draped in a signboard proclaiming MARTIN LUTHER KING A TOOL OF THE COMMUNISTS; and tapped a tall bald man on the shoulder. "Remember me? Dick Maple, Plato to Dante, B-plus."

The section man turned, bespectacled and pale. It was shocking; he had aged.

The march was slow to start. Trucks and police cars appeared and disappeared at the playground gate. Officious young seminarians tried to organize the crowd into lines. Unintelligible announcements crackled within the loudspeakers. Martin Luther King was a dim religious rumor on the playground plain—now here, now there, now dead, now

: 228 :

alive. The sun showed as a kind of sore spot burning through the clouds. Carol nibbled her popsicle and shivered. Richard and Joan argued whether to march under the Danvers banner with the psychiatrist or with the Unitarians because her father was one. In the end it did not matter; King invisibly established himself at their head, a distant truck loaded with singing women lurched forward, a far corner of the crowd began to croon, "Which side are you on, boy?," and they were marching.

On Columbus Avenue they were shuffled into lines ten abreast. The Maples were separated. Joan turned up between her psychiatrist and a massive, doleful African wearing tribal scars, sneakers, and a Harvard Athletic Association sweatshirt. Richard found himself at the end of the line ahead, with Carol beside him. The man behind him, a forward-looking liberal, stepped on his heel, giving the knit of his loafer such a wrench that he had to walk the three miles through Boston with a floppy shoe and a dragging limp. He had been born in West Virginia, near the Pennsylvania line, and did not understand Boston. In ten years he had grown familiar with some of its districts, but was still surprised by the quick curving manner in which these districts interlocked. For a few blocks they marched between cheering tenements from whose topmost windows hung banners that proclaimed END DE FACTO SEGREGATION and RETIRE MRS. HICKS. Then the march turned left, and Richard was passing Symphony Hall, within whose rectangular vault he had often dreamed his way along the deep-grassed meadows of Brahms and up the agate cliffs of Strauss. At this corner, from the Stygian subway kiosk, he had emerged with Joan, Orpheus and Eurydice, when both were students; in this restaurant, a decade later, he and she, on four drinks apiece, had decided not to get a divorce that week. The new Prudential Tower, taller and somehow fainter than any other building, haunted each twist of their march, before their faces like a mirage, at their backs like a memory. A leggy nervous colored girl wearing the orange fireman's jacket of the Security Unit shepherded their section of the line, clapping her hands, shouting freedom-song lyrics for a few bars. These songs struggled through the miles of the march, overlapping and eclipsing one another. "Which side are you on, boy, which side are you on . . . like a tree-ee planted by the wah-ha-ter, we shall not be moved . . . this little light of mine, gonna shine on Boston, Mass., this little light of mine . . ." The day continued cool and without shadows. Newspapers that he had folded inside his coat for warmth slipped and slid. Carol beside him plucked at her little sweater, gathering it at her breast but unable, as if under a spell, to button it. Behind him, Joan, serenely framed between her id and superego, stepped along masterfully, swinging her arms, throwing her ballet slippers alternately outward in a confident splaying stride. ". . . let 'er shine, let 'er shine . . ."

Incredibly, they were traversing a cloverleaf, an elevated concrete arabesque devoid of cars. Their massed footsteps whispered; the city yawned beneath them. The march had no beginning and no end that Richard could see. Within him, the fever had become a small glassy scratching on the walls of the pit hollowed by the detonating pills. A piece of newspaper spilled down his legs and blew into the air. Impalpably medicated, ideally motivated, he felt, strolling along the curve of the cloverleaf, gathered within an irresistible ascent. He asked Carol, "Where are we going?"

"The newspapers said the Common."

"Do you feel faint?"

Her gray braces shyly modified her smile. "Hungry."

"Have a peanut." A few still remained in his pocket.

"Thank you." She took one. "You don't have to be paternal."

"I want to be." He felt strangely exalted and excited, as if destined to give birth. He wanted to share this sensation with Carol, but instead he asked her, "In your study of the labor movement, have you learned much about the Molly Maguires?"

"No. Were they goons or finks?"

"I think they were either coal miners or gangsters."

"Oh. I haven't studied about anything earlier than Gompers."

"I think you're wise." Suppressing the urge to tell her he loved her, he turned to look at Joan. She was beautiful, like a poster, with far-seeing blue eyes and red lips parted in song.

Now they walked beneath office buildings where like mounted butterflies secretaries and dental technicians were pressed against the glass. In Copley Square, stony shoppers waited forever to cross the street. Along Boylston, there was Irish muttering; he shielded Carol with his body. The desultory singing grew defiant. The Public Garden was beginning to bloom. Worthy statues—Channing, Kosciusko, Cass, Phillips—were trundled by beneath the blurring trees; Richard's dry heart cracked like a book being opened. The march turned left down Charles and began to press against itself, to link arms, to fumble for love. He lost sight of Joan in the crush. Then they were treading on grass, on the Common, and the first drops of rain, sharp as needles, pricked their faces and hands.

"Did we have to stay to hear every damn speech?" Richard asked. They were at last heading home; he felt too sick to drive and huddled, in his soaked slippery suit, toward the heater. The windshield wiper seemed to be squeaking *free-dom, free-dom.*

"I wanted to hear King."

"You heard him in Alabama."

"I was too tired to listen then."

"Did you listen this time? Didn't it seem corny and forced?"

"Somewhat. But does it matter?" Her white profile was serene; she passed a trailer truck on the right, and her window was spattered as if with applause.

"And that Abernathy. God, if he's John the Baptist, I'm Herod the Great. 'Onteel de Frenchman go back t'France, onteel de Ahrishman go back t'Ahrland, onteel de Mexican he go back tuh—' "

"Stop it."

"Don't get me wrong. I didn't mind them sounding like demagogues; what I minded was that God-awful boring phony imitation of a revival meeting. 'Thass right, yossuh. Yoh-*suh!*' "

"Your throat sounds sore. Shouldn't you stop using it?"

"*How* could you crucify me that way? *How* could you make this miserable sick husband stand in the icy rain for hours listening to boring stupid speeches that you'd heard before anyway?"

"I didn't think the speeches were that great. But I think

it was important that they were given and that people listened. You were there as a witness, Richard."

"Ah witnessed. Ah believes. Yos-suh."

"You're a very sick man."

"I know, I *know* I am. That's why I wanted to leave. Even your pasty psychiatrist left. He looked like a dunked doughnut."

"He left because of the girls."

"I loved Carol. She respected me, despite the color of my skin."

"You didn't have to go."

"Yes I did. You somehow turned it into a point of honor. It was a sexual vindication."

"How you go on."

" 'Onteel de East German goes on back t'East Germany, onteel de Luxembourgian hies hisself back to Luxembourg—"

"Please stop it."

But he found he could not stop, and even after they reached home and she put him to bed, the children watching in alarm, his voice continued its slurred plaint. "Ah'ze all riaight, Missy, jes' a tech o' double pneu*mon*ia, don't you fret none, we'll get the cotton in."

"You're embarrassing the children."

"Shecks, doan min' me, chilluns. Ef Ah could jes' res' hyah foh a spell in de shade o' de watuhmelon patch, res' dese ol' bones . . . Lawzy, dat do feel good!"

"Daddy has a tiny cold," Joan explained.

"Will he die?" Bean asked, and burst into tears.

"Now, effen," he said, "bah some un*foh*-choonut chayance, mah spirrut should pass owen, bureh me bah de levee, so mebbe Ah kin heeah de singin' an' de banjos an' de cotton bolls a-bustin' . . . an' mebbe even de whaat folks up in de Big House kin shed a homely tear er two . . ." He was almost crying; a weird tenderness had crept over him in bed, as if he had indeed given birth, birth to this voice, a voice crying for attention from the depths of oppression. High in the window, the late afternoon sky blanched as the storm lifted. In the warmth of the bed, Richard crooned to himself, and once started up, crying out, "Missy! Missy! Doan you worreh none, ol' Tom'll see anotheh sun-up!"

But Joan was downstairs, talking firmly on the telephone.

The Taste of Metal

METAL, strictly, has no taste; its presence in the mouth is felt as disciplinary, as a *No* spoken to other tastes. When Richard Maple, after thirty years of twinges, jagged edges, and occasional extractions, had all his remaining molars capped and bridges shaped across the gaps, the gold felt chilly to his cheeks and its regularity masked holes and roughnesses that had been a kind of mirror wherein his tongue had known itself. The Friday of the final cementing, he went to a small party. As he drank a variety of liquids that tasted much the same, he moved from feeling slightly less than himself (his native teeth had been ground to stumps of dentine) to feeling slightly more. The shift in tonality that permeated his skull whenever his jaws closed corresponded, perhaps, to the heightened clarity that fills the mind after a religious conversion. He saw his companions at the party with a new brilliance—a sharpness of vision that, like a camera's, was specific and restricted in focus. He could see only one person at a time, and found himself focussing less on his wife Joan

: 235 :

than on Eleanor Dennis, the long-legged wife of a municipal-bond salesman.

Eleanor's distinctness in part had to do with the legal fact that she and her husband were "separated." It had happened recently; his absence from the party was noticeable. Eleanor, in the course of a life that she described as a series of harrowing survivals, had developed the brassy social manner that converts private catastrophe into public humorousness; but tonight her agitation was imperfectly converted. She listened as if for an echo that wasn't there, and twitchily crossed and recrossed her legs. Her legs were handsome and vivid and so long that, after midnight, when parlor games began, she hitched up her brief shirt and kicked the lintel of a doorframe. The host balanced a glass of water on his forehead. Richard, demonstrating a headstand, mistakenly tumbled forward, delighted at his own softness, which felt to be an ironical comment upon flesh that his new metal teeth were making. He was all mortality, all porous erosion save for these stars in his head, an impervious polar cluster at the zenith of his slow whirling.

His wife came to him with a face as neat and unscarred as the face of a clock. It was time to go home. And Eleanor needed a ride. The three of them, plus the hostess in her bangle earrings and coffee-stained culottes, went to the door, and discovered a snowstorm. As far as the eye could probe, flakes were falling in a jostling crowd through the whispering lavender night. "God bless us, every one," Richard said.

The hostess suggested that Joan should drive.

Richard kissed her on the cheek and tasted the metal of her bitter earring and got in behind the wheel. His car was a brand-new Corvair; he wouldn't dream of trusting anyone else to drive it. Joan crawled into the back seat, grunting to emphasize the physical awkwardness, and Eleanor serenely arranged her coat and pocketbook and legs in the space beside him. The motor sprang alive. Richard felt resiliently cushioned: Eleanor was beside him, Joan behind him, God above him, the road beneath him. The fast-falling snow dipped brilliant—explosive, chrysanthemumesque—into the car headlights. On a small hill the tires spun—a loose, reassuring noise, like the slither of a raincoat.

In the knobbed darkness lit by the green speed gauge, Eleanor, showing a wealth of knee, talked at length of her separated husband. "You have no *idea*," she said, "you two are so sheltered you have no idea what men are capable of. I didn't know myself. I don't mean to sound ungracious, he gave me nine reasonable years and I wouldn't *dream* of punishing him with the children's visiting hours the way some women would, but that *man!* You know what he had the crust to tell me? He actually told me that when he was with another woman he'd sometimes close his eyes and pretend it was *me*."

"Sometimes," Richard said.

His wife behind him said, "Darley, are you aware that the road is slippery?"

"That's the shine of the headlights," he told her.

Eleanor crossed and recrossed her legs. Half the length of a thigh flared in the intimate green glow. She went on, "And his *trips*. I wondered why the same city was always putting out bond issues. I began to feel sorry for the mayor, I thought they were going bankrupt. Looking back at myself, I was so *good*, so wrapped up in the children and the house, always on the phone to the contractor or the plumber or the gas company trying to get the new kitchen done in time for Thanksgiving when his silly, *silly* mother was coming to visit. About once a day I'd sharpen the carving knife. Thank

God that phase of my life is over. I went to his mother for sympathy I suppose and very indignantly she asked me, What had I done to her boy? The children and I had tuna-fish sandwiches by ourselves and it was the first Thanksgiving I've ever enjoyed, frankly."

"I always have trouble," Richard told her, "finding the second joint."

Joan said, "Darley, you know you're coming to that terrible curve?"

"You should see my father-in-law carve. Snick, snap, snap, snick. Your blood runs cold."

"On my birthday, my *birth*day," Eleanor said, accidentally kicking the heater, "the bastard was with his little dolly in a restaurant, and he told me, he solemnly told me—men are incredible—he told me he ordered cake for dessert. That was his tribute to me. The night he confessed all this, it was the end of the world, but I had to laugh. I asked him if he'd had the restaurant put a candle on the cake. He told me he'd thought of it but hadn't had the guts."

Richard's responsive laugh was held in suspense as the car skidded on the curve. A dark upright shape had appeared in the center of the windshield, and he tried to remove it, but the automobile proved impervious to the steering wheel and instead drew closer, as if magnetized, to a telephone pole that rigidly insisted on its position in the center of the windshield. The pole enlarged. The little splinters pricked by the linemen's cleats leaped forward in the headlights, and there was a flat whack surprisingly unambiguous, considering how casually it had happened. Richard felt the sudden refusal of motion, the *No*, and knew, though his mind was deeply cushioned in a cottony indifference, that an event had occurred which in another incarnation he would regret.

. . .

"You jerk," Joan said. Her voice was against his ear. "Your pretty new car." She asked, "Eleanor, are you all right?" With a rising inflection she repeated, "Are you all right?" It sounded like scolding.

Eleanor giggled softly, embarrassed. "I'm fine," she said, "except that I can't seem to move my legs." The windshield near her head had become a web of light, an exploded star.

Either the radio had been on or had turned itself on, for mellow, meditating music flowed from a realm behind time. Richard identified it as one of Handel's oboe sonatas. He noticed that his knees distantly hurt. Eleanor had slid forward and seemed unable to uncross her legs. Shockingly, she whimpered. Joan asked, "Sweetheart, didn't you know you were going too fast?"

"I am very stupid," he said. Music and snow poured down upon them, and he imagined that, if only the oboe sonata were played backwards, they would leap backwards from the telephone pole and be on their way home again. The little distances to their houses, once measured in minutes, had frozen and become immense. Galactic.

Using her hands, Eleanor uncrossed her legs and brought herself upright in her seat. She lit a cigarette. Richard, his knees creaking, got out of the car and tried to push it free. He told Joan to come out of the back seat and get behind the wheel. Their motions were clumsy, wriggling in and out of darkness. The headlights still burned, but the beams were bent inward, toward each other. The Corvair had a hollow head, its engine being in the rear. Its face, an unimpassioned insect's face, was inextricably curved around the pole; the bumper had become locked mandibles. When Richard pushed and Joan fed gas, the wheels whined in a vacuum. The smooth encircling night extended around them, above and beyond the snow. No window light had acknowledged their accident.

Joan, who had a social conscience, asked, "Why doesn't anybody come out and help us?"

Eleanor, the voice of bitter experience, answered, "This pole is hit so often it's just a nuisance to the neighborhood."

Richard announced, "I'm too drunk to face the police." The remark hung with a neon clarity in the night.

A car came by, slowed, stopped. A window rolled down and revealed a frightened male voice. "Everything O.K.?"

"Not entirely," Richard said. He was pleased by his powers, under stress, of exact expression.

"I can take somebody to a telephone. I'm on my way back from a poker game."

A lie, Richard reasoned—otherwise, why advance it? The boy's face had the blurred pallor of the sexually drained. Taking care to give each word weight, Richard told him, "One of us can't move and I better stay with her. If you could take my wife to a phone, we'd all be most grateful."

"Who do I call?" Joan asked.

Richard hesitated between the party they had left, their babysitter at home, and Eleanor's husband, who was living in a motel on Route 128.

The boy answered for him: "The police."

Iphigenia redeemed the becalmed fleet at Aulis: so Joan got into the stranger's car, a rusty red Mercury. The car faded through the snow, which was slackening. The storm had been just a flurry, an illusion conjured to administer this one rebuke. It wouldn't even make tomorrow's newspapers.

Richard's knees felt as if icicles were being pressed against the soft spot beneath the caps, where the doctor's hammer searches for a reflex. He got in behind the wheel again, and switched off the lights. He switched off the ignition. Eleanor's cigarette glowed. Though his system was still adrift in liquor, he could not quite forget the taste of metal in his teeth. That utterly flat *No:* through several dreamlike thicknesses something very hard had touched him. Once, swimming in surf, he had been sucked under by a large wave. Tons of sudden surge had enclosed him and, with an implacable downward shrug, thrust him deep into dense green bitterness and stripped him of weight; his struggling became nothing, he was nothing within the wave. There had been no hatred. The wave simply hadn't *cared*.

He tried to apologize to the woman beside him in the darkness.

She said, "Oh, please. I'm sure nothing's broken. At the worst I'll be on crutches for a few days." She laughed and added, "This just isn't my year."

"Does it hurt?"

"No, not at all."

"You're probably in shock. You'll be cold. I'll get the heat back." Richard was sobering, and an infinite drabness was dawning for him. Never again, never ever, would his car be new, would he chew on his own enamel, would she kick so high with vivid long legs. He turned the ignition back on and started up the motor, for warmth. The radio softly returned, still Handel.

Moving from the hips up with surprising strength, Eleanor turned and embraced him. Her cheeks were wet; her lipstick tasted manufactured. Searching for her waist, for the smallness of her breasts, he fumbled through thicknesses of cloth. They were still in each other's arms when the whirling blue light of the police car broke upon them.

Your Lover Just Called

THE TELEPHONE RANG, and Richard Maple, who had stayed home from work this Friday because of a cold, answered it: "Hello?" The person at the other end of the line hung up. Richard went into the bedroom, where Joan was making the bed, and said, "Your lover just called."

"What did he say?"

"Nothing. He hung up. He was amazed to find me home."

"Maybe it was *your* lover."

He knew, through the phlegm beclouding his head, that there was something wrong with this, and found it. "If it was *my* lover," he said, "why would she hang up, since I answered?"

Joan shook the sheet so it made a clapping noise. "Maybe she doesn't love you anymore."

"This is a ridiculous conversation."

"You started it."

"Well, what would you think, if you answered the phone on a weekday and the person hung up? He clearly expected you to be home alone."

"Well, if you'll go to the store for cigarettes I'll call him back and explain what happened."

"You think I'll think you're kidding but I know that's really what *would* happen."

"Oh, come on, Dick. Who would it be? Freddie Vetter?"

"Or Harry Saxon. Or somebody I don't know at all. Some old college friend who's moved to New England. Or maybe the milkman. I can hear you and him talking while I'm shaving sometimes."

"We're surrounded by hungry children. He's fifty years old and has hair coming out of his ears."

"Like your father. You're not adverse to older men. There was that Chaucer section man when we first met. Anyway, you've been acting awfully happy lately. There's a little smile comes into your face when you're doing the housework. See, there it is!"

"I'm smiling," Joan said, "because you're so absurd. I have no lover. I have nowhere to put him. My days are consumed by devotion to the needs of my husband and his many children."

"Oh, so I'm the one who made you have all the children? While you were hankering after a career in fashion or in the exciting world of business. Aeronautics, perhaps. You could have been the first woman to design a nose cone. Or to crack the wheat futures cycle. Joan Maple, girl agronomist. Joan Maple, lady geopolitician. But for that fornicating brute she mistakenly married, this clear-eyed female citizen of our ever-needful republic—"

"Dick, have you taken your temperature? I haven't heard you rave like this for years."

"I haven't been betrayed like this for years. I hated that

click. That nasty little I-know-your-wife-better-than-you-do
click."

"It was some child. If we're going to have Mack for dinner
tonight, you better convalesce now."

"It *is* Mack, isn't it? That son of a bitch. The divorce isn't
even finalized and he's calling my wife on the phone. And
then proposes to gorge himself at my groaning board."

"I'll be groaning myself. You're giving me a headache."

"Sure. First I foist off children on you in my mad desire
for progeny, then I give you a menstrual headache."

"Get into bed and I'll bring you orange juice and toast
cut into strips the way your mother used to make it."

"You're lovely."

As he was settling himself under the blankets, the phone
rang again, and Joan answered it in the upstairs hall. "Yes
. . . no . . . no . . . good," she said, and hung up.

"Who was it?" he called.

"Somebody wanting to sell us the *World Book Encyclopedia*," she called back.

"A very likely story," he said, with self-pleasing irony,
leaning back onto the pillows confident that he was being
unjust, that there was no lover.

Mack Dennis was a homely, agreeable, sheepish man their
age, whose wife, Eleanor, was in Wyoming suing for divorce.
He spoke of her with a cloying tenderness, as if of a favorite
daughter away for the first time at camp, or as a departed
angel nevertheless keeping in close electronic touch with the
scorned earth. "She says they've had some wonderful thunder-
storms. The children go horseback riding every morning,
and they play Pounce at night and are in bed by ten. Everybody's health has never been better. Ellie's asthma has cleared

up and she thinks now she must have been allergic to *me*."

"You should have cut all your hair off and dressed in cellophane," Richard told him.

Joan asked him, "And how's *your* health? Are you feeding yourself enough? Mack, you look thin."

"The nights I don't stay in Boston," Mack said, tapping himself all over for a pack of cigarettes, "I've taken to eating at the motel on Route 33. It's the best food in town now, and you can watch the kids in the swimming pool." He studied his empty upturned hands as if they had recently held a surprise. He missed his own kids, was perhaps the surprise.

"I'm out of cigarettes too," Joan said.

"I'll go get some," Richard said.

"And a thing of Bitter Lemon at the liquor store."

"I'll make a pitcher of Martinis," Mack said. "Doesn't it feel great, to have Martini weather again?"

It was that season which is late summer in the days and early autumn at night. Evening descended on the downtown, lifting the neon tubing into brilliance, as Richard ran his errand. His sore throat felt folded within him like a secret; there was something reckless and gay in his being up and out at all after spending the afternoon in bed. Home, he parked by his back fence and walked down through a lawn loud with fallen leaves, though the trees overhead were still massy. The lit windows of his house looked golden and idyllic; the children's rooms were above (the face of Judith, his bigger daughter, drifted preoccupied across a slice of her wallpaper, and her pink square hand reached to adjust a doll on a shelf) and the kitchen below. In the kitchen windows, whose tone was fluorescent, a silent tableau was being enacted. Mack was holding a Martini shaker and pouring it into a vessel, eclipsed by an element of window sash, that Joan was offering with a long white arm. Head tilted winningly, she was talking with the slightly pushed-forward mouth that Richard recognized as peculiar to her while looking into mirrors, conversing with her elders, or otherwise seeking to display herself to advantage. Whatever she was saying made Mack laugh, so that his pouring (the silver shaker head glinted, a drop of greenish liquid spilled) was unsteady. He set the shaker down and displayed his hands—the same hands from which a little while ago a surprise had seemed to escape—at his sides, shoulder-high. Joan moved toward him, still holding her glass, and the back of her head, done up taut and oval in a bun, with blond down trailing at the nape of her neck, eclipsed all of Mack's face but his eyes, which closed. They were kissing. Joan's head tilted one way and Mack's another to make their mouths meet tighter. The graceful line of her shoulders was carried outward by the line of the arm holding her glass safe in the air. The other arm was around his neck. Behind them an open cabinet door revealed a paralyzed row of erect paper boxes whose lettering Richard could not read but whose coloring advertised their contents—Cheerios, Wheat Honeys, Onion Thins. Joan backed off and ran her index finger down the length of Mack's necktie (a summer tartan) ending with a jab in the vicinity of his navel that might have expressed a rebuke or a regret. His face, pale and lumpy in the harsh vertical light, looked mildly humorous but intent, and moved forward, toward hers, an inch or two. The scene had the fascinating slow motion of action underwater, mixed with the insane silent suddenness of a television montage glimpsed from the street. Judith came to the window upstairs, not noticing her father standing in the massy shadow of the tree. Wearing a nightie of lemon gauze, she innocently scratched her armpit while studying a moth beating on her screen; and this too gave Richard a momentous sense, crowding his heart, of having been brought by the mute act of witnessing— like a child sitting alone at the movies—perilously close to the hidden machinations of things. In another kitchen window a neglected teakettle began to plume and to fog the panes with steam. Joan was talking again; her forward-thrust lips seemed to be throwing rapid little bridges across a narrowing gap. Mack paused, shrugged; his face puckered as if he were speaking French. Joan's head snapped back with laughter and triumphantly she threw her free arm wide and was in his embrace again. His hand, spread starlike on the small of her back, went lower to what, out of sight behind the edge of formica counter, would be her bottom.

Richard scuffled loudly down the cement steps and kicked the kitchen door open, giving them time to break apart before he entered. From the far end of the kitchen, smaller than children, they looked at him with blurred, blank expressions. Joan turned off the steaming kettle and Mack shambled forward to pay for the cigarettes. After the third round of Martinis, the constraints loosened and Richard said, taking pleasure in the plaintive huskiness of his voice, "Imagine my discomfort. Sick as I am, I go out into this bitter night to get my wife and my guest some cigarettes, so they can pollute the air and aggravate my already grievous bronchial condition, and coming down through the back yard, what do I see? The two of them doing the Kama Sutra in my own kitchen. It was like seeing a blue movie and knowing the people in it."

"Where do you see blue movies nowadays?" Joan asked.

"Tush, Dick," Mack said sheepishly, rubbing his thighs with a brisk ironing motion. "A mere fraternal kiss. A brotherly hug. A disinterested tribute to your wife's charm."

"Really, Dick," Joan said. "I think it's shockingly sneaky of you to be standing around spying into your own windows."

"Standing around! I was transfixed with horror. It was a real trauma. My first primal scene." A profound happiness was stretching him from within; the reach of his tongue and wit felt immense, and the other two seemed dolls, homunculi, in his playful grasp.

"We were hardly doing anything," Joan said, lifting her head as if to rise above it all, the lovely line of her jaw defined by tension, her lips stung by a pout.

"Oh, I'm sure, by your standards, you had hardly begun. You'd hardly sampled the possible wealth of coital positions. Did you think I'd never return? Have you poisoned my drink and I'm too vigorous to die, like Rasputin?"

"Dick," Mack said, "Joan loves you. And if I love any man, it's you. Joan and I had this out years ago, and decided to be merely friends."

"Don't go Irish on me, Mack Dennis. 'If I love any mon, 'tis thee.' Don't give me a thought, laddie. Just think of poor Eleanor out there, sweating out your divorce, bouncing up and down on those horses day after day, playing Pounce till she's black and blue—"

"Let's eat," Joan said. "You've made me so nervous I've probably overdone the roast beef. Really, Dick, I don't think you can excuse yourself by trying to make it funny."

Next day, the Maples awoke soured and dazed by hangovers; Mack had stayed until two, to make sure there were no hard feelings. Joan usually played ladies' tennis Saturday mornings, while Richard amused the children; now, dressed in white shorts and sneakers, she delayed at home in order to quarrel. "It's desperate of you," she told Richard, "to try to make something of Mack and me. What are you trying to cover up?"

"My dear Mrs. Maple, I *saw*," he said, "I *saw* through my own windows you doing a very credible impersonation of a female spider having her abdomen tickled. Where did you learn to flirt your head like that? It was better than finger puppets."

"Mack always kisses me in the kitchen. It's a habit, it means nothing. You know for yourself how in love with Eleanor he is."

"So much he's divorcing her. His devotion verges on the quixotic."

"The divorce is her idea, you know that. He's a lost soul. I feel sorry for him."

"Yes, I saw that you do. You were like the Red Cross at Verdun."

"What I'd like to know is, why are you so pleased?"

"Pleased? I'm annihilated."

"You're delighted. Look at your smile in the mirror."

"You're so incredibly unapologetic, I guess I think you must be being ironical."

The telephone rang. Joan picked it up and said, "Hello," and Richard heard the click across the room. Joan replaced the receiver and said to him, "So. She thought I'd be playing tennis by now."

"Who's she?"

"You tell me. Your lover. Your loveress."

"It was clearly yours, and something in your voice warned him off."

"Go to her!" Joan suddenly cried, with a burst of the same defiant energy that made her, on other hungover mornings, rush through a mountain of housework. "Go to her like a man and stop trying to maneuver me into something I don't understand! I have no lover! I let Mack kiss me because he's lonely and drunk! Stop trying to make me more interesting than I am! All I am is a beat-up housewife who wants to go play tennis with some other tired ladies!"

Mutely Richard fetched from their sports closet her tennis racket, which had recently been restrung with gut. Carrying it in his mouth like a dog retrieving a stick, he laid it at the toe of her sneaker. Richard Jr., their older son, a wiry nine-year-old presently obsessed by the accumulation of Batman cards, came into the living room, witnessed this pantomime, and laughed to hide his fright. "Dad, can I have my nickel for emptying the waste baskets?"

"Mommy's going to go out to play, Dickie," Richard said, licking from his lips the salty taste of the racket handle. "Let's all go to the five-and-ten and buy a Batmobile."

"Yippee," the small boy said limply, glancing wide-eyed from one of his parents to the other, as if the space between them had gone treacherous.

Richard took the children to the five-and-ten, to the playground, and to a hamburger stand for lunch. These blameless activities transmuted the residue of alcohol and phlegm into a woolly fatigue as pure as the sleep of infants. Obligingly he nodded while his son described a boundless plot: ". . . and then, see Dad, the Penguin had an umbrella smoke came out of, it was neat, and there were these two other guys with funny masks in the bank, filling it with water, I don't know why, to make it bust or something, and Robin was climbing up these slippery stacks of like half-dollars to get away from the water, and then, see Dad . . ."

Back home, the children dispersed into the neighborhood on the same mysterious tide that on other days packed their back yard with unfamiliar urchins. Joan returned from tennis glazed with sweat, her ankles coated with dust. Her body was swimming in the rose afterglow of exertion. He suggested they take a nap.

"Just a nap," she warned.

"Of course," he said. "I met my mistress at the playground and we satisfied each other on the jungle gym."

"Maureen and I beat Alice and Judy. It can't be any of those three, they were waiting for me half an hour."

In bed, the shades strangely drawn against the bright afternoon, a glass of stale water standing bubbled with secret light, he asked her, "You think I want to make you more interesting than you are?"

"Of course. You're bored. You left me and Mack alone deliberately. It was very uncharacteristic of you, to go out with a cold."

"It's sad, to think of you without a lover."

"I'm sorry."

"You're pretty interesting anyway. Here, and here, and here."

"I said really a nap."

In the upstairs hall, on the other side of the closed bedroom door, the telephone rang. After four peals—icy spears hurled from afar—the ringing stopped, unanswered. There was a puzzled pause. Then a tentative, questioning *pring*, as if someone in passing had bumped the table, followed by a determined series, strides of sound, imperative and plaintive, that did not stop until twelve had been counted; then the lover hung up.

Eros Rampant

THE MAPLES' HOUSE is full of love. Bean, the six-year-old baby, loves Hecuba, the dog. John, who is eight, an angel-faced mystic serenely unable to ride a bicycle or read a clock, is in love with his Creepy Crawlers, his monster cards, his dinosaurs, and his carved rhinoceros from Kenya. He spends hours in his room after school drifting among these things, rearranging, gloating, humming. He experiences pain only when his older brother, Richard Jr., sardonically enters his room and pierces his placenta of contemplation. Richard is in love with life, with all outdoors, with Carl Yastrzemski, Babe Parelli, the Boston Bruins, the Beatles, and with that shifty apparition who, comb in hand, peeps back shiny-eyed at him out of the mirror in the mornings, wearing a moustache of toothpaste. He receives strange challenging notes from girls—*Dickie Maple you stop looking at me*—which he brings home from school carelessly crumpled along with his spelling papers and hectographed notices about eye, tooth, and lung inspection. His feelings about young Mrs. Brice, who confronts his section of the fifth grade with the enamelled poise and studio diction of an airline hostess, are so guarded as to be suspicious. He almost certainly loves, has always deeply loved, his older sister, Judith. Verging on thirteen, she has become difficult to contain, even within an incestuous passion. Large and bumptious, she eclipses his view of the television screen, loudly Frugs while he would listen to the Beatles, teases, thrashes, is bombarded and jogged by powerful rays from outer space. She hangs for hours by the corner where Mr. Lunt, her history teacher, lives; she pastes effigies of the Monkees on her walls, French-kisses her mother good-night, experiences the panic of sleeplessness, engages in long languorous tussles on the sofa with the dog. Hecuba, a spayed golden retriever, races from room to room, tormented as if by fleas by the itch for adoration, ears flattened, tail thumping, until at last she runs up against the cats, who do not love her, and she drops exhausted, in grateful defeat, on the kitchen linoleum, and sleeps. The cats, Esther and Esau, lick each other's fur and share a bowl. They had been two of a litter. Esther, the mother of more than thirty kittens mostly resembling her brother, but with a persistent black minority vindicating the howled appeal of a neighboring tom, has been "fixed"; Esau, sentimentally allowed to continue unfixed, now must venture from the house in quest of the bliss that had once been purely domestic. He returns scratched and battered. Esther licks his wounds while he leans dazed beside the refrigerator; even his purr is ragged. Nagging for their supper, they sit like bookends, their backs discreetly touching, an expert old married couple on the dole. One feels, unexpectedly, that Esau still loves Esther, while she merely accepts and understands him. She seems scornful of his merely dutiful attentions. Is she puzzled by her abrupt surgical lack of what drastically attracts him? But it is his big square tomcat's head that seems puzzled, rather than her triangular feminine feline one. The children feel a difference; both Bean and John cuddle Esau more, now that Esther is sterile. Perhaps, obscurely, they feel that she has deprived them of a miracle, of the semiannual miracle of her kittens, of drowned miniature piglets wriggling alive from a black orifice vaster than a cave. Richard Jr., as if to demonstrate his superior purchase on manhood and its righteous compassion, makes a point of petting the two cats equally, stroke for stroke. Judith claims she hates them both; it is her chore to feed them supper, and she hates the smell of horsemeat. She loves, at least in the abstract, horses.

Mr. Maple loves Mrs. Maple. He goes through troublesome periods, often on Saturday afternoons, of being unable to take his eyes from her, of being captive to the absurd persuasion that the curve of her solid haunch conceals, enwraps, a precarious treasure confided to his care. He cannot touch her enough. The sight of her body contorted by one of her yoga exercises, in her elastic black leotard riddled with runs, twists his heart so that he cannot breathe. Her gesture as she tips the dregs of white wine into a potted geranium seems infinite, like one of Vermeer's moments frozen in an eternal light from the left. At night he tries to press her into himself, to secure her drowsy body against his breast like a clasp, as if without it he will come undone. He cannot sleep in this position, yet maintains it long after her breathing has become steady and oblivious: can love be defined, simply, as the refusal to sleep? Also he loves Penelope Vogel, a quaint little secretary at his office who is recovering from a disastrous affair with an Antiguan; and he is in love with the memories of six or so other women, beginning with a seven-year-old playmate who used to steal his hunter's cap; and is half in love with death. He as well seems to love, perhaps alone in the nation, President Johnson, who is unaware of his existence. Along the same lines, Richard adores the moon; he studies avidly all the photographs beamed back from its uncongenial surface.

And Joan? Whom does she love? Her psychiatrist, certainly. Her father, inevitably. Her yoga instructor, probably. She has a part-time job in a museum and returns home flushed and quick-tongued, as if from sex. She must love the children, for they flock to her like sparrows to suet. They fight bitterly for a piece of her lap and turn their backs upon their father, as if he, the source and shelter of their life, were a grotesque intruder, a chimney sweep in a snow palace. None of his impersonations with the children—scoutmaster, playmate, confidant, financial bastion, factual wizard, watchman of the night—win them over; Bean still cries for Mommy when hurt, John approaches her for the money to finance yet more monster cards, Dickie demands that hers be the last good-night, and even Judith, who should be his, kisses him timidly, and saves her open-mouthed passion for her mother. Joan swims through their love like a fish through water, ignorant of any other element. Love slows her footsteps, pours upon her from the radio, hangs about her, in the kitchen, in the form of tacked-up children's drawings of houses, families, cars, cats, dogs, and flowers. Her husband cannot touch her: she is solid but hidden, like the World Bank; presiding yet immaterial, like the federal judiciary. Some cold uncoördinated thing pushes at his hand as it hangs impotent; it is Hecuba's nose. Obese spayed golden-eyed bitch, like him she abhors exclusion and strains to add her warmth to the tumble, in love with them all, in love with the smell of food, in love with the smell of love.

Penelope Vogel takes care to speak without sentimentality; five years younger than Richard, she has endured a decade of amorous ordeals and, still single at twenty-nine, preserves herself by speaking dryly, in the flip phrases of a still younger generation.

"We had a good thing," she says of her Antiguan, "that became a bad scene."

She handles, verbally, her old affairs like dried flowers; sitting across the restaurant table from her, Richard is made jittery by her delicacy, as if he and a grandmother are together examining an array of brittle, enigmatic mementos. "A very undesirable scene," Penelope adds. "The big time was too much for him. He got in with the drugs crowd. I couldn't see it."

"He wanted to marry you?" Richard asks timidly; this much is office gossip.

She shrugs, admitting, "There was that pitch."

"You must miss him."

"There is that. He was the most beautiful man I ever saw. His shoulders. In Dickinson's Bay, he'd have me put my hand on his shoulder in the water and that way he'd pull me along for miles, swimming. He was a snorkel instructor."

"His name?" Jittery, fearful of jarring these reminiscences, which are also negotiations, he spills the last of his Gibson, and jerkily signals to order another.

"Hubert," Penelope says. She is patiently mopping with her napkin. "Like a girl friend told me, Never take on a male beauty, you'll have to fight for the mirror." Her face is small and very white, and her nose very long, her pink nostrils inflamed by a perpetual cold. Only a Negro, Richard thinks, could find her beautiful; the thought gives her, in the restless shadowy restaurant light, beauty. The waiter, colored, comes and changes their tablecloth. Penelope continues so softly Richard must strain to hear, "When Hubert was eighteen he had a woman divorce her husband and leave her children for him. She was one of the old planter families. He wouldn't marry her. He told me, If she'd do that to him, next thing she'd leave me. He was very moralistic, until he came up here. But imagine an eighteen-year-old boy having an effect like that on a mature married woman in her thirties."

"I better keep him away from my wife," Richard jokes.

"Yeah." She does not smile. "They *work* at it, you know. Those boys are *pros*."

Penelope has often been to the West Indies. In St. Croix, it delicately emerges, there was Andrew, with his goatee and his septic-tank business and his political ambitions; in Guadeloupe, there was Ramon, a customs inspector; in Trinidad, Castlereigh, who played the alto pans in a steel band and also did the limbo. He could go down to nine inches. But Hubert was the worst, or best. He was the only one who had followed her north. "I was supposed to come live with him in this hotel in Dorchester but I was scared to go near the place, full of cop-out types and the smell of pot in the elevator, I got two offers from guys just standing there pushing the Up button. It was not a healthy scene." The waiter brings them rolls; in his shadow her profile seems wan and he yearns to pluck her, pale flower, from the tangle she has conjured. "It got so bad," she says, "I tried going back to an old boy friend, an awfully nice guy with a mother and a nervous stomach. He's a computer systems analyst, very dedicated, but I don't know, he just never impressed me. All he can talk about is his gastritis and how she keeps telling him to move out and get a wife, but he doesn't know if she means it. His mother."

"He is . . . white?"

Penelope glances up; there is a glint off her halted butter knife. Her voice slows, goes drier, "No, as a matter of fact. He's what they call an Afro-American. You mind?"

"No, no, I was just wondering—his nervous stomach. He doesn't sound like the others."

"He's not. Like I say, he doesn't impress me. Don't you find, once you have something that works, it's hard to back up?" More seems meant than is stated; her level gaze, as she munches her thickly buttered bun, feels like one tangent in a complicated geometrical problem: find the point at which she had switched from white to black lovers.

The subject is changed for him; his heart jars, and he leans forward hastily to say, "See that woman who just came in? Leather suit, gypsy earrings, sitting down now? Her name is Eleanor Dennis. She lives down our street from us. She's divorced."

"Who's the man?"

"I have no idea. Eleanor's moved out of our circles. He looks like a real thug." Along the far wall, Eleanor adjusts the great loop of her earring; her sideways glance, in the shuffle of shadows, flicks past his table. He doubts that she saw him.

Penelope says, "From the look on your face, that was more than a circle she was in with you."

He pretends to be disarmed by her guess, but in truth considers it providential that one of his own old loves should appear, to countervail the dark torrent of hers. For the rest of the meal they talk about *him*, him and Eleanor and Marlene Brossman and Joan and the little girl who used to steal his hunter's cap. In the lobby of Penelope's apartment house, the elevator summoned, he offers to go up with her.

She says carefully, "I don't think you want to."

"But I *do*." The building is Back Bay modern; the lobby is garishly lit and furnished with plastic plants that need never be watered, Naugahyde chairs that were never sat upon, and tessellated plaques no one ever looks at. The light is an absolute presence, as even and clean as the light inside a freezer, as ubiquitous as ether or as the libido that, Freud says, permeates us all from infancy on.

"No," Penelope repeats. "I've developed a good ear for sincerity in these things, I think you're too wrapped up back home."

"The dog likes me," he confesses, and kisses her good-night there, encased in brightness. Dry voice to the contrary, her lips are shockingly soft, wide, warm, and sorrowing.

"So," Joan says to him. "You slept with that little office mouse." It is Saturday; the formless erotic suspense of the afternoon—the tennis games, the cartoon matinees—has passed. The Maples are in their room dressing for a party, by the ashen light of dusk, and the watery blue of a distant streetlamp.

"I never have," he says, thereby admitting, however, that he knows who she means.

"Well you took her to dinner."

"Who says?"

"Mack Dennis. Eleanor saw the two of you in a restaurant."

"When do they converse? I thought they were divorced."

"They talk all the time. He's still in love with her. Everybody knows that."

"O.K. When do he and *you* converse?"

Oddly, she has not prepared an answer. "Oh—" His heart falls through her silence. "Maybe I saw him in the hardware store this afternoon."

"And maybe you didn't. Why would he blurt this out anyway? You and he must be on cozy terms."

He says this to trigger her denial; but she mutely considers and, sauntering toward her closet, admits, "We understand each other."

How unlike her, to bluff this way. "When was I supposedly seen?"

"You mean it happens often? Last Wednesday, around eight-thirty. You *must* have slept with her."

"I couldn't have. I was home by ten, you may remember. You had just gotten back yourself from the museum."

"What went wrong, darley? Did you offend her with your horrible pro-Vietnam stand?"

In the dim light he hardly knows this woman, her broken gestures, her hasty voice. Her silver slip glows and crackles as she wriggles into a black knit cocktail dress; with a kind of determined agitation she paces around the bed, to the bureau and back. As she moves, her body seems to be gathering bulk from the shadows, bulk and a dynamic elasticity. He tries to placate her with a token offering of truth. "No, it turns out Penelope only goes with Negroes. I'm too pale for her."

"You admit you tried?"

He nods.

"Well," Joan says, and takes a half-step toward him, so that he flinches in anticipation of being hit, "do you want to know who *I* was sleeping with Wednesday?"

He nods again, but the two nods feel different, as if,

transposed by a terrific unfelt speed, a continent had lapsed between them.

She names a man he knows only slightly, an assistant director in the museum, who wears a collar pin and has his gray hair cut long and tucked back in the foppish English style. "It was *fun*," Joan says, kicking at a shoe. "He thinks I'm *beau*tiful. He cares for me in a way you just *don't*." She kicks away the other shoe. "You look pale to me too, buster."

Stunned, he needs to laugh. "But we *all* think you're beautiful."

"Well you don't make me *feel* it."

"*I* feel it," he says.

"You make me feel like an ugly drudge." As they grope to understand their new positions, they realize that she, like a chess player who has impulsively swept forward her queen, has nowhere to go but on the defensive. In a desperate attempt to keep the initiative, she says, "Divorce me. Beat me."

He is calm, factual, admirable. "How often have you been with him?"

"I don't know. Since April, off and on." Her hands appear to embarrass her; she places them at her sides, against her cheeks, together on the bedpost, off. "I've been trying to get out of it, I've felt horribly guilty, but he's never been at all pushy, so I could never really arrange a fight. He gets this hurt look."

"Do you want to keep him?"

"With you knowing? Don't be grotesque."

"But he cares for you in a way I just don't."

"Any lover does that."

"God help us. You're an expert."

"Hardly."

"What *about* you and Mack?"

She is frightened. "Years ago. Not for very long."

"And Freddy Vetter?"

"No, we agreed not. He knew about me and Mack."

Love, a cloudy heavy ink, inundates him from within, suffuses his palms with tingling pressure as he steps close to her, her murky face held tense against the expectation of a blow. "You whore," he breathes, enraptured. "My virgin bride." He kisses her hands; they are corrupt and cold. "Who else?" he begs, as if each name is a burden of treasure she lays upon his bowed serf's shoulders. "Tell me all your men."

"I've told you. It's a pretty austere list. You know *why* I told you? So you wouldn't feel guilty about this Vogel person."

"But nothing happened. When you do it, it happens."

"Sweetie, I'm a woman," she explains, and they do seem, in this darkening room above the muted hubbub of television, to have reverted to the bases of their marriage, to the elemental constituents. Woman. Man. House.

"What does your psychiatrist say about all this?"

"Not much." The triumphant swell of her confession has passed; her ebbed manner prepares for days, weeks of his questions. She retrieves the shoes she kicked away. "That's one of the reasons I went to him, I kept having these affairs—"

"*Kept* having? You're killing me."

"Please don't interrupt. It was somehow very innocent. I'd go into his office, and lie down, and say, 'I've just been with Mack, or Otto—'"

"Otto. What's that joke? Otto spelled backwards is 'Otto.' Otto spelled inside out is 'toot.'"

"—and I'd say it was wonderful, or awful, or so-so, and then we'd talk about my childhood masturbation. It's not his business to scold me, it's his job to get me to stop scolding myself."

"The poor bastard, all the time I've been jealous of him, and he's been suffering with this for years; he had to listen every *day*. You'd go in there and plunk yourself still warm down on his couch—"

"It wasn't every day at all. Weeks would go by. I'm not Otto's only woman."

The artificial tumult of television below merges with a real commotion, a screaming and bumping that mounts the stairs and threatens the aquarium where the Maples are swimming, dark fish in ink, their outlines barely visible, known to each other only as eddies of warmth, as mysterious animate chasms in the surface of space. Fearing that for years he will not again be so close to Joan, or she be so open, he hurriedly asks, "And what about the yoga instructor?"

"Don't be silly," Joan says, clasping her pearls at the nape of her neck. "He's an elderly vegetarian."

The door crashes open; their bedroom explodes in shards of electric light. Richard Jr. is frantic, sobbing.

"Mommy, Judy keeps *teas*ing me and getting in front of the *tele*vision!"

"I did not. I did not." Judith speaks very distinctly. "Mother and Father, he is a retarded liar."

"She can't help she's growing," Richard tells his son, picturing poor Judith trying to fit herself among the intent childish silhouettes in the little television room, pitying her for her size, much as he pities Johnson for his Presidency. Bean bursts into the bedroom, frightened by violence not on TV, and Hecuba leaps upon the bed with rolling golden eyes, and Judith gives Dickie an impudent and unrepentant sideways glance, and he, gagging on a surfeit of emotion, bolts from the room. Soon there arises from the other end of the upstairs an anguished squawk as Dickie invades John's room and punctures his communion with his dinosaurs. Downstairs, a woman, neglected and alone, locked in a box, sings about *amore*. Bean hugs Joan's legs so she cannot move.

Judith asks with parental sharpness, "What were you two talking about?"

"Nothing," Richard says. "We were getting dressed."

"Why were all the lights out?"

"We were saving electricity," her father tells her.

"Why is Mommy crying?" He looks, disbelieving, and discovers that indeed, her cheeks coated with silver, she is.

At the party, amid clouds of friends and smoke, Richard resists being parted from his wife's side. She has dried her tears, and faintly swaggers, as when, on the beach, she dares wear a bikini. But her nakedness is only in his eyes. Her head beside his shoulder, her grave polite pleasantries, the plump unrepentant cleft between her breasts, all seem newly treasurable and intrinsic to his own identity. As a cuckold, he has grown taller, attenuated, more elegant and humane in his opinions, airier and more mobile. When the usual argument about Vietnam commences, he hears himself sounding like a dove. He concedes that Johnson is unlovable. He allows that Asia is infinitely complex, devious, ungrateful, feminine: but must we abandon her therefore? When Mack Dennis, grown burly in bachelorhood, comes and asks Joan to dance, Richard feels unmanned and sits on the sofa with such an air of weariness that Marlene Brossman sits down beside him and, for the first time in years, flirts. He tries to tell her with his voice, beneath the meaningless words he is speaking, that he loved her, and could love her again, but that at the moment he is terribly distracted and must be excused. He goes and asks Joan if it isn't time to go. She resists; "It's too rude."

Eros Rampant

She is safe here among proprieties and foresees that his exploitation of the territory she has surrendered will be thorough. Love is pitiless. They drive home at midnight under a slim moon nothing like its photographs—shadow-caped canyons, gimlet mountain ranges, gritty circular depressions around the metal feet of the mechanical intruder sent from the blue ball in the sky.

They do not rest until he has elicited from her a world of details: dates, sites, motel interiors, precisely mixed emotions. They make love, self-critically. He exacts the new wantonness she owes him, and in compensation tries to be, like a battered old roué, skillful. He satisfies himself that in some elemental way he has never been displaced; that for months she has been struggling in her lover's grasp, in the gauze net of love, her wings pinioned by tact. She assures him that she seized on the first opportunity for confession; she confides to him that Otto spray-sets his hair and uses perfume. She, weeping, vows that nowhere, never, has she encountered his, Richard's, passion, his pleasant bodily proportions and backwards-reeling grace, his invigorating sadism, his male richness. Then why . . . ? She is asleep. Her breathing has become oblivious. He clasps her limp body to his, wasting forgiveness upon her ghostly form. A receding truck pulls the night's silence taut. She has left him a hair short of satiety; her confession feels still a fraction unplumbed. The lunar face of the electric clock says three. He turns, flips his pillow, restlessly adjusts his arms, turns again, and seems to go downstairs for a glass of milk.

To his surprise, the kitchen is brightly lit, and Joan is on the linoleum floor, in her leotard. He stands amazed while she serenely twists her legs into the lotus position. He asks her again about the yoga instructor.

"Well, I didn't think it counted if it was part of the exercise. The whole point, darley, is to make mind and body one. This is Pranayama—breath control." Stately, she pinches shut one nostril and slowly inhales, then pinches shut the other and exhales. Her hands return, palm up, to her knees. And she smiles. "This one is fun. It's called the Twist." She assumes a new position, her muscles elastic under the black cloth tormented into runs. "Oh, I forgot to tell you, I've slept with Harry Saxon."

"Joan, no. How often?"

"When we felt like it. We used to go out behind the Little League field. That heavenly smell of clover."

"But sweetie, why?"

Smiling, she inwardly counts the seconds of this position. "You know why. He asked. It's hard, when men ask. You mustn't insult their male natures. There's a harmony in everything."

"And Freddy Vetter? You lied about Freddy, didn't you?"

"Now *this* pose is wonderful for the throat muscles. It's called the Lion. You mustn't laugh." She kneels, her buttocks on her heels, and tilts back her head, and from gaping jaws thrusts out her tongue as if to touch the ceiling. Yet she continues speaking. "The whole theory is, we hold our heads too high, and blood can't get to the brain."

His chest hurts; he forces from it the cry, "Tell me everybody!"

She rolls toward him and stands upright on her shoulders, her face flushed with the effort of equilibrium and the downflow of blood. Her legs slowly scissor open and shut. "Some men you don't know," she goes on. "They come to the door to sell you septic tanks." Her voice is coming from her belly.

Worse, there is a humming. Terrified, he awakes, and sits up. His chest is soaked.

He locates the humming as a noise from the transformer on the telephone pole near their windows. All night, while its residents sleep, the town communes with itself electrically. Richard's terror persists, generating mass as the reality of his dream sensations is confirmed. Joan's body seems small, scarcely bigger than Judith's, and narrower with age, yet infinitely deep, an abyss of secrecy, perfidy, and accepting-ness; acrophobia launches sweat from his palms. He leaves the bed as if scrambling backward from the lip of a vortex. He again goes downstairs; his wife's revelations have steepened the treads and left the walls slippery.

The kitchen is dark; he turns on the light. The floor is bare. The familiar objects of the kitchen seem discovered in a preservative state of staleness, wearing a look of tension, as if they are about to burst with the strain of being so faithfully themselves. Esther and Esau pad in from the living room, where they have been sleeping on the sofa, and beg to be fed, sitting like bookends, expectant and expert. The clock says four. Watchman of the night. But in searching for signs of criminal entry, for traces of his dream, Richard finds nothing but—clues mocking in their very abundance—the tacked-up drawings done by children's fingers ardently bunched around a crayon, of houses, cars, cats, and flowers.

Sublimating

THE MAPLES agreed that, since sex was the only sore point in their marriage, they should give it up: sex, not the marriage, which was eighteen years old and stretched back to a horizon where even their birth pangs, with a pang, seemed to merge. A week went by. On Saturday, Richard brought home in a little paper bag a large raw round cabbage. Joan asked, "What is *that?*"

"It's just a cabbage."

"What am I supposed to *do* with it?" Her irritability gratified him.

"You don't have to do *any*thing with it. I saw Mack Dennis go into the A & P and went in to talk to him about the new environment commission, whether they weren't muscling in on the conservation committee, and then I had to buy something to get out through the check-out counter so I bought this cabbage. It was an impulse. You know what an impulse is." Rubbing it in. "When I was a kid," he went on, "we always used to have a head of cabbage around; you could cut a piece off to nibble instead of a candy. The hearts were best. They really burned your mouth."

"O.K., O.K." Joan turned her back and resumed washing dishes. "Well I don't know where you're going to put it; since Judith turned vegetarian the refrigerator's already so full of vegetables I could cry."

Her turning her back aroused him; it usually did. He went closer and thrust the cabbage between her face and the sink. "*Look* at it, darley. Isn't it beautiful? It's so perfect." He was only partly teasing; he had found himself, in the A & P, ravished by the glory of the pyramided cabbages, the mute and glossy beauty that had waited thirty years for him to rediscover it. Not since preadolescence had his senses opened so innocently wide: the pure sphericity, the shy cellar odor, the solid heft. He chose, not the largest cabbage, but the roundest, the most ideal, and carried it naked in his hand to the check-out counter, where the girl, with a flicker of surprise, dressed it in a paper bag and charged him 33¢. As he drove the mile home, the secret sphere beside him in the seat seemed a hole he had drilled back into reality. And now, cutting a slice from one pale cheek, he marveled across the years at the miracle of the wound, at the tender compaction of the leaves, each tuned to its curve as tightly as a guitar string. The taste was blander than his childhood memory of it, but the texture was delicious in his mouth.

Bean, their baby, ten, came into the kitchen. "What is Daddy eating?" she asked, looking into the empty bag for cookies. She knew Daddy as a snack-sneaker.

"Daddy bought himself a cabbage," Joan told her.

The child looked at her father with eyes in which amusement had been pre-prepared; there was a serious warmth that Mommy and animals, especially horses, gave off, and everything else had the coolness of comedy. "That was silly," she said.

"Nothing silly about it," Richard said. "Have a bite." He offered her the cabbage as if it were an apple. Inside her round head he envisioned leaves and leaves of female psychology, packed so snugly the wrinkles dovetailed.

Bean made a spitting face and harshly laughed. "That's nasty," she said. Bolder, brighter-eyed, flirting: "*You're* nasty." Trying it out.

Hurt, Richard said to her, "I don't like you either. I just like my cabbage." And he kissed the cool pale dense vegetable once, twice, on the cheek; Bean gurgled in astonishment.

Her back still turned, Joan continued from the sink, "If you *had* to buy something, I wish you'd remembered Calgonite. I've been doing the dishes by hand for days."

"Remember it yourself," he said. "Where's the Saran Wrap for my cabbage?" But, as the week wore on, the cabbage withered; the crisp planar wound of each slice by the next day had browned and loosened. Stubbornly loyal, Richard cut and nibbled his slow way to the heart, which burned on his tongue so sharply that his taste buds even in their adult dullness were not disappointed; he remembered how it had been, the oilcloth-covered table where his grandmother used to "schnitz" cabbage into strings for sauerkraut and give him the leftover raw hearts for a snack. He did not buy another cabbage, once the first was eaten; analogously, he never returned to a mistress, once Joan had discovered and mocked her. Their eyes, that is, had married and merged to three, and in the middle shared one her dry female-to-female clarity would always oust his erotic mists.

Her lovers, on the other hand, he never discovered while she had them. Months or even years later she would present an affair to him complete, self-packaged as nicely as a cabbage, the man remarried or moved to Seattle, her own wounds licked in secrecy and long healed. So he knew, coming home one evening and detecting a roseate afterglow in her face, that he would discover only some new wrinkle of innocence. Nevertheless, he asked, "What have *you* been up to today?"

"Same old grind. After school I drove Judith to her dance lesson, Bean to the riding stable, Dickie to the driving range."

"Where was John?"

"He stayed home with me and said it was boring. I told him to go build something so he's building a guillotine in the cellar; he says the sixth grade is studying revolution this term."

"What's he using for a blade?"

"He flattened an old snow shovel he says he can get sharp enough."

Richard could hear the child banging and whistling below him. "Jesus, he better not lose a finger." His thoughts flicked from the finger to himself to his wife's even white teeth to the fact that two weeks had passed since they gave up sex.

Casually she unfolded her secret. "One fun thing, though."

"You're taking up yoga again."

"Don't be silly; I was never anything to him. No. There's an automatic car wash opened up downtown, behind the pizza place. You put three quarters in and stay in the car and it just happens. It's hilarious."

"*What* happens?"

"Oh, you know. Soap, huge brushes that come whirling around. It really does quite a good job. Afterwards, there's a little hose you can put a dime in to vacuum the inside."

"I think this is very sinister. The people who are always washing their cars are the same people behind our boys in

Vietnam. Furthermore, it's bad for it. The dirt protects the paint."

"It needed it. We're living in the mud now."

Last fall, they had moved to an old farmhouse surrounded by vegetation that had been allowed to grow wild. This spring, they attacked the tangle of Nature around them with ominously different styles. Joan raked away dead twigs beneath bushes and pruned timidly, as if she were giving her boys a haircut. Richard scorned such pampering and attacked the problem at the root, or near the root. He wrestled vines from the barn roof, shingles popping and flying; he clipped the barberries down to yellow stubble; he began to prune some overweening yews by the front door and was unable to stop until each branch became a stump. The yews, a rare Japanese variety, had pink soft wood maddeningly like flesh. For days thereafter, the stumps bled amber.

The entire family was shocked, especially the two boys, who had improvised a fort in the cavity under the yews. Richard defended himself: "It was them or me. I couldn't get in my own front door."

"They'll never grow again, Dad," Dickie told him. "You didn't leave any green. There can't be any photosynthesis." The boy's own eyes were green; he kept brushing back his hair from them, with that nervous ladylike gesture of his generation.

"Good," Richard stated. He lifted his pruning clippers, which had an elbow hinge for extra strength, and asked, "How about a haircut?"

Dickie's eyes rounded with fright and he backed closer to his brother who, though younger, had even longer hair. They looked like two chunky girls, blocking the front door. "Or why don't you both go down to the cellar and stick your

heads in the guillotine?" Richard suggested. In a few powerful motions he mutilated a flowering trumpet vine. He had
a vision, of right angles, clean clapboards, unclouded windows,
level and transparent spaces from which the organic—the
impudent, importunate, unceasingly swelling organic—had
been finally scoured.

"Daddy's upset about something else, not about your hair,"
Joan explained to Dickie and John at dinner. As the pact wore
on, the family gathered more closely about her; even the cats,
he noticed, hesitated to take scraps from his hand.

"What about then?" Judith asked, looking up from her
omelette. She was sixteen and Richard's only ally.

Joan answered, "Something grown-up." Her older daughter
studied her for a moment, alertly, and Richard held his breath,
thinking she might *see*. Female to female. The truth. The
translucent vista of scoured space that was in Joan like a
crystal tunnel.

But the girl was too young and, sensing an enemy, attacked
her reliable old target, Dickie. "*You*," she said. "I don't
ever see *you* trying to help Daddy, all you do is make
Mommy drive you to golf courses and ski mountains."

"Yeah? What about *you*," he responded weakly, beaten
before he started, "making Mommy cook two meals all the
time because you're too *pure* to sully your lips with *an*imal
matter."

"At least when I'm here I try to help; I don't just sit around
reading books about dumb Billy Caster."

"Casper," Richard and Dickie said in unison.

Judith rose to her well-filled height; her bell-bottom hip-
hugging Levis dropped an inch lower and exposed a mingled
strip of silken underpants and pearly belly. "I think it's
*atro*cious for some people like us to have too many bushes

and people in the ghetto don't even have a weed to look at, they have to go up on their rooftops to breathe. It's *true*, Dickie; don't make that face!"

Dickie was squinting in pain; he found his sister's body painful. "The young sociologist," he said, "flaunting her charms."

"You don't even know what a sociologist is," she told him, tossing her head. Waves of fleshly agitation rippled down toward her toes. "You are a very *spoiled* and *self*ish and *lim*ited person."

"Puh puh, big mature," was all he could say, poor little boy overwhelmed by this blind blooming.

Judith had become an optical illusion in which they all saw different things: Dickie saw a threat, Joan saw herself of twenty-five years ago, Bean saw another large warmth-source that, unlike horses, could read her a bedtime story. John, bless him, saw nothing, or, dimly, an old pal receding. Richard couldn't look. In the evening, when Joan was putting the others to bed, Judith would roll around on the sofa while he tried to read in the chair opposite. "Look, Dad. See my stretch exercises." He was reading *My Million-Dollar Shots*, by Billy Casper. The body must be coiled, tension should be felt in the back muscles and along the left leg at top of backswing. Illustrations, with arrows. The body on the sofa was twisting into lithe knots; Judith was double-jointed and her prowess at yoga may have been why Joan stopped doing it, outshone. Richard glanced up and saw his daughter arched like a staple, her hands gripping her ankles; a glossy bulge of supple belly held a navel at its acme. At the top of the back-swing, forearm and back of the left hand should form a straight line. He tried it; it felt awkward. He was a born wrist-collapser. Judith watched him pondering his own wrist

and giggled; then she kept giggling, insistently, flirting, trying it out. "Daddy's a narcissist." In the edge of his vision
she seemed to be tickling herself and flicking her hair in circles.

"*Judith!*" He had not spoken to her so sharply since, at the
age of three, she had spilled sugar all over the kitchen floor.
In apology he added, "You are driving me crazy."

The fourth week, he went to New York, on business. When
he returned, Joan told him during their kitchen drink, "This
afternoon, everybody was being so cranky, you off, the
weather lousy, I piled them all into the car, everybody except
Judith; she's spending the night at Margaret Leonard's—"

"You *let* her? With that little bitch and her druggy crowd?
Are there going to be boys there?"

"I didn't ask. I hope so."

"Live vicariously, huh?"

He wondered if he could punch her in the face and at the
same time grab the glass in her hand so it wouldn't break. It
was from a honeymoon set of turquoise Mexican glass of
which only three were left. With their shared eye she saw his
calculations and her face went stony. Break his fist on that
face. "Are you going to let me finish my story?"

"Sure. *Dites-moi,* Scheherazade."

"The dog was hilarious, she kept barking and chasing the
brushes around and around the car trying to defend us. It took
her three rotations to figure out that if it went one way it
would be coming back the other. Everybody absolutely
howled; we had Danny Vetter in the car with us, and one of
Bean's horsy friends; it was a real orgy." Her face was pink,
recalling.

"That is a truly disgusting story. Speaking of disgusting, I
did something strange in New York."

"You slept with a prostitute."

"Almost. I went to a blue movie."

"How scary for you, darley."

"Well, it was. Wednesday morning I woke up early and didn't have any appointment until eleven so I wandered over to 42nd Street, you know, with this innocent morning light on everything, and these little narrow places were already open. So—can you stand this?"

"Sure. All I've heard all week are children's complaints."

"I paid three bucks and went in. It was totally dark. Like a fun house at a fairground. Except for this very bright pink couple up on the screen. I could hear people breathing but not see anything. Every time I tried to slide into a row I kept sticking my thumb into somebody's eye. But nobody groaned or protested. It was like those bodies half-frozen in whatever circle it was of Hell. Finally I found a seat and sat down and after a while I could see it was all men, asleep. At least most of them seemed to be asleep. And they were spaced so no two touched; but even at this hour, the place was half full. Of motionless men." He felt her disappointment; he hadn't conveyed the fairy-tale magic of the experience: the darkness absolute as lead, the undercurrent of snoring as from a single dragon, the tidy way the men had spaced themselves, like checkers on a board. And then how he had found a blank square, had jumped himself, as it were, into it, had joined humanity in stunned witness of its own process of perpetuation.

Joan asked, "How was the movie?"

"Awful. Exasperating. You begin to think entirely in technical terms: camera position, mike boom. And the poor cunts, God, how they work. Apparently to get a job in a blue movie a man has to be A, blond, and B, impotent."

"Yes," Joan said and turned her back, as if to conceal a train of thought. "We have to go to dinner tonight with the new Dennises." Mack Dennis had remarried, a woman much like Eleanor only slightly younger and, the Maples agreed, not nearly as nice. "They'll keep us up forever. But maybe tomorrow," Joan was going on, as if to herself, timidly, "after the kids go their separate ways, if you'd like to hang around . . ."

"No," he took pleasure in saying. "I'm determined to play golf. Thursday afternoon one of the accounts took me out to Long Island and even with borrowed clubs I was hitting the drives a mile. I think I'm on to something; it's all up here." He showed her the top of his backswing, the stiff left wrist. "I must have been getting twenty extra yards." He swung his empty arms down and through.

"See," Joan said, gamely accepting his triumph as her own, "you're sublimating."

In the car to the Dennises, he asked her, "How is it?"

"It's quite wonderful, in a way. It's as if my senses are jammed permanently open. I feel all one with Nature. The jonquils are out behind the shed and I just looked at them and cried. They were so beautiful I couldn't stand it. I can't keep myself indoors, all I want to do is rake and prune and push little heaps of stones around."

"You know," he told her sternly, "the lawn isn't just some kind of carpet to keep sweeping, you have to make some decisions. Those lilacs, for instance, are full of dead wood."

"Don't," Joan whimpered, and cried, as darkness streamed by, torn by headlights.

In bed after the Dennises (it was nearly two; they were numb on brandy; Mack had monologued about conservation and Mrs. Dennis about interior decoration, of "her" house, that the Maples still thought of as Eleanor's), Joan confessed to Richard, "I keep having this little vision—it comes to me anywhere, in the middle of sunshine—of me dead."

"Dead of what?"

"I don't know that, all I know is that I'm dead and it doesn't much matter."

"Not even to the children?"

"For a day or two. But everybody manages."

"Sweetie." He repressed his strong impulse to turn and touch her. He explained, "It's part of being one with Nature."

"I suppose."

"I have it very differently. I keep having this funeral fantasy. How full the church will be, what Spence will say about me in his sermon, who'll be there." Specifically, whether the women he has loved will come and weep with Joan; in the image of this, their combined grief at his eternal denial of himself to them, he glimpsed a satisfaction for which the transient satisfactions of the living flesh were a flawed and feeble prelude; love is merely the backswing. In death, he felt, as he floated on his back in bed, he would grow to his true size.

Joan with their third eye may have sensed his thoughts; where usually she would roll over and turn her back, whether as provocation or withdrawal it was up to him to decide, now she lay paralyzed, parallel to him. "I suppose," she offered, "in a way, it's cleansing. I mean you think of all that energy that went into the Crusades."

"Yes, I think," Richard agreed, unconvinced, "we may be on to something."

ILLUSTRATION CREDITS

p. 157: Neck girth pressing on horse's windpipe. From *Histoire de la locomotion terrestre*.

p. 189: Cyclops from "Some Pond Creatures and Their Sizes," sheet printed by the Massachusetts Audubon Society, Lincoln, Mass.

p. 189: Daphnia, *ibid*.

p. 190: Water-mite (*Hydrachna geographica*), from *Field Book of Ponds and Streams*, by Ann Haven Morgan. Copyright 1930 by Ann Haven Morgan, renewed 1958. Reprinted by permission of G. P. Putnam's Sons, New York.

p. 190: Fairy shrimp, *ibid*.

p. 191: Diatoms (*Meridion, Tabellaria*), *ibid*.

p. 191: Volvox, *ibid*.

p. 191: Anatomy of a rotifer (after F. J. Myers), *ibid*.

p. 191: Stentor, *ibid*.

p. 191: Spirostumum, *ibid*.

p. 192: Brown hydra (*Hydra oligactis*), *ibid*.

p. 192: *Hydra oligactis* after eating, *ibid*.

p. 194: Jurassic high life (left to right, Plateosaurus, Polacanthus, and Rhamphorynchus), from *Le Monde après le création de l'homme*, by Louis Fingier, 1870. Artist: Antoine Jobin. Engraver: Vermoreken.

p. 195: Skull of *Stegosaurus Stenops* from "Osteology of the Armored Dinosauria in the United States National Museum, with Special Reference to the Genus Stegosaurus," by Charles Whitney Gilmore, Washington, D.C.: Govt. Printing Office; 1914.

p. 197: Skeleton of Brontosaurus from Webster's New International Dictionary; Second Edition, © 1959 by G. & C. Merriam Co., publishers of the Merriam-Webster Dictionaries.

Illustration Credits

p. 201: Skeleton of *Iguanodon bernissartensis* (after Dollo), from Encyclopædia Britannica, Eleventh Edition, article on "Iguanodon."

p. 202: Baluchitherium, from *La Grand Larousse Encyclopédie Larousse*, Volume I, Librairie Larousse.

p. 203: Baluchitherium foot (upraised in admonition), from *The Vertebrate Story*, by Alfred S. Romer. Illinois: University of Chicago Press; 1959.

p. 207: First picture of a horse collar. From a Frankish manuscript, tenth century. Reproduction from *A History of Technology*, edited by Singer, Holmyard, Hall and Williams, Volume II, New York: Oxford University Press; 1956.

p. 207: Ancient Egyptian double yoke with neck and body girths. From *Die Wägen und Fahrwerke der Griechen und Römer*, by Johann Ginzrot, Volume I, München: J. Lentner; 1817.

p. 208: Front view of chariot horses, with strap passing between legs from girth-band to breast-band. From a Greek vase of c. 500 B.C. Reproduction from *A History of Technology*, Volume II, New York: Oxford University Press; 1956.

p. 208: Side view of chariot horses, with horizontal breast-band. Bone carving from a Byzantine casket, ninth century A.D. Reproduction *ibid*.

p. 210: Mule and horse working fields; horse (right) in newly invented horse collar. From the Bayeux tapestry, eleventh century. Reproduction from *A History of Western Technology*, by Frederich Klemm. Mass.: M. I. T. Press.

p. 212: Perfected medieval harness, being used to haul the sun up the sky. From *Hortus delicarum*, by Herrad von Landsperg, early twelfth century. Reproduction *ibid*.

p. 279: Vorticella, from *Field Book of Ponds and Streams*, by Ann Haven Morgan. Copyright 1930 by Ann Haven Morgan, renewed 1958. Reprinted by permission of G. P. Putnam's Sons, New York.

ABOUT THE AUTHOR

JOHN UPDIKE was born in 1932, in Shillington, Pennsylvania. He was graduated from Harvard College in 1954, and spent a year in England on the Knox Fellowship, at the Ruskin School of Drawing and Fine Art in Oxford. From 1955 to 1957 he was a member of the staff of *The New Yorker*, to which he has contributed short stories, poems, and book reviews. He is the author of six collections of short fiction, nine novels, four volumes of poetry, and two of criticism. Mr. Updike lives in Massachusetts.

VINTAGE FICTION, POETRY, AND PLAYS

VINTAGE CRITICISM: LITERATURE, MUSIC, AND ART

VINTAGE BELLES—LETTRES